Dedication

To my wife, Stacey J.
Here's to Jazz,
Coffee on the patio,
Rainy days and castles in the hills.

1X2

The Shopkeeper's Journal

Chapter 1

The key turning in the antique lock on the door made the same rustic sound it had years before, when the shopkeeper first inserted it. No one could recall how long the shop had been there, but most of the townspeople claimed the shopkeeper had been its only resident—an odd notion, since the building was one of the first built in the town over a hundred years before.

The shop, a historic building constructed from cut limestone, was like many of the buildings found in old towns, built to meet the demands of industry or trade, but now left to tourism and the faster pace of a new generation. The skilled, artistic craftsmen of a time and dedication long past painstakingly chiseled each of the fifty-pound stones to fit together in a seamless, four-story edifice.

Aside from the front door, one of the building's most impressive architectural designs was a set of six large plate glass windows positioned, three each, on either side of the door: four-by-eight-foot spans of arched leaded glass, designed for a single purpose—to let in the morning and evening light. Watching the light and the passersby was where the shopkeeper could most often be found. Light was different, softer, more diffused when streaming through such portals, especially since the shopkeeper rarely cleaned them. *Too tall*, he reasoned. And so they remained, the outsides washed only by summer rains.

Although orderly, the inside of the shop was cleaned about as often as the windows. The wood floors were swept regularly, but little else received the same care.

1

Troy W. Rasmussen

The books, stacked on shelves in no particular order, gained much of their character from layers of dust. Countless treasures lay scattered around the shop with numerous antiques strewn throughout. Costly and rare artifacts from past eras graced an old table or a hand-carved sideboard: a small cameo brooch, an oil painting of a sailboat battling the rages of a storm, a small bust of Beethoven with a chip in the back of his head. Each found a temporary lodging among well-worn leather and tapestry furniture.

Comfort was the order of the shop, additionally enhanced when the shopkeeper added the brass coffee machine several years prior. Little else, except maybe the scent of his pipe tobacco, said "comfort" like the smell of coffee. Small tables and weathered couches placed in front of the windows encouraged visitors to relax into themselves and enjoy a cup of java. Besides coffee, other treats such as a hot cocoa—made thick and smooth from ancient Mayan recipes—were available for customers to enjoy.

The most ornate (some would say imposing) element in the shop was the counter from which the shopkeeper greeted visitors. Carved from a two-hundred-year-old oak and inlaid with teak, grand in its Old World manner and artistry, it rarely failed to elicit comments from shop visitors. The counter didn't require dusting: nearly all ran their hands along its timeworn top and verdigris edges, even as their eyes followed the grain of wood sculpted into Victorian detail.

Monday
Had an interesting visitor today. A young boy by the name of Chester, claiming to be all of eight years old, walked in and proceeded to inspect the

The Shopkeeper's Journal

place as if he was the proprietor. A fine bluff, but a bluff all the same. Watching someone who knows they are being watched provides its own entertainment...

Sideways glances followed by a few more tentative steps deeper into an unknown world...an attempt to touch the forbidden artifact...another glance. A slow stroll turns into a walk of amazement as large rooms, high ceilings, and furniture the size of monsters begin to take on the wonder that lives in the imagination of the small creatures that are boys. It's not long before tentative steps gain purpose, and hesitant touches become a mindless drag of the hand across the marble top of a table or curve of a lamp. Dusting!

Chester stopped at the base of the wooden circular staircase, with ornately carved handrails and well-worn steps leading to rows of books two and three stories up. His slow approach to the "gates of the kingdom," and all the wonder that lay beyond, was apparent in his eyes. Chester's thoughts went to the question boys often ask themselves: *Does the first step end it all (the shopkeeper is watching), or does it start the magic?*

Music came from somewhere—starting, he was sure, the moment his foot landed on the step. The magic began.

Wooden steps became ancient stone leading up the side of a great castle, and he a knight, stealing in the dark to rescue a beautiful maiden. Would he ever reach her?

Troy W. Rasmussen

The Mighty Chester breathed in silently, so the seventy-five guards lying in wait at the top would not know of his coming. A pretty girl could not—should not—be kept in such places against her will, especially when the knight of her heart was lurking about to save the day.

Halfway there and, still, he was undetected; it had to remain so. All depended on his reaching her in time. With magic on his side, Sir Chester bounded the final few steps, his sword drawn, and his heart pounding with the rhythm of—

"Chester?" His mother's voice, laced with the conditioned understanding of his antics and what it took to gain his attention, wafted through the air and up the stairs to him.

Foiled. All of it, gone with just one word. Chester turned to see his mother at the bottom of what had moments ago been the only entrance to the castle, but the shopkeeper noticed his mother's interruption didn't seem to faze the boy much. And why should it? It was a common thing for boys to wander and mothers to hunt them down. Less reluctantly than the shopkeeper expected, Chester descended the steps, bounding the last few, and the shopkeeper smiled to himself.

The magic held.

With no other words spoken, Chester's mother escorted him out of the shop to yet another destination where dragons and bad guys were sure to lurk. As they passed the counter, Chester turned toward his compatriot in crime—magic. The shopkeeper responded with a secretive gleam in his eye and the sly movement of his finger against his lips: "Shh."

Chester knew he would be back, and so did the shopkeeper. Castle steps could be found anywhere in a

The Shopkeeper's Journal

boy's imagination. Someone who understood the magic was not so easily discovered.

> *Wednesday*
> Trudy came as she always does, with a short wave hello accompanied by a look of longing and remembrance about her face. It's the same each time when Trudy comes to play the piano. I recall the first time she came in, a woman finding something she had been looking for, yet with no interest to buy.

"Hello," said Trudy.

"Mmmm." The shopkeeper acknowledged his guest with a nod of his head. There was something about her greeting that caught his attention, a hello less a greeting than a reason. He had observed this same thing many times and was continually intrigued by how this one word caused the speaker to feel he or she had gained an unneeded acceptance to browse.

Trudy wasn't browsing, though. She had long since found the object of her interest during the many times she'd passed through the shop.

The piano sat at the far end of the shop, just to the other side of the last plate glass window. Each morning, the light caught the tufted leather bench that topped graceful, yet sturdy, Victorian carved legs. Before reaching the pinnacle of the window, the light slowly moved across the faded, worn keys of the instrument, illuminating for a few moments the grandeur that once was.

The shopkeeper watched the trek each day, entertaining the idea that the morning light creeping

5

Troy W. Rasmussen

across the piano started the music and the evening light, in retreat across a similar path, slowly closed the lid on the keys.

Exactly who created the piano was knowledge that had been lost, but the small price tag hanging from its edge notified visitors it was the most costly piece in the shop.

The rich wood bending gracefully around the body was polished smooth, highlighting detailed carvings of curved fleurs-de-lis. One's glance couldn't help but follow the elaborate carvings, sloping gently down to nestle behind the necks of swans, each of which comprised one of the piano legs. The swans' wings reached upward and back, resting flat against the side of the instrument; in a depiction of flight about to begin, the birds' necks dipped low, graceful, caught in the final moment of ease before taking to the air.

In contrast to other such instruments the shopkeeper had seen over the years, the piano's craftsman had elected not to coat the piece in layers of lacquer, but to polish it smooth with endless hours of hand-rubbing with oil. The effect caused an onlooker to gently draw his hand across its surface, exactly what the craftsman had in mind. Its beauty was enhanced, made all the richer, for the polishing—dusting, really—it received from so many imparting the oil from their hands deeper into its surface.

When people enquired about it, the shopkeeper explained: the piano came from a grand eighteenth-century chateau in Eastern Europe, where it had graced the halls of a large ballroom with inlaid parquet floors. Legend held that the piano was commissioned as a gift to the bride of a wealthy landowner. Although a centerpiece to the ballroom, it was rarely played during such occasions. Instead, the landowner's wife would play her chords privately, intimately, for the man she loved.

The Shopkeeper's Journal

The hours they spent together in the hall, her fingers touching each key in a rhythmic flow of sound, had a way of easing his day and enhancing hers. Women of her class were raised to play an instrument as part of their education—albeit playing an instrument and mastering it were two different things.

The music stopped the day she lost her love.

He had been riding his favorite horse through the hills when the horse's foreleg caught in the hole of some ground-dwelling creature, one the rider had failed to see. With the horse's leg shattered, his rider was thrown headlong, and his neck snapped on impact. The horse died shortly after—as did, in a way, the landowner's wife, her heart unable to withstand the same force that took her lover. Like a rose bush without blooms, she continued living, but without glory.

The shopkeeper kept music on in the background, except when Trudy came. Just as the first notes of her playing sounded, the shopkeeper would reach behind the counter and turn the music off.

Trudy played as if no one else was present; clearly, she didn't consider the shopkeeper intruding, for which he was glad. The way she played reminded him of the rage of ocean tides calmed by the setting sun into a gentle rush across the sand.

Thursday
Opened the shop early today. Not uncommon. I glanced through the windows and calculated it would still take several more minutes for the sun to tell the world another day was beginning. Time to start the coffee.

7

Troy W. Rasmussen

> The rays of new light found me
> standing in wait for the first shaft to break
> the hills and pierce the room. Yet another
> reminder someone needs to dust. The
> scent of coffee began to permeate the air
> just as a couple entered the shop. That
> they arrived wasn't the surprise; that they
> arrived together was. The strain and
> discord toward one another was as
> palpable as the dust in the air. As usual,
> they noticed the counter. Not so much for
> the work of art it is, but for the mutual
> distraction it provided for two people
> whom had long since failed to find
> something to talk about.

After a polite greeting and halfhearted smile, the two began the trek though the shop; she looked one way, he the other. Little except an elegant wood sculpture, hand carved by an artisan in Malaysia, caught their eyes.

"Well," she said, and looked at her husband as if to ask, *does this piece meet the mark?* His shrug was all the answer she received. Their browsing didn't last long, but as they were about to leave, the woman commented on the counter. The shopkeeper explained the counter was made by a craftsman, the sculpture, by an artist.

At that moment the man turned toward the shopkeeper with a look of question—or, the shopkeeper speculated, a challenge? Noting his sudden turn, the woman spoke up.

"What can you tell us about the wood sculpture over there?" She pointed toward it.

"It was created by an aged artisan in Malaysia many years ago. It took three years to complete." The shopkeeper explained how the artisan followed the grain

The Shopkeeper's Journal

of the wood to release the shape of the piece. "There were no images from the artist's mind, only the grain."

"There isn't any shape to the thing," the man said.

"All things have shape, sir," said the shopkeeper. "The artisan of the piece noted only this: 'Many things bring shape. Here, the wind, and rain, and sun bring all that is needed to shape the tree. The tree may grow or die, but either way its shape is formed by the force of another.'"

"That sounds rather ephemeral," the man said sarcastically. "What is it this 'artisan' is suggesting?"

The shopkeeper met the man's eyes for a moment before he went on.

"His meaning will come differently to you than to me." The shopkeeper moseyed a short distance to an antique cabinet and withdrew a bottle of merlot. Handing it to the couple, he added, "Enjoy this while you ponder his meaning…or not."

The couple stood still for a moment, but accepted the bottle of wine, added a hesitant "thank you," and left.

A few days later, the couple returned, noticeably more at ease with each other—but also, seemingly on a mission. With a quick "hello," they proceeded to the back of the shop as if predestined to go to exactly that spot. Moments later the woman, her husband well in tow, approached the counter with a look of dismay.

"Sir," she said anxiously," the wood piece that was just over there, the one by the Malaysian artist. Has it sold?"

"Mmmm," replied the shopkeeper. His eyebrows knitted together.

Thinking the situation required further insight, the man added, "Surely you recall it. You told us of its story and creation, how the artisan—"

Troy W. Rasmussen

"How was the wine?" the shopkeeper interrupted.

With sheepish grins, the couple looked at each other like teenagers reliving a night of parking in the woods.

"I'm not a fan of wine," the man said, "but the bottle you gave us seemed to have worked a bit of magic."

"We bought two more bottles at the store across the street from our hotel," the woman said.

"Spent a lot of time in the Jacuzzi tub."

The woman gave a satisfied sigh and, after checking the position of her wedding ring, said, "Added some bubbles."

"Oh, my God," the man said, looking toward the shopkeeper, "bubbles everywhere. Nearly broke my neck getting out of the damn thing."

"You weren't out long," she said.

Caught in her meaning, the man leaned toward the shopkeeper, "Should have brought the extra bottle with us to begin with."

The shopkeeper reached under the counter and pulled out a nondescript box wrapped in plain paper, making due note of the woman's hands involuntarily stroking the counter top. *No dusting again today,* he thought.

The shopkeeper handed the package to the couple. "The piece you were looking for. Keep it clear of bubbles."

The amazed clarity of its contents spread across their faces.

"But—how? How did you—?" the man stammered.

Accepting the package, the woman gave the shopkeeper a soft smile. "Thank you."

To all things is the right time given.

The Shopkeeper's Journal

Friday

Chester arrived again this afternoon. It was good to see him. He was unmistakably here for a purpose. Once inside the door, he stopped a few feet in front of the counter. Our stares met each other and held for a minute or two; then, I nodded my head to the left. Chester turned and started walking in that direction. It's amazing, the trust and understanding of children, especially when curiosity rules the moment.

Chester walked to the back of the shop taking in the new sights, his destination a large wardrobe nestled in the corner at the back of the shop. Turning his head upward, he thought the piece of furniture seemed more like a fort than a place to store clothing.

The shopkeeper stood at Chester's left side, his expression a mirror of the boy's excitement. Not so much that the wardrobe was a fort; rather, the treasures it held would become all the more potent to a boy whose imagination needed a place to run.

"There are two locks," the shopkeeper said.

As he looked the front of the wardrobe over, Chester shook his head. "There's only one, mister."

"Mmmm, only to those who don't know the secret location of the other. Once you discover the hidden lock, you're honor bound to keep its location a secret. "

The wonder grew in Chester's eyes with the thrill of a mystery. The shopkeeper stepped back, enjoying a child's wonder in a few moments of reflection. Chester didn't hesitate; he immediately began looking the wardrobe over for some hint of the lock's location. How

11

Troy W. Rasmussen

he would open it was a problem he'd solve when the time came.

The shopkeeper returned to the counter just as Chester's mother stepped through the door.

"Has Chester come in here, by chance?" she asked. The shopkeeper noticed an urgency about the woman, as if she were running late.

"Mmmm." Using his pipe as a pointer, the shopkeeper indicated where Chester could be found. As the boy's mother moved in that direction, the shopkeeper went on, "There are places a boy can be and places he shouldn't."

The shopkeeper's statement left a look of confusion on the woman's face as she deliberated its meaning. *Was it okay for Chester to be here or not?* The shopkeeper wasn't fond of questions, even those unspoken. He offered only, "The shop doesn't close until everyone has left."

The young woman remained where she stood, weighing his words until it became apparent that she understood what he meant. Chester was safe in this place.

The shopkeeper kept a stack of cards on the corner of the counter, and he picked up one off the top and gave it to her.

Glancing at the card, she saw, stamped in a plain font, ten digits of a phone number.

The woman introduced herself as Sheila.

"Mmmm." The shopkeeper merely raised his eyebrows in reply.

"I have a meeting I can't miss." She glanced toward the back of the shop. "I'll be back as soon as I can."

The shopkeeper took a long draw on his pipe.

"Here." Finally, the woman took a pen from her purse and wrote her phone number on the back of the

The Shopkeeper's Journal

card then handed it to the shopkeeper. "If anything happens, dial that number. It's my cell phone."

The shopkeeper nodded.

Chester walked to the counter a few moments later, clearly exasperated.

"The key worked?" asked the shopkeeper.

Chester was reluctant to admit he hadn't turned it. "Does it help find the hidden lock?" he asked instead.

"Mmmm."

Boys firmly locked in the grip of challenge and the pursuit of hidden treasures need little motivation to continue their search. Chester turned swiftly and headed back the way he came. Once he arrived at the wardrobe, he wasted little time turning the gilded key protruding from the lock.

Click.

To a boy in the midst of discovery, it was a heart-stopping sound. With eyes wide in wonder and concentration, Chester slowly pulled on the old handle— but nothing happened. Not the slightest budge. He paused, thinking. The key was a given. It was the hidden lock he sought, and he wasn't going to stop until he found it.

Glaring at the door as if intimidation would cause it to magically spring open, Chester pondered his dilemma. He examined the lock again, and then discovered what he'd missed the first time: turning the key had caused a small oval piece, located a few inches from the lock, to pop out. Chester noticed the protruding piece of wood— another heart-stopping moment. He'd done it! The secret was discovered, and he was the victor!

Reaching his hand to the left, Chester took hold of the piece of wood and turned it back and forth, waiting for something to catch…and it did. He pulled again on

13

Troy W. Rasmussen

the door and, with a release of musty dampness and a creek of hinges long in need of oil, it swung open.

From behind the counter, the shopkeeper raised a knowing brow. With that telltale sound, he had all the information he needed to know where Chester would be found for some time.

The shopkeeper's revelry was interrupted by the appearance of a weathered man strolling by the shop. People strolling by were not uncommon, but their displaying an interest in the flowerbeds just outside the door was. Other than weeds and the creeping phlox wedged firmly between the stones, there were no other plants someone would notice enough to pause, let alone stop.

This man, however, was different.

As the shopkeeper watched, the man sat down on the edge of the flowerbeds and slowly, gently, pulled the weeds. His wide-brimmed hat was the only shade to his deeply tanned skin. As the shopkeeper watched, he heard the man mumbling something incoherent. Whatever it was, the words seemed to compel the man to continue.

The inside of the wardrobe looked like any other, but to Chester, the cavernous space found behind the two large doors extended much further than the wall of the shop it stood against, and the object he sought now lay just inside. Centered on a pedestal resembling a column from ancient Rome sat a rectangular wood box. Oversized nails with odd-shaped square heads held the old box together. He stared, mesmerized for a moment. He had never seen such a thing.

As his eyes adjusted to the darkness within, Chester also noticed the box had a drawer.

14

The Shopkeeper's Journal

There was no question in his young mind what to do next. Stepping into the wardrobe, he reached out, slowly turned the box's latch, and lifted the lid. Awed, he whispered, "The dagger of Prince Shahzada."

Resting on a plain piece of muslin cloth, the ornate weapon with its carved ivory handle became, in his imagination, the key to solving the ills of the world——and Chester the heir apparent for having found it. The blade of the dagger was too long for someone his age to handle, yet the desire to do just that won the short battle between the equally heart-stopping notions of *should I* and *shouldn't I.*

In the twinkle of an eye, he was a hero, surrounded by cheers ringing loud in the square. The parade continued for hours, with the conquering hero carried through the streets. Chester, "Discoverer of the Dagger," was about to take his place in history when a strange sensation prickled the hairs on his neck.

Turning slowly around, Chester found himself not in the streets of a far-off land, but standing face to face with the shopkeeper.

"Hidden locks are created for keeping things safe," said the shopkeeper.

"I know where the hidden lock is, and how it works. I'll keep it safe."

"Mmmm."

"There's a drawer." Chester turned toward the box and pointed with his elbow. It was half statement, half question.

"To all things is the right time given," the shopkeeper replied.

Chester wasn't sure what the shopkeeper meant. But he understood enough to know the dagger should be placed back in the box and the contents of the drawer left

Troy W. Rasmussen

to another time. When Sheila arrived back at the store, she found her son sitting calmly on the sofa, sipping a cold drink.

When he left the shop that evening, the shopkeeper noticed the freshly turned soil in the flowerbed where weeds had once been.

"Mmmm."

Saturday
The man who has been pulling weeds in the flowerbed was at the shop again today. For days he's been coming by, pulling weeds, tending the soil, and mumbling to himself.

Today, he brought along a small cart loaded with a variety of plants and flowers. His visit was longer than usual. Not surprising, since the time to plant is here. I watched, as often as visitors to the shop allowed, his methodical movements: selecting, bending, planting, and mumbling. Such ease of purpose.

After filling a glass with water, the shopkeeper approached the man, still entrenched in his work, and set the refreshment on the edge of the flowerbed. Without missing a beat to his well-established rhythm, the man picked up the glass of water and gently began pouring it over the plants recently placed into the rich soil.

To all things is the right time given.

The following morning the man tending the flowerbeds arrived early, as morning light made its ritualistic pass over the face of the piano and the coffee machine's brew alarm sounded. The shopkeeper poured a

The Shopkeeper's Journal

cup of the rich blend and set it on the edge of the flowerbed. At first the man didn't say anything, so the shopkeeper followed suit.

As the shopkeeper headed back to the counter, the man nodded, brushed his hands together, and spoke. "You could add some real taste to that with a good splash of rum."

Troy W. Rasmussen

Chapter 2

Monday
Bacardi—a fitting name for someone with an affinity for the liquor by the same name—has finished the flowerbed. He continues to stop by, though, checking the flowers, banishing weeds, mumbling, and sipping a cup of coffee with a "good splash of rum" in it.

The shopkeeper, a cup of coffee and rum in his hand, stood in the doorway. "Per your request."

"Umphf."

The shopkeeper was undeterred by the man's indifference. "No charge."

The man set aside his trowel and stood to face the shopkeeper. "You prone to givin' stuff away?"

"As the situation demands, I am."

The man wiped his hands on his pants before taking the cup and tasting the brew. "It'll do."

"The town's flower beds are all the better for your care of them, and now, those here…"

"Ain't nothin'. It's what I do. People like lookin' at a nice garden, but most don't care for the work it takes to keep them that way."

"Mmmm."

The man gulped the remainder of his drink and wiped his mouth with the back of his hand. "Bacardi's the name. Not the one I was given, but the one I go by."

"And how does one come by such a name?"

The Shopkeeper's Journal

"That goes back a ways. We were a lot younger with too much time on our hands."

"We?"

"Me and two other guys grew up together. Prowlin' about with a bottle of rum and up to no good." Bacardi scratched his chin. "Can't say I remember it all, but I was braggin' about bein' able to finish that bottle off. Start chugging what's left with them other two chantin' 'Bacardi'. I did what I said I would. Never no mind that it all came back up a few minutes later. Been Bacardi ever since."

"And this is why you add it to your coffee?"

"Nah. Just like the taste, that's all. Like coffee and I like rum. Figure a guy can't go wrong putting the two together."

> *Tuesday*
> Chester was in again today, the lure of the dagger and the mysteries a young boy's imagination creates proving too much to resist. To date, his coming and going is marked only by a quick wave as he passes the counter on his way to the wardrobe. The newness of the wonder has yet to dull; he approaches slowly, eyes widening, as the story in his mind unfolds. The familiar click of one lock, followed by the pop of the second, and the inevitable creak of hinges, together write a new chapter.

The crowds continued their revelry as the young explorer progressed through the streets. Young and old put their days on hold to come and see the one who had

Troy W. Rasmussen

returned with the dagger of Prince Shahzada. The human throng opened before him like gates as Chester the Great moved forward toward his destiny.

The hero's welcome concluded with Chester standing before two enormous gates, their heavy carvings showing wear. Twelve guards in brightly colored costumes stood immovable and strong, six to a side. As Chester stood before the aperture, the cheers of the crowd stilled. Only the quiet of the desert breeze could be heard.

A large metal rod hung heavily over a thick, richly carved and scarred metal plate. All heroes instinctively knew what the scars were from—the banging of the rod, demanding entrance.

Stepping forward, Chester took hold of the rod and with three mighty swings banged the rod against the plate. Those present held their breath, all attention on the gates; in the stillness of the moment, each contact with the door sent a reverb of sound through the ancient posts. Soon after, the gates moved, breaking the crowd's suspense, and they responded with deafening cheers. The adventurer had been granted access. Chester, a powerful presence of calm nobility, continued on his path toward the temple.

Trumpets sounded as the doors to the temple began to open seemingly of their own accord.

All such things happen in the magic kingdoms eight-year-old boys create. What doesn't are things like the gentle tap on the shoulder Chester felt as a turned to see the shopkeeper.

With a knowing stare, the shopkeeper held out a weathered leather satchel, the kind every explorer needs to carry his discoveries. Taking hold of the strap, Chester placed the satchel across his shoulder and felt the weight

The Shopkeeper's Journal

of the gift as it settled at his side. He turned back to the box, slowly lifting the latch and lid to gaze again at the dagger. The sun breaking through the window caught the glint of the blade and the artistry of the handle.

Chester moved forward to lift the dagger from its encasement and place it in the satchel, the realization of the miracle of the satchel now firmly understood: he and his prize were no longer bound by the confines of the wardrobe.

Chester stood before the temple doors, the dagger of Prince Shahzada resting safely in his satchel. Moving amongst yet more well-wishers chanting his praise, he found himself focusing on an elevated platform illuminated at the far wall. Standing at the top of the twenty-four steps leading up to the platform was the richly dressed, enormously powerful Prince Shahzada.

The Mighty Chester moved as if in a dream. Aware of hands and fingers reaching out to touch him as he passed by...children, scrambling here and there, poking their heads between the legs of taller adults in an effort to gain a better glimpse of him. Reaching the base of the steps, Chester began his ascent. Only a few had made this journey, and only one carried with him the hope and promise the return of the lost dagger would bring.

Reaching the pinnacle, he met Prince Shahzada's gaze and paused only long enough for a brief bow before he reached into his satchel and pulled out the dagger. Lowering his head, Chester held the dagger out to the Prince, who received the weapon in his hands and raised it above his head. A roar rose from the crowd, growing ever more powerful as the Prince turned to set the dagger in its rightful place.

Troy W. Rasmussen

The hero's code, something all explorers instinctively know, governed Chester's actions in all things—among them, that he knew he would seek no reward. He merely bowed in homage once more to the prince and then turned to descend the platform when a weighty hand gripped his shoulder.

"Chester."

The sound of the voice brought him slowly back to reality, but even so, Chester took a few moments to realize he was no longer standing in front of the wardrobe, but on the landing of the circular stairway— the former sole entrance to a certain castle. The shopkeeper stood at the foot of the staircase, his expression somber.

"A hero's reward," the shopkeeper said quietly, "must be paid."

What did those words mean? Chester could hardly fathom them, and he thought them over as he took his time descending the stairs. As he reached the base of the staircase, the shopkeeper turned and led him once more toward the back of the shop. Chester's curiosity and caution held as they approached the wardrobe, its doors still open, when he felt panic well up within him.

It was time to return the dagger to the box.

With sad understanding, he began to open his satchel to retrieve the dagger, but the gentle touch of the shopkeeper's hand stayed him mid-motion.

Tilting his head toward the box, the shopkeeper gave a quiet "Mmmm" before looking back at Chester, who hardly dared to breathe at what he sensed in that single word...

Magic restored.

The drawer of the box was to be opened.

22

The Shopkeeper's Journal

Chester needed no further prodding to move forward and seize the knob on the drawer. The drawer slid open, revealing what was to every young boy a reward of unfathomable awesomeness—fireworks. Almost afraid to hope, Chester looked toward the shopkeeper, who merely nodded.

Snatching the fireworks up, Chester proceeded to the shop's front door and stepped out into the day, his heart beating with excitement. Laying the string of fireworks on the sidewalk, he stepped back to allow the shopkeeper to bend forward and set the fuse alight.

The roar and smoke of a string of two hundred fireworks was almost too much for him. The canal of buildings made the noise much bigger than the little explosives could have made on their own, and hearing it, he couldn't stand still.

"Woohoo!" he cried out, as the fireworks bounced madly around him. Passersby, seeing the event, thought that the boy danced as madly as the sparks flew in the air.

As the noise subsided and the smoke and shards of paper drifted away in the breeze, Chester turned to the shopkeeper and gave him a high five. Such a salute wasn't lost on the shopkeeper, and he heartily returned it.

"Those are illegal, you know," came an irritated voice.

Chester and the shopkeeper turned to see Mrs. Thrilkil across the street. Contrary to what her name portrayed, however, she didn't diminish their joy.

Troy W. Rasmussen

Chapter 3

Tuesday

Mrs. Thrilkil. Most pronounced it "Thrill Kill," and when they did so within her hearing, were promptly informed, "It's pronounced *Thrulkul*." One wonders, though. It wasn't surprising that yesterday's fireworks elicited the response they did. People of a "thrill-killing" nature are often discomfited by such spectacles. (The fireworks probably bothered her, too.)

Mrs. Thrilkil lived in the apartment above the shop she owned and worked in. Throughout the day she could be seen sweeping the walk, stopping only to stretch her back and adjust an apron invariably encrusted with clay.

Mrs. Thrilkil was a potter of extraordinary talent, with the work of her potter's wheel on display and for sale throughout her shop. Some pieces, the rare ones, were formed by hand and not on the pottery wheel. Had anyone actually seen Mrs. Thrilkil in the process of creating one of these pieces, they would have the impression it was more an act of bludgeoning rather than the intricate steps of creating a piece of art.

The clay was first kneaded by hand, then thrown countless times into the unyielding wood of an old butcher block table. The assault didn't stop there. Mrs. Thrilkil then began pounding away at the mass with gnarled, unforgiving blows of her fist. Passersby couldn't

24

The Shopkeeper's Journal

help but stop and wonder at the sounds the process produced, which was often accompanied by unintelligible words spoken in what was assumed her native tongue. Once the battering came to a halt, Mrs. Thrilkil would sit, often for long periods of time, staring at the lump. When the inspiration took hold though, she remained at the task of creation, sometimes for days, until the final work emerged. And there it would sit under the damp cloth shroud until the kiln was to the required degree to bake the soft compound into its hardened form. The next step, glazing, was an art in itself, and therein lay the mastery of the craftsmanship of Mrs. Thrilkil.

Friday
The talent of the young man who came into the shop this evening is remarkable. The music emitted from the easy strums of his guitar strings was of such quality as to cause those within hearing to stop and listen, to reflect and wonder, to dream and wish; longing for his talent, thankful he had it.

Choosing a caved-in, slouching couch, the young man arranged a few cushions, sat back, then raised and rested his Borelli-encased feet on the table. From his perch, some distance from the counter, he ordered a Viennese coffee, thanked me as politely as he asked, then began to play.

Throughout the evening, visitors to the shop periodically stopped to listen, make comments about the grandeur of the guitar player's talent, or content themselves with quiet conversation. Small groups formed

25

Troy W. Rasmussen

amongst the tables and old furniture in the front of the shop; whether they knew it or not, the music had already begun creating the new social event Friday evenings would become.

> *Saturday*
> Chester wandered in today, his usual curiosity and excitement for the wonders of life noticeably dimmed. No far-off travels today, apparently, only the particular sadness young boys show when their world has taken a turn they don't understand.

Noticing his mood, the shopkeeper approached Chester and set a bottle of soda on the table next to him. (An ice-cold soda cures many ills.) Chester took a deep swig, then slumped forward, staring at the ice crystals snaking down the side of the bottle for a few moments before he spoke.

"Mom got a call, and she's crying," he murmured. Another chunk of ice slid down the bottle onto Chester's hand. "Something happened. Something about my dad, but I don't know exactly what." Absentmindedly, he took another gulp.

The shopkeeper merely nodded his head and waited.

Chester looked up into the shopkeeper's eyes. "What's a national hero?"

The Shopkeeper's Journal

Chapter 4

Wednesday

Does the pain of a loved one's loss ever dim? The shop was closed today, in honor of the man Chester called Dad. Sheila was in earlier, expressing her concern for the lad. I assured her that he would make it through, but when grief is new and raw, words meant to comfort don't always have that effect.

Chester's father was a military man, part of a band of men operating covertly in situations of which few know the reality but all enjoy the resultant freedom. Chester came into the shop earlier this morning without speaking a word; after spending a few short moments in the back of the store, he solemnly walked out.

The honors bestowed on Chester's father were met with blank stares by those present. Few had met the man, but where tragedies in small communities are concerned, that didn't matter. Chester stared at a bouquet of flowers as the colonel approached his mother, bearing the neatly folded flag that had draped his father's casket.

"On behalf of the President of the United States, a grateful nation, and a proud Marine Corps, this flag is presented...." Chester didn't hear the rest of the colonel's words. His mind was working out the timing of his plan

Troy W. Rasmussen

to say goodbye to his father. He took a deep breath and stood up.

Standing opposite Chester, the shopkeeper sensed something seemingly resolving itself in the mind of the young boy. As the minister concluded the service and people began to leave, Chester walked to the end of his father's casket, with one hand in his satchel. Before the crowd had dispersed, he pulled out a fistful of fireworks and said quietly, "The rewards of a hero must be paid."

Nodding in understanding, the shopkeeper walked over and lit the string of fireworks.

This time, the boy didn't jump around or cheer, only stood silently, tears rolling down his cheeks. The noise subsided, the solemnness returned, and the mourners finished their exit, save Mrs. Thrilkil.

"Those are illegal, you know."

> *Thursday*
> The flower bed has a new tenant:
> Bacardi planted a Poppy in memory of
> Chester's father.
>
> He stayed longer than normal,
> uncharacteristically asking me to add a
> double portion of rum to his coffee. His
> work complete, Bacardi sat quietly for a
> few moments before downing the hot
> mixture in what seemed a single gulp.
> With a nod of his head, he raised the cup
> to the sky in a gesture of respect, then
> smashed it to the ground—honor given.

The shopkeeper collected the shards of Bacardi's cup and placed them in the alabaster box containing the charred remains of the fireworks Chester brought to his father's funeral. (To this day, it can be found sitting in

The Shopkeeper's Journal

the wardrobe, next to the box containing the dagger of Prince Shahzada—honor given.)

> *Friday*
> Time and the incomparable chords
> from the guitar of an accomplished
> musician possess the ability, it would
> seem, to heal the wounds of community
> loss. Although the mood of the evening
> was more subdued, the rejuvenation was
> apparent and welcome, as was the arrival
> of Gordo. If the universe possessed a
> young man more comfortable in his own
> skin, it surely is a wonder.

Gordo entered the shop that evening as if he had been doing so for some time. Indeed, a familiar lift of the chin from the guitar player made it seem he had. Wearing tattered jeans, leather flip-flops, and a shirt that defined "comfortable," Gordo strolled to the counter and ordered what would become his "usual"—a Mayan hot cocoa, hold the cinnamon.

Unlike the guitar player, Gordo was a traveler. The light in his eyes, the tanned skin, the ease among others in the room were visible indicators that such a lifestyle suited him. His dreadlocks—a story in themselves—hung heavy and thick down his back, adding yet another layer of "mod" to his presence.

Leaning forward, Gordo moved his head from side to side, noting the detail work of the counter. "Nice piece," he said. No dusting for Gordo. "This your place?" he asked the shopkeeper.

"Mmmm."

Troy W. Rasmussen

Gordo nodded, picked up his cup of cocoa and drank the thick mixture in full, smacking his lips in contentment. He soon made his way toward the guitar player, picking up a chair for himself as he went. Straddling the chair backward, he leaned into it and drummed his fingers to the beat of the music. When the song ended, he and the guitar player caught up with each other's travels since they'd last met up, a little under a year before.

Gordo, returning from an excursion in South Africa, was on his way to visit family. He arrived unannounced, as was his custom, to find his sister Julia and her husband Bart sitting on the back patio of their home in the hills, Julia with a Mai Tai and Bart sipping iced tea.

"You look fantastic." With that greeting, Gordo leaned into his sister to kiss her on the forehead, a gesture that made her squeal in delight.

"We had no idea you were coming!" she exclaimed. "We didn't even know you were in the country. And why would we? When have we? You've been gone a long time."

"The worlds a big place, Jules, lots to see," Gordo replied.

Releasing her death grip from his neck, Julia stepped back and left Gordo free to shake Bart's hand. Bart, not content with a handshake, embraced his brother-in-law instead.

"Good to see you," he said with a grin.

They spent the rest of the afternoon in the yard as Gordo, his long hair tied back with a leather strap, recounted life since last he'd seen Julia. He'd traveled the Southern Hemisphere, trekked through Australia, and met an aboriginal sage. From there, he'd sailed to the small island of Tristan, discovering a society not very

30

The Shopkeeper's Journal

receptive to newcomers—but all too willing to welcome his unassuming self.

A few months later, Gordo was on the plains of Tanzania, to see for himself the power and magnitude of the Wildebeest migration. Leaving camp one day, ignoring the danger, he'd lain on the ground too close to the moving mass of animals and had been nearly trampled. When a local guide asked what he was doing, he simply said, "Have you ever wondered what the ground feels like when they're rushing by?"

Morocco found Gordo a perfect fit to its bright colors, energetic markets, and exotic atmosphere. He shared the love of a local woman while there and learned, to a degree, how to charm a snake out of a basket. The laughter of the locals rang loud when he'd asked, "Why don't you just reach in and take it out?"

A short safari in Namibia, including bouldering and cave camping in the Namib Desert, proved the ideal location for Gordo to spend some time to himself. His mind and body were tight friends, but every now and then, one demanded a break from the other.

Giza was a temptation that didn't last long on his itinerary. Not that the grandeur wasn't impressive, but a more esoteric experience beckoned.

Esoteric or not, hiking Kilimanjaro was an excursion not to be missed. The nine-inch scar running from his hip to mid-thigh had been a gift from the mountain, eliciting many a question from those seeing it—which were many. Gordo was not fond of clothes, preferring to feel the elements directly on his skin. Thus, his time in Africa concluded with his face turned toward the heavens, taking in the grandeur of the Southern Cross, without apparel.

Troy W. Rasmussen

Chapter 5

Wednesday
Although more affable, Trudy still showed a sadness about her. On a day warmer than most, she asked for a cold melon drink before taking her seat at the piano. The moment she played, I could tell the piece meant something special to her, and the tears rolling down her cheeks confirmed my suspicions.

Trudy and her husband of many years were out on the town celebrating their wedding anniversary. The evening began with a bouquet of azaleas, Trudy's favorite flower, plus a handwritten card her love had given her expressing his thanks for all she was to him; it ended with dinner at an exclusive fine dining establishment. The meal wasn't a financial burden, but it was more extravagant than either had allowed themselves through the years.

As the evening progressed, the band struck up a rendition of "their song," and Trudy's husband asked her to dance. The lack of a dance floor didn't deter them; they stood to one side of their table and swayed to the music, with steps of their own they'd made up long ago.

The world around them faded, leaving just the two of them, speaking softly to one another. Only after the song finished did they realize others in the restaurant had stopped to watch them and were applauding. It was a night to remember.

The Shopkeeper's Journal

Later, as the two were walking down the street deep in the experience of the other, a young man walking by bumped into Trudy.

"Watch where you're going, bitch."

"Hey! Watch your mouth," Trudy's husband called out. "How about you apologize?"

"What for? I ain't done nothin' wrong. Sidewalk ain't yours. How 'bout you get outta my way?"

Incensed by the young man's rudeness, Trudy's husband placed himself protectively in front of her. "There's no call for this. Apologize to my wife."

"What are you gonna do about it, old man?"

Trudy took hold of her husband's arm. "It's nothing. Let's go."

"I will not. Not until this young man apologizes."

"You're in for a long wait, mister."

Trudy's husband pulled free from her grasp and stepped toward the young man, who took this as an affront and punched him in the face.

"Stop it!" Trudy cried out.

Although the punch was not enough to do serious harm, her husband stumbled backward, and fearing he would slam into Trudy, shifted his weight and fell head-first against a street sign.

The young man ran down the street as Trudy bent to check on her husband. She shifted her weight to cradle his head and began calling out his name, but there was no response.

Patrons in the restaurant rushed outside to assist.

Trudy rocked her husband as the blood from his head wound soaked into her dress. "Wake up. Please wake up." *We were just dancing. How is this happening? We were just dancing.*

"Ma'am. The paramedics are here."

33

Troy W. Rasmussen

Trudy took the man's hand and stood shaking as she watched the emergency medical team rush to her husband's aid.

"Is he okay?" Trudy turned to the man who had helped her up. "We were just dancing. He was just a boy. It was nothing—nothing."

"I know. We saw it from inside."

"Just an ugly name, that's all. How did it come to this?"

To Trudy, the minutes turned into hours as she watched the paramedics rip open packets of gauze to stop the bleeding.

"Please tell me he's all right."

At the hospital, Trudy's husband was rushed into emergency surgery to relieve the pressure from the blunt force trauma to his head. She spent the next three days at her husband's bedside waiting for him to wake up. He never did.

Trudy's tears fell against his face as she leaned over him one last time. "Goodbye, my love. I'll always remember the music and how we danced."

Each Wednesday, as Trudy sat at the piano to play her memories, she would do so with a periodic glance at the bouquet of azaleas arranged in a lead crystal vase atop the piano.

She never asked where they came from.

Tonight, Trudy concluded her playing, wiped her tears, and stood to go. She thanked the shopkeeper for the cool drink, then left without another word.

As the shopkeeper went through the motions of closing the shop for the day, he stopped at the piano and removed its price tag. As long as Trudy came to play, the instrument was not for sale.

To all things is the right time given.

34

The Shopkeeper's Journal

Thursday

There's a certain fascination about those who wander. The freedom, I suppose, or maybe a primal call to the spirit of something we were meant to experience to a greater capacity than we ever do, or ever will. Gordo is a very real reminder of this. Although not prone to long conversations, he seems to understand others' curiosity, and so can often be found indulging those vicariously fulfilling a void in their own lives with the adventure of his.

The three visitors found Gordo, wearing only a loose-fitting pair of linen pants, sitting on Julia's back patio strumming an unknown tune on a guitar. Somehow the network of people who inevitably found their way to Gordo discovered he was stateside and were making their own sojourn to Julia's backyard.

These situations were not strange to Julia. Accustomed as she was to the "groupies"—as she affectionately called them—who showed up whenever Gordo was around, she filled several glasses of tea and brought them out to the patio.

As the day went on, the number of visitors grew. By midafternoon, the backyard looked as if Bart and Julia were hosting a weekend barbeque. The field at the edge of their mountain property slowly filled with old topless Jeeps, rusted-out VW vans, and other vehicles of an age no longer identifiable.

By evening, the festivities had grown, too. The music had gone from Gordo's singular guitar to something resembling more of a band, loudspeakers

Troy W. Rasmussen

included. Bart and Julia sat on the porch watching the goings-on unconcerned, assuming it wouldn't be long before things quieted down and people would begin to leave. Unbeknownst to them, or anyone at the time, what was occurring in their backyard was about to turn into an event drawing hundreds of people, and lasting several days.

By nightfall, the music picked up its pace. Those present swayed back and forth, then jumped up down in rhythmic unison, hands in the air, smiling and cheering their approval. Julia's foot tapped to the beat, causing the ice in her drink to jingle and clink. Bart's remained the same.

In the darkness, a small glow at the top of the rise grew larger and flowed down the small hill toward those dancing about. In an explosion of light, the flood of people holding sparklers raced toward the rest of the group, surrounding them in a spectacular shower of sparks.

The spectacle lasted only a few moments, but for Julia, it was the highlight of another grand experience brought on by Gordo's presence. Bart stood to go inside; practical issues with the number of people in his backyard outweighed any rush of enjoyment he may have felt.

The morning sun found Gordo and Julia once again on the back patio, surveying the remains of the previous night's activities. Numerous bodies, some in makeshift tents, lay about the property. Those prone to an early rise could be seen reluctantly stirring about.

"It's good to have you back," Julia said.

Knowing her statement meant more than the bare words, Gordo responded with a kind smile and a quick nod of his head.

The Shopkeeper's Journal

"There are quite a few people..." Her voice trailed away. "I'm not sure what to do."

Gordo waited.

"With work and all..." Shrugging, she looked at Gordo.

"It's nothing more than a choice, Jules," he said. "You can call in and be part of something, or not."

Gordo knew that the right and wrong of Julia's inner struggle was best handled with few words versus a long dialogue about indulgence.

"What do you suppose will happen now?" she asked.

"Who knows, Jules? That's the beauty of letting life happen. Could be nothing, could be everything."

Julia uncharacteristically decided to bank on "everything" and called off work for the weekend.

By midafternoon, things began happening again in earnest. Hippies—and otherwise—used their cell phones and social media connections to send notice it was "going down," noted the location, and pressed *send*.

After that, the hillside across the road from Bart and Julia's place began to fill with hundreds of people. A makeshift stage was erected, allowing those with talent (some more than others) to take turns entertaining the horde.

Julia took up residence in a lounger next to Gordo. Bart, although present, was preoccupied with the activities going on around him. As Julia and Gordo conversed, a couple of groupies approached and hugged Gordo's neck, effusive in their pleasure at seeing him. He only smiled and continued his conversation with Julia.

Undeterred, the girls began working Gordo's hair into thick, irregular bunches of dreadlocks. They sat back to assess their handiwork, heads tilting this way, then that, then ran their fingers over various wood beads entwined in his hair. Finally, the two gave him a quick kiss on the cheek and sauntered off.

Julia watched the event, reflectively sipping her Mai Tai. Bart's stare registered something different. Turning to Bart, Gordo said, "How many trash bags you got?"

An odd question, Bart thought.

Gordo didn't elaborate, just stood and started walking toward the field where people were assembling around the stage.

"Make a run to town, Bart. Get what you think is needed." With a knowing glance at Julia, he disappeared into the crowd.

Even in the oppressive afternoon heat, the goings-on continued. Sweating sunbaked bodies, pressed close together, gyrated to the tunes of the Welded Roses, an up-and-coming band, whose guitar player was a close friend of Gordo's.

Gordo strolled onto the stage; familiar with his style, the band members just nodded to him nonchalantly. Fist bumping each member, in turn, Gordo picked up a tambourine and began knocking it against his hip. The music crescendo matched the rising excitement from the crowd as he turned, raised his hands over his head, and sent the crowd into a frenzy.

Gordo danced, his lean body swaying from side to side, to the beat of the reggae-infused number, his dreadlocks bouncing heavily on his shoulders.

As the set progressed, however, so did the cloudbank forming above the hills. Undeterred, the music and Gordo pressed on, until rain poured down in welcome relief from the heat. The rains and the song ended at about the same time and, bowing slightly, Gordo left the stage as calmly as he had taken it.

The Shopkeeper's Journal

Caught up in the excitement, Julia had stepped off the porch, tilted her face toward the sky, and remained so until drenched.

As evening drew near, the people relaxed as well—sitting around campfires, with flames in the patio fire pit burning high and bright. Gordo, guitar in hand, began strumming and singing a ditty about two lovers whose hearts mimicked the flames, and Julia felt Bart's hand slip over hers. Blinking back tears, she mirrored her husband's smile, then caught a knowing glance from Gordo.

The following day the revelers packed their paltry belongings in preparation for moving on to the next event. To Bart's surprise, all the oversized trash bags he purchased had found their way, full and bulging, to a designated place where it would be easy for them to be collected and discarded. *Hippies ain't all bad,* he thought.

Julia brought out three mugs of coffee for them to enjoy as the morning progressed in its stillness. Numerous people came by to extend their appreciation to Bart and Julia for hosting the occasion. One individual with two half-asleep groupies trailing in his wake approached Bart and said, "These things can sometimes turn into more than what people are prepared for. That's the coolness of it—really."

"It was the quite the event," Julia said.

Bart gave her a look as if to ask, *you're kidding, right?*

"Yeah. Gordo—man, he's the real thing." The young man put his arms around the girls. "Things happen when he's around."

"So we've seen," Bart added less enthusiastically. "Appreciate your cleaning the place up, though."

39

Troy W. Rasmussen

"Ah, no problem there, man. Some of the new crowd doesn't get it, but they will."

"Get it?"

"Yeah. No worries getting together, but cleaning up's part of the deal. Everyone does their part or it doesn't work."

"Well," Julia said. "It was wonderful to have you."

"Thanks. One of the V-dubs won't start. Don't mind if we leave it, do ya? Someone will be back to haul it off."

Julia shook her head.

The young man placed a wad of collected bills in Bart's palm. "Took up a collection. Don't want to be freeloaders. Have to pay anywhere else. Just 'cuz you're Gordo's fam doesn't mean it's any different."

Somewhat stunned, Bart remained still as the three turned to leave, waving goodbye to those remaining.

To all things is the right time given.

> *Friday*
> The shop takes on a different air when
> the guitar player arrives, similar to when a
> guest of honor walks in and everyone
> takes note. Tonight was no exception,
> Melanie included. Melanie, that gentle
> breeze settling itself softly where it
> chooses. She's the butterfly flitting to rest,
> briefly or not, slowly moving its wonder
> to catch the light. Do such creatures know
> of the effect they have on the world?
> Doubtful.

Melanie's first visit to the shop was quiet and unassuming. Her coy approach to the counter, attempting to conceal her curiosity, brought a smile to the
40

The Shopkeeper's Journal

shopkeeper's face. Her gentle stroking of the counter—dusting—had a soothing effect beyond any the shopkeeper noticed when other visitors partook in the same ritual. Gentler, somehow. More subtle.

The shopkeeper gave Melanie a tour of the shop, her glance following his voice as it described various pieces of art or antiques. The books seemed to fascinate Melanie the most; so, after providing a brief description of the categories, the shopkeeper left her amongst the many worlds the books offered within their pages.

Melanie spent most of an hour perusing the books. Settling on a particular novel that would take the reader on an adventure in Marrakesh, she approached the counter and ordered a cool mint and fruit drink. The rest of her visit was spent curled up in the corner of a couch, reading—seemingly oblivious to the rest of the world.

What brought Melanie into the shop Friday night, the shopkeeper could only guess. A late evening stroll, perhaps? Regardless, the night's activities were only beginning when he noticed her sitting quietly in front of the windows, her bare feet curled underneath her legs, book in hand. Shortly thereafter, the guitar player arrived, greeting those he knew and giving a slight nod to those he didn't.

The guitar player, settling in, caught a glance of Melanie's curled up figure, her head resting easily on her bent arm as she leaned against the back of the couch, and he smiled. Throughout the evening, he indulged in periodic and intentional bouts of watching Melanie as she read, until the music took on something of her essence.

Saturday
The usual ruckus from Mrs. Thrilkil's place took on an extra vigor today. Instead

of the sounds of pounding and the
occasional words spoken in anger, people
in the vicinity of her shop were astounded
to see several pieces of art thrown out the
door, ending up in a heap at the curb. I
couldn't help but smile to myself, not only
at the look on people's faces, but at the
mental picture of what Mrs. Thrilkil's face
must have looked like as she sent various
objects hurtling through space!

At the time of the incident, the shopkeeper was
sweeping the steps of his shop, and at first, he just kept
on working; it wasn't uncommon for him to hear Mrs.
Thrilkil, even from across the street. However, that all
changed as the first object hit the ground. The
shopkeeper raised his head and looked toward her shop,
his attention piqued.

Mrs. Thrilkil seemed to care for little in this world
except for her work. Seeing her so violently destroy
several pieces in such a manner left the shopkeeper
sensing something was wrong.

He waited another moment, his attention fixed on the
door of her shop. The shopkeeper caught the enraged
look of Mrs. Thrilkil as she stepped into the same
doorway through which her pottery had flown. Anger,
maddening anger, was etched into the crevices of her
face, her eyes hot with it. She offered no explanation,
however, merely turned to go back inside, but the
shopkeeper sensed something more sinister at the root of
it, a darkness that shook him. Mrs. Thrilkil had
acknowledged the reality of something dark and ugly.
The rage she'd unleashed was in a vain attempt to accept
its cause.

The Shopkeeper's Journal

Chapter 6

Monday
Mrs. Thrilkil's shop was closed today. I've only seen her once since the outburst, and then but a brief glimpse as she turned the shop sign from *open* to *closed.* I have to say, the street seemed eerily strange without the familiar sounds of pounding and cursing. It's one of those things you don't realize have become a part of life until it's gone.

The morning rays of the sun found Bacardi and Gordo sitting side by side on the edge of the flowerbed; some time ago, the two had formed a friendship. As the shopkeeper approached to unlock the door, Bacardi lifted his head in acknowledgement, and Gordo gave a familiar, "Hey, Keep," his nickname for the proprietor.

After a short while, Gordo came in to order his usual—what he now referred to as a cup of mud.

"Bacardi says Mrs. Thrilkil's closed today," he said, "and he hasn't seen that in a long time." His brow creased. "Wonder if anything's wrong?"

"Mmmm," replied the shopkeeper, glancing at Mrs. Thrilkil's shop door.

Thursday
Mrs. Thrilkil came into the shop this evening.

To all things is the right time given.

43

Just as the shopkeeper was finishing closing for the day, he turned to see Mrs. Thrilkil standing in the doorway. In all his time at the shop, he'd never know her to visit.

Setting aside his broom, the shopkeeper offered her a seat at one of the tables stationed in front of the large plate glass windows. She accepted his offer and, as she approached, the shopkeeper politely pulled out the chair for her to sit. Mrs. Thrilkil sat quietly looking out the window, her strong callused hands lying in her lap. Seemingly she was fascinated by the view from his side of the street.

The shopkeeper, having left Mrs. Thrilkil to herself for a moment, returned with a bowl of broth and eased himself into the chair next to hers. As she turned her gaze to the bowl of warm liquid, the shopkeeper noticed a tear falling slowly down her weathered cheek. With no other prompting, he ladled a small amount of the broth into an antique silver spoon and lifted it to her lips. She accepted his offering with eyes closed, swallowing the rich mixture. He repeated the gesture in like fashion for several minutes. No words were exchanged, no glances shared. Only the slow dipping of a silver spoon into a bowl of broth, followed by its elevation to the mouth of its recipient.

A celebration of some sort was gearing up its firework finale somewhere in the community, the small explosives showering their rays of sparks and light into the night sky. Mrs. Thrilkil turned her head toward the commotion, silent at first. Then, at last, she uttered, "Those are illegal, you know."

"Mmmm," he replied, sliding the bowl and spoon out of the way.

The Shopkeeper's Journal

He was still watching the fireworks display as the spirit of Mrs. Thrilkil left its place of residence. It seemed to the shopkeeper most fitting that she should pass away with such a celebration.

Troy W. Rasmussen

Chapter 7

Monday

No one knew if Mrs. Thrilkil had any family, so the disposal of items in her shop was left to town officials and a few members of the community. Not knowing what to do with the pieces of her work, the City Attorney announced to those present—all of whom knew Mrs. Thrilkil—that they should take what they wanted. Few people accepted his offer, so an auction date was set for the rest. A bowl of a certain size—a reminder of the one containing some broth—caught my attention.

It was midafternoon and the shop was busy, unusual for the beginning of the week. Visitors came and went in a steady stream, most taking note of an elderly figure slumped a few feet from the shop door, yet none stopping to interact.

Save Gordo.

Gordo noticed the man on the sidewalk and approached him with ease. Tapping his leg to arouse him, Gordo merely told the man, "Come with me." Lifting the figure to his unsteady feet, Gordo assisted the man in gaining his balance before walking with him into the shop.

"Hey Keep, how 'bout a cup of mud?"

46

The Shopkeeper's Journal

Seeing the situation, the shopkeeper nodded to a table in front of the windows, then went about creating the rich mixture. Moments later, the man roused and sipped the chocolaty richness. As Gordo engaged the man in conversation, the shopkeeper left briefly, then returned to set down a sandwich and a bowl of soup.

Looking sideways, the vagrant commented, "A man such as this should not be so privileged as to eat his soup from a silver spoon."

"The bowl is where the privilege lies," the shopkeeper replied.

From that time forward Mrs. Thrilkil's bowl, filled with soup, and the silver spoon were placed before anyone in need of sustenance.

> *Tuesday*
> A most distinguished man visited the shop today, introducing himself as Redmond. The Old World grandeur he projected seemed, uncannily, to make one feel as if all in the universe was right for having him in their midst. I've seen Redmond strolling about town. Amazing how someone can say so little and yet capture so much attention.

Redmond stepped into the shop and remained there a few moments, taking in his surroundings. He was clearly seeking something and not finding it. When asked about it, he told the shopkeeper he was in need of a working pocket watch and fob, preferably in gold. Raising his eyebrow, the shopkeeper walked a few paces further down the counter where the finely carved wood took on more regular patterns with a row of protruding knobs.

47

Troy W. Rasmussen

The shopkeeper pulled on one of the knobs, sliding open a felt lined drawer embedded in the counter.

Redmond stepped forward and beheld five finely crafted gold antique watches and fobs. He took only a brief glance before he selected his timepiece: a notable specimen with layers of filigree encompassed by swirls and various engravings, culminating around a cherub.

"This will do," he said. "I have a mind for a bit of coffee, if you please, sir."

Redmond took a seat at one of the higher bar tables and spent a few moments apparently reflecting. Sensing his guest's penchant for finer things, the shopkeeper returned a few moments later with a bone china cup of steaming Kopi Luwak. With a brisk whip of his hand, the shopkeeper cleared a few crumbs of pastry off the table and set a matching saucer with two biscuits next to the coffee. Redmond nodded in acknowledgement, then reached into the pocket of his blazer to retrieve a pack of Ark Royal Sweets.

Redmond remained in repose for some time, watching the passersby on the street, the smoke rising slowly through the streams of light coming in the windows.

> *Thursday*
> The harp has finally arrived! The auction was an abysmal mess. Why do I expect it to be different? The travel, the crowds inspecting their finds, mumbling one to the other what they feel this or that selection will go for, the endless waiting. The bidding brings a certain level of enthusiasm, I suppose, something to break the tedium. The purchase of the harp, an

The Shopkeeper's Journal

exquisite piece of artistry, made the trip worth it in the end.

Such grand instruments, harps. The graceful curves of maple and spruce, chosen for their strength and natural ability to respond to string vibration and produce the rich sounds for which the instrument is known. The specimen arriving at the shop displayed a distinct, intricately carved pillar designed to resemble a fluted Greek column. No sooner had the shopkeeper stepped back to gaze at the work of art than he heard the unmistakable sound of someone behind him gasping.

Tameril was an accomplished harpist, and the amazed look on her face left little doubt she fully understood the caliber of the instrument before her. The shopkeeper stepped to the side and motioned her toward the harp with an unmistakable "be my guest" gesture, and watched with a sort of tenderness as she approached the harp—as excitedly, even reverently, as a young person who's just been handed the keys to their first vehicle.

Sitting astride the stool, Tameril pulled the instrument toward her and rested it gently on her shoulder. Her fingers caressed the strings in fluid plucking movements; taking a slow pull on his pipe, the shopkeeper stood listening to the melodious chords as they filled the shop.

Friday

Even when they sit in the palm of your hand or dance on the end of an extended finger, it seems butterflies remain unaware of their own captivating powers. Such is the case with Melanie to the guitar player. Poor wretch.

Troy W. Rasmussen

The shopkeeper noted, with a bit of irony that the guitar player arrived earlier than usual. Several of the Friday night crowd had already begun to gather, mingling, discussing the week's work or current events. Sliding the coffee toward his new arrival, the shopkeeper nodded his welcome.

Melanie was sitting, legs crossed, by the window. The shopkeeper noticed a hesitation when the musician turned toward the couch and saw her. He sat down and plucked one of the strings of his guitar, leaning his ear closer to the neck, then adjusting the appropriate tuner to get the pitch. After checking each string, he leaned back and began to play, the first chords drawing attention— and a quick hush—from those gathered. But Melanie's gaze remained pointed toward the street, apparently oblivious.

As the evening and the music continued, the shopkeeper noticed the communication between the two become a seduction of the spirit, deeper than mere sideways glances or repositioning of hair. When he played slowly, romantically, Melanie's movements from one position to the next followed suit. Once during a particularly lively number, her mouth turned up in a slight, knowing smile. The guitar player's emotion at her response came through in his breathing.

When Melanie left for the evening, the musical communication between the two ended; the shopkeeper could tell, however, that the guitar player's fascination did not.

> *Saturday*
> Redmond was in today, seemingly deep in thought. As I set his coffee and ashtray next to him, he asked about the

The Shopkeeper's Journal

> shop across the street and why it remained
> empty. A self-made man of wealth,
> Redmond has little tolerance for idleness
> in people or buildings, it would seem. He
> concluded, simply, that someone ought to
> open another business there.

Redmond, a man of few words, gazed at the empty shop across the street.

"A private investor is often the key to the success of new endeavors," he observed.

"Mmmm."

Apparently, that was the extent of what Redmond was willing to share on the subject of commerce.

Visitors streamed in and out, and the shopkeeper kept busy answering questions and providing details on the history of the pieces located throughout the shop. After a conversation about his recent acquisition of the harp, the shopkeeper noticed the space next to it as if for the first time—it was empty. This took him temporarily aback, as he made a conscious effort not to have vacant space in the shop.

He took a few minutes away from the front of the shop and walked to the back storage area, where he kept numerous antiques, the inventory of which was stored in his memory. Making his way through the space, he stopped briefly to consider first one piece, then another. Finally, he came across an artist's easel he'd purchased several years before.

Unlike other examples of this style, the easel had a unique design: it folded down on itself, forming the top of a table. Its legs weren't as lavishly detailed as its top, but were formed well and provided sturdy support. And, although the tabletop itself showed the wear of use by a

Troy W. Rasmussen

previous artist, even that didn't hide the craftsmanship of gold filigree inlay in each of the corners. Two center drawers, one larger than the other, provided storage space for paint and brush. On either side of those center drawers, three additional smaller drawers, stacked one on top of the other, gave the piece a thick, rounded appearance.

Giving in to the perennial desire to open a drawer, the shopkeeper bent over and pulled each of the drawers out, in turn, noting as he did that the entire stack also pivoted out. All but one still functioned smoothly.

Mmmm. Personally, he was of the opinion that any old table should have a drawer or two that stuck. Then, laughing at his own whimsy, he decided the easel would be the perfect piece to move into the space out front.

After the shop closed, the shopkeeper cleaned and polished the easel and placed it in the area to the side of the harp—one drawer still requiring a bit more force to open.

The Shopkeeper's Journal

Chapter 8

Monday

Natalia—quite possibly one of the saddest, most downtrodden people I've ever met—came into the shop this evening. Her pensive nature, downcast eyes, and arms folded tightly against her chest caught my attention. She huddled close to the door like a vagabond coming in out of the cold, hoping no one would send them away. If it hadn't been for my saying hello, she probably would have left as soon as she arrived.

The shopkeeper motioned for Natalia to sit, but she didn't move at first, only reached out a hand to place a loose strand of her hair behind her ear, her glance nervous. Barely twenty years of age, she was clearly a refugee of public systems that didn't always help and the victim of too many people using her for something she'd ceased to be able to give.

Natalia had spent all her money on bus tickets to get this far and was now stranded. It wasn't uncommon to have such travelers come through town and stay a few days or weeks, working odd jobs, before moving on. Those electing to stay became regulars in one of the town parks, selling their homemade wares to tourists. What was to happen with Natalia was of far greater magnitude.

Hesitantly, she moved toward the table indicated and sat down. The shopkeeper brought the bowl and silver

Troy W. Rasmussen

spoon, along with a frosty glass of an iced drink. As she sipped, the shopkeeper explained about the bowl and how it came to be in his shop.

"She sounds like a miserable person," Natalia said flatly.

"There are many who would agree with you."

Natalia ate another spoonful of soup.

"What brings you to these parts?"

"Same as most. I'm traveling around…"

The shopkeeper gave her a questioning look.

"Well, if you must know, I got tired of putting up with all the bullshh…crap back home and decided to leave."

"And how long ago was that?"

"I don't know. Five or six years. Foster care can get rough, and so I decided life on my own couldn't be any worse. Didn't have a car, so I hitched as far as I could until I thought it was safe. Got a job in a restaurant waiting tables." Natalia shrugged. "Wasn't the best money in the world, but since I didn't have anything else to do, I covered extra shifts. It was enough to pay for a motel room. The boss let us eat for free."

"Sounds like a nice guy."

"Yeah. Not very many of them, though."

"So you stayed there awhile?"

"About a year. If the town's big enough, people don't ask questions about where you're from or who your family is." Natalia stirred her soup. "Once that starts, it's time to head out again."

"And so here you are. What's next?"

"Next? You make it sound like I have an option."

"You do."

"Listen, mister, I'm done with dreams. Life has a way of killing those."

"Mmmm."

54

The Shopkeeper's Journal

"What?" She wiped her mouth with a napkin.

"Let's see. You've had a rough few years, spent most of them going from place to place, have ended up here to start the cycle over again, and…"

"And what?"

"And are prepared to just continue?"

"It's worked so far."

"No doubt, but what kind of a life is it?"

Natalia sat still for a moment. "It isn't, but when you've had the life I have…"

"You begin to feel that's all there is, and so resign yourself to the false assumption there's nothing more."

"You're saying that's not true?"

"The fact you've asked that question shows you haven't given up altogether. You mentioned that you've spent the last few years working in restaurants."

"Once they find out you've done it before, most places will hire you right away," she said. "I don't mind it, really. It's just that most of them don't know anything about how to do it right. And when you tell them what you think, they yell—or fire you."

"Interesting," he said. "What's the right way to run a restaurant?"

"What?"

"You mentioned most of the owners you worked for didn't know how to run a restaurant. You have ideas about it. What are they?"

After some consideration, Natalia sat back and said, "Ambiance. I know, you wouldn't think I know what that word means, but I do. I think people would like a nice place to go. The food's a big deal. You have to get that right."

"Ambiance. When you picture this, what comes to mind?"

55

Troy W. Rasmussen

Natalia's eyes sparkled a bit. "A small place—not too small, though. Big enough so people feel they're part of something—the popular place in town. There would be some tables outside, maybe with plants and funky dishes."

"Funky dishes."

"Yeah. None of them matching. And tablecloths blowing in the breeze. I'd walk around and talk with the customers, get to know them, ask how their days have gone, and if they were enjoying their experience. The inside would be open with soft lighting, maybe some big windows in the front. I'd figure out a way to involve the people living in the town so they felt like my place was theirs, too."

The shopkeeper smiled. "Your ideas needed refining and some guidance, yet are feasible."

"Yeah, well, ideas cost money."

"How much money do you suppose it would take to create a place like what you've described?"

Natalia looked dumbfounded. "More than I have, mister." Abruptly, she stood to leave.

"Is it what you really want? A restaurant?"

Natalia stopped. "No. A bistro. That's what I'd have."

"How much?"

"Why are you doing this?"

"My dear, I'm asking you the same question."

Natalia's shook her head and shrugged as if to ask 'what' again.

"You have some experience and plenty of good ideas. Why are you still running?" The shopkeeper stood and took her hands in his. "You've conquered greater battles. Running is familiar, and so it feels safe, but it's not what you desire. Why not stop it and instead put the energy into creating a life that makes you happy?"

56

The Shopkeeper's Journal

A tear slid down her cheek. "How?"

The shopkeeper put his hand on her shoulder and looked across the street at Mrs. Thrilkil's old shop.

Even as he spoke to Natalia, the shopkeeper noticed another young woman, dressed in a trendy getup, tentatively running her fingers over the top of the easel—dusting. Something was different about the woman, her study of the easel more than the casual visitor admiring a fine work of art. It was as if she knew the piece, how it functioned, where to place the guide to lift the surface to the correct height. As the shopkeeper observed her, she pulled the stool closer, making her communication with the piece more personal.

Excusing himself from Natalia, the shopkeeper approached the woman. "It appears you're familiar with easels?"

The woman didn't respond.

The shopkeeper cleared his throat.

Nothing.

Placing his hand gently on her shoulder, he posed a questioning look to her. But instead, the woman timidly looked away.

The shopkeeper glanced down at her loosely woven handbag, dropped haphazardly on the floor, and noticed the ends of a few paint brushes and the unmistakable smeared palette of watercolor paints.

"You are an artist?" he asked.

The woman smiled, then tapped her ear lightly with her fingers, signaling she was deaf.

He nodded and then held up his finger to get her attention. The woman watched as he wrote 'Artist?' on a piece of paper and held it up for her to read.

The woman smiled.

Troy W. Rasmussen

The shopkeeper left and returned with a small bowl of water, paper towels, and several pieces of thick handmade paper. He placed the bowl and towels on the extended turnout of the side drawers, then slid the paper underneath the lip of the tilted tabletop. Hesitantly, the woman reached for her paints and brushes, dampened the paper with a splash of the water, and began to paint.

She remained at the easel for some time before collecting her tools and quietly leaving. Returning to the easel, the shopkeeper saw a simple, yet exquisite depiction: a hand, resting on a woman's shoulder.

Wednesday
Chester, that light of the world, came to visit again today, with his satchel slung over his shoulder. The stick of an oversized lollipop protruding out of his mouth only added to his air of mischief.

He's been into the shop several times since his father's passing, but not with the same purpose as today: this time, he was on the prowl. What better place to prowl, than a favorite haunt that consistently delivers the fuel to a young boy's imagination?

"Hey, Mister," came Chester's frank greeting. As if nothing else was necessary, the boy remained where he was with a look of expectation.

The shopkeeper's "Mmmm" brought grins to both their faces. Sliding his pipe from between his lips and letting the aromatic smoke drift away, the shopkeeper moved from behind the counter and walked through the shop. Chester followed reluctantly, still apparently

58

The Shopkeeper's Journal

waiting to be impressed—but knowing that remaining behind meant he'd miss out.

He needed something new, something big, something to call his own, and the shop itself no longer sufficed. Stopping in front of the wood-paneled wall of the bookcase, the shopkeeper turned toward the boy with a pointed look. In return, Chester only raised his eyebrows, as if to say, *well?*

The shopkeeper reached toward the seemingly solid panel and pressed an (until now) unnoticed antiqued button. Hearing a *click* snapped Chester's attention from the shopkeeper to the object making such a glorious sound. (Clicks, to Chester, were the beginnings of great things.) With no further prompting, the boy stepped forward to investigate.

Chester ran his fingers along the raised paneling, moving back and forth like a blind man seeking something out. Then, as he leaned forward to take a closer look, his weight caused the panel to give.

He slid the four-foot-high section to the right and stepped back to survey the black hole before him ...

Arius, the discoverer of ancient caves, ducked cautiously into the gaping hole his chisel had created, his eyes taking a few minutes to adjust to the darkness. All such places are booby-trapped, as every explorer knows.

Reaching into his satchel, Arius took out his always-fueled Zippo lighter. His thumb flipped the metal lid up with a familiar click and then slid over the grooved wheel, grinding it against the flint to ignite the gas.

In its light, cobwebs hung thick in the cave, clinging heavily to the stone walls, but Arius also noticed a torch, balanced in a rusted sheath. He set it alight, took the

59

Troy W. Rasmussen

torch in hand, and pressed forward into the depths of the cave.

The sounds of Trudy playing her piano drew the shopkeeper away from watching Chester disappear into the space behind the panel.

"Good morning," he said to her.

"Yes, it is," she replied.

"It'd be better if a guy had his coffee," Bacardi declared, from his perch at the door.

After filling the heavy clay mug with Bacardi's preferred mixture, the shopkeeper stepped outside to hand it to the gardener.

"Time for a change," Bacardi declared, with more spirit than usual. "Yep, things are a-changin', that's for sure."

With that, he began to uproot old and overgrown plants from the flowerbed; the shopkeeper looked across the street to Mrs. Thrilkil's place and understood the gardener's meaning.

Natalia was busy at work, in the process of supervising workmen turning Mrs. Thrilkil's pottery shop into a bistro-style eatery.

The shopkeeper allowed his imagination to picture it: the cement sidewalk dug up and replaced with smooth stone…the windows washed clean and their old wood frames scraped clear of paint to give the façade a worn, trendy look. He smiled to himself. Small wrought-iron tables and chairs would sit atop the stone, with waiters coming in and out serving their guests. Inside, hungry tourists and townsfolk would sit at bench-style tables, draped with patterned tablecloths, viewing the artwork of local artists as they ate—most notably, the work of the watercolor painter.

The Shopkeeper's Journal

Time spent at Natalia's would be time spent at leisure. He could see guests now, enjoying the food, and the experience, with open expressions of pleasure…

He'd just ambled back behind the counter when the shopkeeper heard a cheery "Good day," from Redmond.

"That it is."

"A cup of your finest."

After taking a few moments to prepare his distinguished guest's drink, the shopkeeper approached Redmond at his table and noticed him watching the activity across the street.

"It appears our entrepreneur has things well in hand."

"That she does," Redmond said. "If things turn out half as grand as you portrayed them…"

"They will," the shopkeeper interrupted.

"I'm counting on it." Redmond raised the cup to his lips.

Arius moved stealthily through the cave, having successfully escaped two traps—one designed to entangle his feet and, under the weight of an unseen pulley, hang him upside-down; the second intended to cut his legs off at the knees and leave him to bleed to death on stumps. All of his senses were on alert, naturally. Explorers have an extra sense about them. They can tell when something isn't right, and without fail know just what to do to thwart the devious designs of wicked rulers who create such obstacles to keep their treasures safe. But Arius the Cunning was not so easily fooled.

Arius wasn't sure what the treasure consisted of, but it must be something of great value for such traps to lie in wait for unsuspecting explorers.

Troy W. Rasmussen

He paused, sitting for a moment on a small outcropping of the cave to consider his next move. As he wiped moisture from his forehead with his shirt, he noticed the corner of a piece of cloth sticking out of a crack in the cave wall. One more effort to do me in.

The code of all explorers was to investigate each piece of the puzzle as it presented itself. So, he rose slowly from his place of rest and leaned forward across the small expanse of the tunnel to see what could be learned.

Further investigation showed a balled-up cloth, resting unobstructed on a small shelf in the cave wall. It struck Arius odd that having supposedly been in its place for centuries, the cloth was void of dust.

Reaching his hand cautiously into the tight space holding the cloth, Arius grabbed hold and yanked it out at lightning speed to avoid the possibility of yet another amputated body part. With a sigh of relief, but suspicions still on alert, Arius began to unfold the bundle. As the last fold of cloth fell to the side, Arius' eyes opened wide at his discovery.

Chester could hardly believe what lay in the palm of his hand. The bright gold medallion was surely a lost treasure; yet now, here it was in his possession. The heartbeats of young boys at such moments can defy medical reasoning.

Lifting the medallion, watching its gold chain follow the upward motion, Chester narrowed his eyes in an attempt to make out the intricate designs carved into the surface. He pulled a flashlight from his satchel and shone the beam onto the uplifted medallion, following its curved engravings in their ancient patterns.

"Wow," he murmured.

The Shopkeeper's Journal

Chester's small fingers traced the face of the medallion; then, breathing onto the metal object, he gave it a good polishing. Then he sat back on his haunches to continue his inspection.

Arius, being the explorer he was, knew the object was by rights his; he promptly stuffed the medallion in his pocket before moving to leave the cave. After covering the entrance of the cave with random branches to disguise its whereabouts, he moved back into the outside world, the wealth of the secret cave firmly his.

Closing the secret panel in the wall, Chester faced a greater dilemma—what the shopkeeper would say about it. As his steps took him closer to the counter, his mind processed any number of scenarios and justifications for keeping this latest treasure. As he stopped at the counter, his eyes met those of his cohort, and he reached into his pocket, his thumb rubbing slowly over the cool metal, about to pull his discovery out.

"A man that finds a thing in a place he calls his own," said the shopkeeper, "is the owner of the thing."

The boy's hand stopped. Looking back toward where he'd come from he asked, "Whose is the place in the wall?"

"Mmmm. There are three requirements that must be met for someone to call a space his own."

Chester's interest grew.

"One, you must know how to enter."

First requirement met. Chester's heart began to race.

"Two, you must enter without crawling on your knees." Chester's mind made the mental check mark of meeting yet another requirement.

63

Troy W. Rasmussen

"Three, you must prove faithful to the explorer's code."

Chester's world stopped. "Code?" he asked, faltering. He knew what he thought the explorer's code was. Did the shopkeeper have a different one?

"Mmmm. To know the value of a thing and that, in time, it may pass—or not."

Chester knew this: what his fingers were wrapped around carried great value.

"How do you know if you meet them all?" the boy asked.

"When a man knows, he knows."

Chester stood for a moment, processing. He knew how to enter, could do so without crawling on his knees, and…the rest could wait. A find was a find.

"I think I meet them all, mister."

"Mmmm. Tell me when you know."

His steps were unsure at first as he moved toward the door of the shop. But then, standing in the doorway, the sun shining on his head, Chester turned toward the shopkeeper with a new resolve.

"I know."

Chester left the shop that day convinced he was taller—but still able to enter the space behind the panel without crawling.

Friday

Everyone is looking forward to the Festival.

The annual celebration has been a part of this community for as long as most of us can recall, with the usual events planned: food, fireworks, street dances, artists displaying their talent, and music. Thanks to Gordo, this year's festival has a

The Shopkeeper's Journal

new focus, though: it's been dubbed the Splash Festival. Although not politically involved, Gordo attended several of the town meetings with the festival on the agenda, his fondness for water is familiar to those who know him. Now that he's spent some time with them, the town's council—and undoubtedly a fair majority of its residents—apparently are at least willing to risk finding out what such an event entails.

During the midafternoon heat of its inaugural day, those attending the festival were exposed to a unique way of beating the high temperature—open fire hydrants.

The hydrants, spanning the six blocks set aside for the festival's activities, were opened without warning to release their contents, in arched canopies high into the air, and rain down on the crowds. People screamed and raised their hands—some to deflect the rush of cold water, others to celebrate and laugh. Young and old, faces turned upwards, jumped and danced about in the cool sprays. Small children darted this way and that, squealing with delight as they ran through what was, in their eyes, the world's largest sprinkler. When the cold water hit the hot pavement, steam rose, creating a surreal atmosphere of hundreds of people dancing in a cloud as speakers, hung by volunteers high above the streets, began spewing music befitting the event.

Gordo, standing near one of the hydrants, grinned in delight. He dropped the wrench he'd used to open his assigned hydrant and jumped as high as he could into the air, landing feet first in one of the many puddles. Several of the town's maintenance team, having completed their

65

Troy W. Rasmussen

final piece of work for the day opening their respective hydrants, did the same. The world struggles to know a more hearty and comforting sound than men laughing.

Young couples twirled in the mayhem, their arms wrapped tight around one another, kissing. Those having more seasons to their lives could be seen smiling, petting one another's faces in strokes of endearment, their faces equally joyous.

With the gutters running slick and full of water, Gordo demonstrated to the children the fine art of gutter surfing. Taking a few steps to gain speed, he threw himself feet first into the current, his momentum propelling him for some distance past the revelers in the street. A photographer captured the moment—Gordo's sleek, toned body awash in a small wave of water as he slid down the street, arms and legs flailing, head thrown back in laughter, with the children doing the same behind him.

Natalia, her hands clapped together in the delight of the moment, sprays of water about her face, couldn't know at the time that someday, a watercolor painting capturing her in that moment would hang in the entryway of her eatery.

Saturday

The streets are clean. Six blocks' worth, anyway. A minor thing to note, I suppose, when compared to the exhibition of life and the freedom to express it to the fullest. So many things to see and behold as the deluge rained down. No tears for Natalia as the cocoon holding her hostage cracked open, releasing the beauty of a creature too long wrapped in her protective shell. There's a magic to it

The Shopkeeper's Journal

all—one beginning her journey into a
world no longer as fearful as before.
Another, prisoner to a world with no
sound, releasing through her talent the
glory in the moment of the first.

The morning found Natalia busy with the details of
building out an old structure; with the heavy construction
now completed, she was ready to begin considering the
décor. Natalia took her time walking through the
restaurant. She checked each spot to ensure the intensity
of light was bright enough to give the place life, yet soft
enough for guests to feel comfortable to linger.

She could see it in her mind's eye…each table with
its own character, fresh flowers or a piece of clay
enthusiastically shaped by the small hands of children
taking part in a contest, the reward being to have their
creation grace the tables of the "new place in town."

The construction of the front of the building created
an elevated, set-apart alcove. This was where Natalia
would put a special table: one available for anyone in
need of a meal, but lacking the means to afford it.

She spent several days visiting the vendors in the
area for lighting, utensils, and artwork. Returning from
one such excursion, she was astonished to see a
watercolor painting of herself from the Splash Festival,
leaning against the frame of the door. Several minutes
passed as she gazed at the colors flowing into the shape
of her likeness. The painting was the perfect size to hang
on the wall just inside the door.

A few days later, everything was in place, and
Natalia was ready for the last task. Locking the door to
ensure she was not disturbed, she turned and picked up
the painting and, with soft music playing around her,

Troy W. Rasmussen

moved in slow circles, gazing at it. One day she would meet the artist, but for now, that didn't matter. What did was that a life once held in the captivity of hurt and anger had released itself into the grandeur of individuality.

Leaning her head against a master's work, Natalia felt the remarkable sensation of tears—tears of hope and promise and possibility. She walked to the entryway and lifted her painting to its place, pausing for a few minutes to appreciate the artistry once more before turning to the locked door. With a click of the deadbolt, she accepted with gratitude her new life.

To all things is the right time given.

By late afternoon, Main Street—or Tourist Lane, as it was referred to by locals—cleared of vendors and their trappings in preparation for the next event of the Splash Festival. Gordo's enthusiasm for body surfing had fueled another idea that, at first, the town council had struggled with. In the end, determined to set a new and favorable precedent for the town, they opted for conditionally approving it, with a "wait and see" approach.

Tourist Lane wound its way from the lower community up through the numerous blocks of shops to residential sections. Those taking the time to study the layout of the street knew each street took a wide, casual turn either right or left—save one. One-third of the way down Tourist Lane, the street turned an abrupt ninety degrees to the right. Traffic had always slowed in this area to a near crawl. Today, the corner would prove a tricky (and somewhat dangerous) obstacle to the brave souls willing to take on the challenge of street surfing.

Once the streets were cleared, the local fire department drove fire trucks the length of Tourist Lane, washing it free of debris, periodically arching the spray from the hoses into the crowd—an action met with screams of surprise from some and cheering from others.

The Shopkeeper' s Journal

Following the trucks were two pickups, their open beds containing people with buckets full of dish soap that they poured onto the street. A few minutes before the event started, several of the hydrants at the top of Tourist Lane were opened, allowing the water to flow the length and breadth of the street. Suspense and, in some cases, grins grew as those lining the street became aware of what was to come.

A large bell in the courtyard of one of the local churches rang out a signal through the hills, and the first brave souls took a few running steps and hurled themselves into the air for a two-and-a-half-minute slide down Tourist Lane on the surface of water and soap.

Gordo, and several others of his age and gender, started down the road face-first, flat on their stomachs—he quickly realized he might not have any skin left by the time he completed the run! A course correction was in order, and Gordo made it fast, maneuvering into a sitting position for more control, especially in the turns. With his bare feet leading the way, he leaned into the first curve, feeling his weight and the centrifugal force pull him to the outside. As he swung back upright, using his legs and backside as rudders, he picked up speed, heading full on into the second curve. Neglecting to account for the buildup of soap, he failed to round the curve smoothly; instead, he spun wildly into the concrete curb. Seconds later, with little more than a grunt, he spun back into position and continued on toward the sharp right turn a block in the distance.

By now, the group Gordo started out with was speeding down the slope in a mass of bodies and bubbles and, like a school of fish that seem to know what the others are about to do, the group leaned heavily to their right in an attempt to make the turn. There would be

Troy W. Rasmussen

many stories told about events at the festival, but few would rival the recitals of when ten to fifteen twenty-somethings overestimated their capabilities of rounding that sharp corner.

The curbs of Tourist Lane were high, but not so high as to keep half the group from careening over them onto the sidewalk and into the storefronts they bordered. More than a few, wiping out at that point, declared themselves done. Continuing on, Gordo and those with him found a sort of equilibrium allowing them to yell and wave at the onlookers. As Gordo approached the shop, he caught sight of Bacardi and the shopkeeper.

"Hey, Keep!" he yelled. "Bacardi, you gotta try this!"

Bacardi raised his clay mug wryly. "Ain't enough sauce in this here cup for that."

Those who persevered had various trophies to show for their efforts. The ones who'd opted to use only clothing as protection earned scrapes and patches of raw skin by the bottom of the lane. Other less daring adrenaline junkies fared better by wrapping themselves in various articles of protection, the most creative of whom decided the trek would be better taken riding on thick plastic lids of trash barrels or toboggans. But in truth, even scrapes and bumps seemed a small price to pay for the exhilaration of arriving at the end of the lane, lungs burning from laughter, with the echoes of excited cheering from the crowd ringing in their ears.

> *Sunday*
> After the rousing success of the Splash Festival's debut, there seemed no end to the ideas people came up with to add to it: water guns, children with water balloons lying in wait for the

The Shopkeeper's Journal

unsuspecting, and the occasional business owner "mistakenly" dousing random customers as they sprayed their walkways off. (Judging by how quickly he came up off the steps and the choice words he used to express his surprise and irritation, clearly, Bacardi wasn't convinced the pot of water soaking him head-to-toe was due to a misjudgment of its weight distribution.)

To all things is the right time given.

The finale couldn't have been more colorful and unique, much like the personality of the one who devised it.

The streets were full of locals and tourists milling from one place to the next, puzzled by the liquid-filled balloons hanging above their heads. The guitar player and the members of the Welded Roses were tuning their instruments and running sound checks. As people gathered around the stage, the band began a heavy rhythm track that soon had people dancing and fist pumping the air.

Gordo, never one to miss an opportunity to express the joy of life, grabbed Chester and lifted him by the waist into the air, who in turn took hold of a balloon, now within reach. Squeezing his fingers into the tightly filled rubbery ball, Chester punctured it, releasing a spray of paint and water on his and Gordo's head. When they heard the laughter and saw what had happened, others did the same and, like a hole in a dam giving way to the pressure of the water behind it, individual bursts of paint-infused water quickly turned into an enormous explosion of liquid fireworks.

Troy W. Rasmussen

The festival ended against the background of actual fireworks, spraying embers of color across the sky. As the display subsided and the merrymakers left, Bacardi, his raspy voice low in the stillness that followed, uttered his own whimsical tribute: "Those are illegal, you know."

The Shopkeeper's Journal

Chapter 9

Monday

Apparently, Nature wanted the Splash Festival to continue longer, and sent soft rains that fell throughout the day. Thinking about it now, I'm not sure the rain came so much for the usual purpose, but as a secondary partner to the experience of Micki, a young girl with a hand full of stillness.

Micki and her mother entered the shop with a pronounced stomping of feet and sighs of relief, both of which he'd heard all day from those coming in out of the rain. Grinning, Micki's mother said hello, then continued, "What a beautiful day!"

Mother and daughter moved as one toward the counter.

"Mmmm," said the shopkeeper, glancing over wire-rimmed glasses, his repair of a vintage coin purse momentarily put on hold. "The kind of day meant for hot chocolate." With that, he looked inquiringly from the mother to child whose bright round eyes met his, yet gave no inclination of response.

"Hot chocolate will do just fine, wouldn't it, Micki?" said the woman.

Micki's eyes followed the shopkeeper as he went about concocting the chocolaty brew while her mother inspected the far wall of antique books. Satisfied there was not much else to gain by watching the shopkeeper,

73

Troy W. Rasmussen

Micki, her gaze and small fingers tracing the intricate lines of the counter to its end, raised her stare to the finely crafted easel, watching the watercolor painter in the initial stages of prepping her canvas.

Micki approached the easel slowly, curious. Sensing the girl's presence, the watercolor painter turned toward her and met the child's gaze with her own. Neither spoke; after a few moments, Micki silently turned and made her way toward an overstuffed couch by the window, where she curled up in the corner of the arm. With a tattered pillow in her lap, Micki leaned her head against the window and traced the trails of raindrops with her fingers.

Through no particular tragedy, yet by conscious decision, Micki decided to experience life without speaking. No one, her mother included, knew if this was to be a permanent arrangement or merely a temporary indulgence Micki devised to entertain herself in a world that seemed better experienced by her presence than her voice.

The shopkeeper approached in the silence he sensed was necessary, setting the hot chocolate on the table, but the girl's tracing didn't stop. Neither did the absentminded plucking of the stuffing from the pillow she held.

Micki's mother returned to the counter with several books she intended to purchase. Micki, her gaze moving from the window, regarded without concern the small cloud of stuffing in her hand. With the imagination of someone her age, Micki gently placed it on top of the hot chocolate.

The watercolor painting of Micki doing just that now hangs on the brick wall between the windows, above the couch where she sat.

The Shopkeeper's Journal

Wednesday

Almost a weekly constant, Trudy's piano playing took on a poignant air today as the notes became the background music for a couple deeply in love.

Trudy had been playing at her piano for half an hour as the shopkeeper went about the periodic ritual of sweeping floors. Hearing the gentle ring of the bell hanging over the door, he looked up to see an older couple walk into the shop arm-in-arm. Approaching the shopkeeper, the man said, "My name is Paul, and this lovely lady is my wife, Claudette. We've just arrived in town, sir, traveling the area on our fifty-second anniversary. We're on the hunt for a natural pearl necklace to mark the fair occasion and wonder if you may have something of that sort."

"Mmmm," the shopkeeper set aside his broom. Beckoning them to follow, he brought them to the row of drawers at the edge of the counter. The pair stepped forward and peered into the velvet-lined tray.

Paul gently placed his hand on her back as Claudette did a closer inspection of one particular necklace. Silence reigned as her aged fingers slowly traced the double strand of fifty identical pearls.

Dusting, the shopkeeper thought. *Profound dusting.*

The strands met one another and were joined together at the base by a sterling silver flower with its leaves gripping the top of a dime-sized natural pearl. Raising the pearls a bit, Claudette caressed them between her thumb and forefinger, as if she, and the necklace, had once met and were now reunited.

Paul took hold of the necklace and placed it around Claudette's neck. "A right nice fit, *Châu.*"

Troy W. Rasmussen

"We spent our honeymoon in Vietnam," Paul said. "I overheard local fishermen referring to the pearls they found as *châu,* and I've called my Claudette that ever since."

The shopkeeper grinned.

Trudy played a bit longer that day and, for the first time, leaned in to smell the azaleas as she turned to go.

The shopkeeper's methodical sweeping was nearly complete when Redmond arrived for his morning coffee.

"I'll be joined momentarily by a guest," he said, settling at his usual table. "Two cups of the Kopi, if you don't mind."

The shopkeeper was pouring the last few drops of the expensive elixir into its small cup when Redmond's guest arrived, greeting Redmond with a congenial smile. The clear resemblance between the older and younger man made it obvious: Redmond was meeting his son.

As the shopkeeper placed both cups on the table, Redmond, a dignified pride in his voice, introduced his son McAlister. A few minutes' discussion provided the information that McAlister was a graduate of Princeton, recently returning from an overseas apprenticeship in the restoration of historical buildings. Redmond and McAlister spent the next several hours discussing Redmond's plans to bring the dilapidated Matfield Greene back to the grandeur for which that area of town was once renowned.

Matfield Greene, a six-hundred-plus-acre expanse of early nineteenth-century homes with yards the size of small parks, was situated a few miles out of town and had been the secluded retreat of the wealthy. Its entry gates, iron ensconced in cut stone, still gave the curious passerby the impression only a select few were welcome.

76

The Shopkeeper's Journal

A full day could be spent driving the overgrown lanes winding their way past and amongst one grand façade after another. Each estate showed the scars of neglect or mistreatment, including the damage from stones cast through hundred-year-old leaded glass windows.

But worse than any damage the bored or unruly caused, time and nature had been the true culprits to the decaying buildings. Moisture seeping into unprotected, rotting sideboards seemed to work in unison with a variety of plants that wound their way through collapsed porches. Those daring to enter the unstable, age-worn buildings found themselves confronted with the ugly grey of decay, and skeleton boards showing through caved-in lath and plaster. Once finely carved and stained woodwork either hung askew or lay fallen among the clutter of forgotten Eastlake furniture.

The grace of Matfield Greene was gone. By commissioning McAlister, Redmond intended to remedy that.

Thursday
Although not overbearing, the afternoon heat was still enough to keep people from lingering outside. Bacardi was the exception. His dedication to the various flower gardens around town was unwavering, regardless of the weather— or, at times, because of it.

It never failed. Each time the shopkeeper brought Bacardi a glass of a cool drink, it either went untouched or ended up poured onto the flowerbed. The shopkeeper left the entryway only to return a few moments later with

Troy W. Rasmussen

Bacardi's preferred drink, even as he noticed the man's contemplation of a plant in less than optimum bloom.

The shopkeeper turned his attention to the afternoon rays of light streaming into a nearby park and allowed his gaze to linger on an individual greeting the rays with an upturned face. The slow communication between the person and light played one with the other, as if in the final caress of a lover's touch. For several moments, the two marveled at one another; then, as gently as the two had met, they parted. One lowered his head; a stream of light faded into darkness, then fell to the ground.

The halting steps of the man as he turned to depart could no longer be sustained alone. He was soon assisted by the steady and trusting arm of a nearby confidant, who handed him a dark pair of glasses and a white stick. As the two continued their stroll down the stone walkway, the shopkeeper, turning his focus again to Bacardi's garden, noticed next to the unfortunate plant a stick tenderly strapped to its stalk.

> *Friday*
> The Friday night characters are a never-ending source of entertainment. The guitar player and his musical dance with Melanie continues; those two seem to accept that, for the time being, nothing more is needed. Gordo, when he arrives, elicits a glance or two from newcomers and a hearty shout from those more accustomed to his energy. Not surprising was the first time arrival of McAlister, and that the Princeton set found themselves comfortably at home at these affairs.

The Shopkeeper's Journal

McAlister had been reacquainting himself with the town, taking early evening walks to clear his head. Hearing the goings-on at the shop, he went to investigate; possibilities lay everywhere.

At the front of the shop, light from inside brought a soft glow to the darkness gathering around it, and McAlister couldn't help but smile as he recalled entering places much like this during his time at Princeton. Joining a fraternity wasn't his forte, but at his father's urging, he'd done so. The shop reminded McAlister of the first time he'd entered a pub, hearing his frat brothers carrying on, the excitement...

Stepping up to the aperture, he noticed again that the carved wood door needed a good sanding and some Tung oil to bring out the richness of the wood.

Inside, the cool of the evening was echoed in a "coolness" from the crowd, at ease with themselves and their surroundings. Even the hippy at the counter seemed to fit in—sort of. Walking to the counter, McAlister recognized the shopkeeper.

"And how are you, sir?" he said cordially.

"Will it be a Kopi then?" asked the shopkeeper with a wink.

"Let's make it something tall and chilled," replied McAlister, a touch more sardonically than he'd intended.

Turning his attention to the activities of the room, McAlister stood, his elbow on the counter, waiting for his drink. Hearing the ice clink against the glass as the shopkeeper gently set the drink on the counter, McAlister turned, his elbow seemingly glued in place, and accepted the soda water and lemon with a tip of the glass.

He spent his time mingling amongst the crowd, introducing himself and providing details here and there

Troy W. Rasmussen

of why he was in town. More than a few eyebrows were raised after learning he was to revitalize Matfield Greene.

"You're redoing Matfield?"

"I am," McAlister said to one woman.

"Wow, that place has been run down for years."

"True. The project is ambitious but well worth the effort."

"How do you mean?" asked her friend.

"The revitalization will not only add to the town's coffers through taxes, but will benefit local trade and businesses."

"Oh."

McAlister grinned at the woman's response. His reply had sounded a little stiff, at that. "It's what I do."

"So, you like redoing old buildings?"

McAlister nodded.

"You know how to do all that?"

"For the most part, yes. The heavy work will be done by local contractors. For this project, I'll be managing operations."

"It's the 'local contractors' part that I'm interested in," a man said, at his elbow.

McAlister turned and shook the man's hand.

"Scott Jacobs. I overheard your comment about redoing Matfield. I work for Hugoton Construction and would be interested in discussing the details of the project with you."

"As would I with you."

McAlister left the shop that evening with two business cards in his pocket: one from a foreman with a local construction company, the other from an enthusiastic young man named Maarten.

The Shopkeeper's Journal

Saturday

Life moves at a quicker pace for some, the young man Parker being a good example. How can he hold so much potential yet so ardently accept the doldrums? Boredom—the millstone to initiative.

Parker had come to the shop often since his teen years. When he was younger, that had more to do with avoiding whatever unfavorable situation he'd gotten himself into than anything else. But, of late, his visits had a different purpose: lounging about, feet up, staring out the windows.

Parker's lounging had little to do with laziness—far from it. Entering the workforce in his mid-teens, he'd eventually found himself a laborer with the city. The physical work of street repair and maintaining the infrastructure of the community was an ideal way to build the physique he currently strutted around. A larger and as yet unknown benefit of Parker's work on the city crews was the development and understanding of the importance of civil engineering to the functioning of a community. His talents in devising plans for common areas or where a street should be routed matched, if not exceeded, many of the formally educated minds of those that enjoyed higher salaries for fewer results. Ironically, therein lay the reason for Parker's current state of mind.

Other than greeting him by name, and nodding as the young man entered the shop, the shopkeeper left Parker to his own thoughts and devices. He always brought over a cup of black coffee and set it within reach; sometimes,

Troy W. Rasmussen

it went untouched. Other times, it seemed the shopkeeper couldn't keep it filled fast enough.

Sometimes, the shopkeeper reflected, *an avalanche starts and gains its momentum of its own accord, and other times not.* With the local newspaper in his hand, he quietly approached Parker.

"Read the news?" the shopkeeper said. "There's an opening on the city council." With that, he set the newspaper on the coffee table.

Parker didn't move. "Good men in that group," he said quietly. "Old, but good." He paused for a deep breath. "Need some fresh ideas in that bunch, though. Took a fair step approving what they did for the Splash Festival, but that won't cut it long-term."

Noting Parker's comment with a nonchalant raise of his eyebrow, the shopkeeper continued on through the shop.

Parker, newspaper in hand, left a few minutes later.

The shopkeeper collected Parker's empty coffee cup and, as he turned toward the counter, caught Bacardi's conspiratorial gaze.

Olivia, a successful realtor, entered the shop displaying all the entrapments of the professional career she enjoyed—a sleekly conservative outfit, cleverly accessorized with trendy jewelry and costly handbag, designed to lend confidence to her customer base. Ever the one for efficiency, she had two reasons for her visit: one, to shop for a piece of glassware for her well-decorated home; the other, a meeting with McAllister to discuss the plans for the development of Matfield Greene.

The click of stiletto heels on a hardwood floor was not a sound the shopkeeper often heard, yet it told him Olivia had arrived, and with purpose. The shopkeeper,

82

The Shopkeeper's Journal

stooped over rearranging stock behind the counter, turned to see her warm smile.

"Good afternoon," she said.

"And to you, Miss Olivia. How does this day find you?" asked the shopkeeper.

She waved her hand. "It finds me well. I have an appointment in a few minutes with McAlister. Until then, I'm looking for a piece of antique glassware."

The shopkeeper raised his finger in an "I have just the piece" gesture, walked from behind the counter, and proceeded to guide Olivia midway into the shop. With a slight bow and a nod of his head, he directed her attention to a Rogaska clear crystal bowl. The moment Olivia saw its heavy, modern lines, she smiled.

"Perfect."

Decision made, she turned and walked back to one of the tables to await McAlister's arrival. The shopkeeper proceeded to the counter to wrap and box Olivia's purchase for delivery to her home. Olivia preferred not to carry anything more than what was necessary and willingly paid for the additional service.

Olivia's meeting with McAlister was every bit as efficient as her shopping. McAlister spent only a few minutes relaying the premise for his vision of resurrecting the wreck of Matfield Greene. She didn't take notes, asked few questions, and, when he finished, gave him a prompt estimate of the properties' proposed values.

"Marketing should begin immediately," she finished matter-of-factly.

"I'm impressed with your approach."

"The future of this project requires a level of immediacy."

Troy W. Rasmussen

McAlister stood to walk Olivia out. "That it does. Thank you for your time."

The shopkeeper noticed neither of them had touched the lemon waters placed before them.

Chester had spent the past few days exploring the far recesses behind the wall and stashing treasures. The shopkeeper was so accustomed to his coming and going that he barely noticed him that day until Chester was standing at the edge of the counter.

Something was missing in the boy's world.

The shopkeeper glanced sideways. "Secret places never lose their magic."

Chester gazed toward the windows, his hands deep in his pockets, and responded only with a small twitch of his mouth.

"There comes a time, though," the shopkeeper went on, "when a man begins to realize there's more to the world."

"Like what?"

"For starters, understanding the value of a job done well. "

"I don't have one of those."

Sliding the newly wrapped package toward the edge of the counter, the shopkeeper asked, "You know Miss Olivia—where she lives?"

"Sure."

The shopkeeper tapped the box as if to ask, "Well…?"

"How much?" Chester may not have fully grasped the concept of a job yet, but his acumen for understanding the value of time and effort needed no fine-tuning.

"Enough to keep a lad such as you in lollipops for a week," said the shopkeeper, grinning.

84

The Shopkeeper's Journal

"Done," Chester said, and without hesitation, he and the boxed crystal were out the door.

Chester had no sooner made his unceremonious exit when in strolled Maarten. *A dandy of a young man,* the shopkeeper thought. *He'll probably amount to more than he realizes once he settles his dreams and expectations.*

"And what may I do for you?" he asked.

Straight to the point—and with more assurance than his twenty-three years gave him experience—Maarten replied. "I've accepted a commission from McAlister to design the interior of the first estate to be revitalized at Matfield Greene, and thought I may find some inspiration perusing your shop."

"Peruse to your content, young man, but inspiration of the sort you seek doesn't come by wandering the dusty aisles of an old man's shop."

Maarten paused, inclining his head.

"Have you walked the halls of the building you're to design?"

"No, I haven't. I drove through the area a few days ago."

"Mmmm."

Maarten joined the shopkeeper at the counter. "It seems to me that until the contractor has done his work, there wouldn't be much 'feel' to the place."

The shopkeeper gave him a steady look. "An artist creates a work from an inner vision. Time and talent brings the piece, whatever its form, into existence."

"Exactly," replied Maarten, although he didn't look like he'd understood.

"What was your involvement in creating the building?"

"Well, none," Maarten stammered. "It's been there for some time."

Troy W. Rasmussen

"Yet you aim to redesign a work of art you've yet to set foot in."

It took a few seconds for the shopkeeper's meaning to sink in. As he went to leave, Maarten turned back toward the counter as if to ask a question, then apparently changed his mind and left.

Chapter 10

Monday
For those destined to wander, the urge to go cannot be denied. Gordo's respite has come to a close, the call of Africa once again sounding in his ears. South Africa, as I understand it. He's been there more than once and is eager to return to further experience what the land offers. Where Gordo goes, Gordo is. The purity of that soul and its connection to the world. How does one explain the ties of a son to a land that knows his name?

With a sigh of contentment, Gordo set the empty "cup of mud" on the counter.

"Safe journey." The shopkeeper retrieved the cup.

"A journey is a journey, Keep—safe or not."

With this, Gordo slung the worn leather pack over his shoulder and strolled out of the shop. Stepping past Bacardi, he said, by way of farewell, "Keep 'em healthy, old man."

"Mmmphhh," Bacardi responded.

As journeys go, the first step starts the process. According to Gordo, life is the journey, the first step taken on barely months-old, unsteady legs, with arms flailing for balance. Gordo maintained that this first-step process, and its accompanying unevenness, yielded a measure of balance to one's life and experience. He didn't deny his journeys were, in part, an effort to ensure

Troy W. Rasmussen

the balance of his life was kept steady through periods of unbalance. After all, isn't that what lies behind the mechanics of walking? The body continually throws itself off-balance with each step, only to have the next one put it right again.

Gordo's time in town—or wherever he happened to be when not wandering—was effectively his life in balance; after a time, the call to accept the next movement to place his life in unbalance would sound. Hesitation in answering this call was not an option, in his mind.

With little more than what he could fit in a leather pack and a deep breath of expectation, Gordo found himself again on the plains of South Africa. Stepping out of a sturdy (albeit road-beaten) Land Rover, he thanked the driver for the lift, slung his pack over his shoulder, and began the last few miles' trek, his destination a small village where he had learned a missions group was working to better the lives of the village inhabitants.

The sun on his shoulders came in thick waves, as did the heat bouncing off the dry tundra across which he walked. To the experienced wanderer, such conditions were more of a welcome than a hindrance. By midday, small children, playing a game of kickball on the outskirts of the village, stopped their activity to herald Gordo's arrival. They did so with the clamor only young children can create when they want to be first to welcome and announce the arrival of a newcomer.

With arms and legs pumping and voices raised in excitement, the small herd set out toward Gordo as if a prize went to the first one to arrive and encircle the traveler. Receptions such as this were not foreign to Gordo. Each one added to his own excitement of arriving at the day's destination.

The Shopkeeper's Journal

As the children and the dust their feet had kicked up encircled him, Gordo couldn't help but laugh and do his best to reach out and touch those so excited to touch him. Doing his best to keep his pace, he turned this way, then that, in a patient effort to engage each of the welcoming party.

In the melee, he caught sight of the smallest of the group, a young boy covered head-to-toe in grime, with well-worn pants held in place by a frayed cord, whose face was marked by the wet streams of frustrated tears. In a silent gesture of understanding, Gordo reached out his hand and, with a knowing grin, motioned for the boy to take hold—which he did eagerly. With the skill of a monkey, he climbed up Gordo's leg and torso and wrapped his arm around Gordo's neck to swing around behind his shoulders, his short legs clinging to either side, then raised one arm and gave a triumphant yell.

With Gordo thoroughly greeted, two of the older children broke from the group to head full speed toward the village in an effort to be the first to announce his arrival. They arrived in a dead heat and broke into excited chatter, imparting their news to a middle-aged man of solemn dignity. The man motioned to quiet the boys, then stepped forward to greet Gordo as the other children arrived. With a clap of his hands and words spoken in a native dialect, the man scattered all but the boy still gripping Gordo's neck.

> *Friday*
> An interesting turn of events tonight: Melanie and the guitar player's dance with each other continues. I'm reminded of those intricate moves and mating ritual documentaries of animals only recently

Troy W. Rasmussen

> acquainted, yet preparing to mate for
> life—dancing, the body's way to express
> itself through movement.
>
> Two dances tonight: one by Melanie's
> suitor, the other by an artist of such fluid
> ability as to cause those watching to feel
> as if a part of themselves, and surely the
> performer, had both lived and died with
> more passion than they may have thought
> possible.

Whether from force of habit or enjoyment of the
space, Melanie was once again on the couch by the front
windows, book in hand. Both by a force greater than
habit and enjoyment of the space, the guitar player was to
be found in the leather chair with collapsing cushions,
not quite straight across from her.

As he settled in, the guitar player caught a quick
glimpse of Melanie and received in return a brief glance
from the eyes of the woman he had yet to speak to. A
quick nod, a slight grin—one, two, three. He adjusted his
guitar and strap; she pulled the hem of her skirt tighter
over her ankle—one, two, three. More tuning of an
instrument that rarely needed it; the idle turn of the page
with words unread—one, two, three; one, two, three. The
dance of love, new love, takes many forms, yet little has
changed in the steps.

The song he played was new. He wrote this
particular piece and thought of the one he meant to play it
for, and so developed a melody many would listen to, but
only one would hear—and she did. As her fingers caused
the page to turn and bow slowly from one side of the
book to the other, the chords of the new song seemed to
follow suit, moving from player to listener. After a few

The Shopkeeper's Journal

minutes, his new song drew to a close, the chords growing slow and soft.

Without moving her eyes from the pages, Melanie asked, "What's it called?"

With his hands coming to a rest across the strings, he replied, *"Something about a Dance."*

Suddenly, dramatic music emerged around them from another source entirely. And, as it did, a woman began to dance, and onlookers took a momentary reprieve from their conversations to watch.

The performer's body moved from just inside the door to the opposite side of the counter, her arms rising and falling in imitation of a bird in flight. Flight without lift. Flight grounded with a broken wing. Her head turned and jerked in the struggle to do that which should come naturally to a creature designed for the air, not the ground. Searching. Searching for a way, any way, to gain the freedom of movement and strength in the lunge of takeoff. Time and again, she attempts, with the same result. With exhaustion setting in, her motions took on the resignation of a creature accepting that today, flight was destined not to be. The artist's body bent slowly backward against itself in imitation of the creature's angered acquiescence, mouth open wide, legs straightened, then collapsed.

Someone in the audience gasped. Two or three of the group standing closest to the performer leaned forward to ensure she was still breathing. After a few tense moments, the artist took an exaggerated breath, threw open her eyes, and rose from her repose on the floor, eliciting applause from all.

Troy W. Rasmussen

Saturday
The young man Parker has all but remade himself to better fit into the next phase of his life. The metamorphosis from a week ago cannot be denied—albeit necessary when seeking election to a public office.

The change in Parker's appearance was noticeable. A conservative suit had replaced the worn jeans; his shaggy hair, although still a bit long, was groomed in a swept-back, professional manner. Approaching the counter, he asked, "What do you think?"

The shopkeeper nodded his approval and noticed the fistful of what looked like pamphlets Parker was holding.

"I gave it some thought and decided who better to run for the Council than a guy like me?"

"I'm not surprised," the shopkeeper responded.

"Oh, it wasn't all me. I had lunch across the street at Natalia's the other day and, well, we got to talking. When I mentioned the open seat on the City Council and some ideas I have, she asked if I was thinking of 'putting my name in the hat.' I decided why not?" Lifting his arms and glancing down at the suit jacket, Parker grinned and continued, "She gave me some recommendations on how to dress the part."

"Good advice."

Parker handed the shopkeeper one of his flyers. "I'll be running a couple of ads in the newspaper as well as posting these around town. If you don't have any objections, I'd like to post this in the shop. Friday nights here draw the crowd I'd most like to reach. I'm planning to be here myself to mingle, let people know I'm running for the Council, and hear their ideas and opinions."

The Shopkeeper's Journal

The shopkeeper nodded toward a glass enclosure hanging just inside the door. "You can post your announcement there."

Parker walked to the enclosure and found it already full of announcements, yet added his own to the mix. "Thanks."

As he turned to leave, the young man noticed Bacardi standing in the doorway. "Good day to you, too, sir," he said, then sauntered off.

Smiling, Bacardi said, "Kid's goin' for it."

The shopkeeper's only response was a slight nod of his head.

Troy W. Rasmussen

Chapter 11

Monday

Death and the fascination it holds for the young. An innate acceptance that life is to be lived, not feared. Interesting that at times, one wishes nothing more than to help ward off inevitability, and at other times simply to watch.

"Don't touch it, Sammy," Sam's sister said in alarm.

Neither the shopkeeper nor Bacardi was sure if it was the words she spoke or the intensity with which she spoke them that caught their attention.

Sam—or Sammy, as his sister called him—was crouched down on his haunches, apparently deep in observation of a mouse lying all but motionless in the crevice where the stones of the walkway met those of the shop. The creature's chest heaved under the strain of breathing that no longer came as easy as before, its small black eyes staring into an unknown place. Sam, a short stick in hand, prodded the creature again in an attempt to elicit movement—nothing.

How do breaths that big go through a nose that small, he wondered?

You're dying, aren't you? Something happened and you got this far before you had to stop and lie down. Now you're waiting and you're not afraid. Not of me, my stick, or what's about to happen, just waiting. I'll stay with you if it doesn't take too long, so you won't die by yourself. I'm not sad, you know, and I don't think you are, either.

The Shopkeeper's Journal

It would have been fun, though, to chase you. You know, before you laid down. I'm fast, but you probably would have gotten away. If I caught you, though, I would have showed you to my sister and watched her scream.

Bacardi noticed the lad grin some, and sucked his teeth. Glancing up and over his shoulder to the shopkeeper, he tapped a small gardening shovel lightly against the palm of his hand. The shopkeeper nodded his understanding and quietly slipped into the shop.

Can you tell how long? How long you'll be there? You don't look like you hurt, but it can't be fun just lying there when you're used to running, and sniffing, and going places. I'll go places. Probably where my mom or sister tells me, but if you don't take too long, I won't go until you have. Maybe I'll go somewhere small and pretend I'm you. I'll crawl in, sniff around some, raise my head like I've seen others like you do, and then disappear inside. Is it fun to disappear? Why don't your eyes move? Can you blink? Is your other eye closed? If not, is it dry or does it have dirt in it? I bet it has dirt in it. I'd check, but my sister would yell again, and I wouldn't be able to stay, for sure. If you take much longer, I'll have to go.

Sam crossed his arms over his knees so he could rest his chin and continue to observe the mouse.

"I'm telling Mom, Sammy." His sister made the threat, but he didn't move.

I haven't touched anything. Even if I did, what would it matter? It would matter to him, maybe, wouldn't it?

Sam reached out his arm and, leaning forward on the balls of his feet, extended his finger and lightly ran it down the length of the dying mouse.

"Ooooo, Sammy. That's gross. Now I'm really telling Mom."

Troy W. Rasmussen

"It's not gross. It's soft—and kind of squishy," Sam replied.

Tell Mom. I don't care, and neither does he. You don't care about much right now, I suppose, 'cept maybe that it's not cold. If it was, I couldn't do much, you know. Where would I find a blanket that small? That wasn't a very big breath, you know. Must be time. When they get smaller, it means it's time, right?

"Is it still breathing?" his sister asked, bending over for a closer look.

"Barely. Not much really. Probably 'bout time."

"Time? Time for what?"

"What do you think?" Sam wrinkled his brow at his sister's silly question.

Is it time? If it is, I won't look away 'cept to check your chest. I can't tell otherwise. I hope you take another one—breath, I mean, 'cuz I want you to know I think I feel bad. Not because you're going—well, maybe, but because we didn't chase. It would have been fun. Yeah, lots of fun.

In the next few moments, Sam's world grew still and quiet as he intently watched the chest of a dying mouse, the intensity of his stare an effort of a young boy to will movement where none would be again.

Bye, mouse.

With his chin more deeply embedded into his folded arms, Sam turned his head and caught a hard—yet oddly understanding—gaze from Bacardi.

"Bring it here, boy."

Sam's sister's eyes, her entire being, froze at the request from the old man, but Sam didn't hesitate. He leaned forward, gently picked the mouse up, and placed it in the palm of his hand.

Sam approached Bacardi with solemn steps as, getting up from the steps and dusting the back of his

The Shopkeeper's Journal

pants, Bacardi moved closer to the flowerbed. He looked askance at the shopkeeper.

"Seems we have a situation here."

Looking at Sam and the still creature he held, the shopkeeper brought one hand forward, proffering an old, frayed piece of cloth. Silently, Sam reached out for the cloth. He placed it gently on the stones of the flowerbed and carefully wrapped the dead mouse within it.

Stepping back, Bacardi handed Sam the garden trowel. Sam took the tool, then bent and dug a place for the mouse to be buried. Once complete, he patted the base of the hole, making it firm; it seemed like the right the thing to do. Sam gently placed the encased mouse into the hole and then completed the work of filling it in. The dirt left a small mound —that, too, he patted firm.

His work complete, Sam stood back and surveyed the mound. With a sigh, he handed the shovel back to Bacardi, thanked him, and turned to take his sister's hand as they walked away.

Tuesday
Some days, all that happens to a being
is a gentle breeze.

The shopkeeper, recently back from an auction, had purchased six antique stools for the counter. He placed one of them at the end; when that one sold, it would be replaced with another.

Moving back behind the counter, he lit his pipe and began the process of cleaning the cappuccino machine, a tedious process, really—but when the shop was slow it could be meditative if one were so inclined. The door to the shop was open, stirring the dust particles each time a breeze came through. One of sorts did—in the form of a little girl named Carlee.

Carlee and her parents entered the shop with all the enthusiasm of a family on vacation, commenting eagerly about how quaint the shop was. To the shopkeeper, the words were like tiny breaks in a silence that had been thickly hanging about.

"Hello," said the woman, while her eyes took in the scenery. Carlee, a few steps behind her parents, was preoccupied with an imaginary game of hopscotch on the shop steps.

"Good afternoon," said the shopkeeper. "How does the world find your family?"

"Oh, wonderful," replied the woman. "What an amazing place. This town seems full of all sorts of places to discover."

"Mmmm. And I see you have one doing just that."

Glancing back, the woman gave a loving smile and a slightly exasperated sigh. "Carlee. Come and say hello to the nice gentleman."

A final hop, landing Carlee firmly in the entryway, was the only "hello" the preoccupied child gave.

"Look about," said the shopkeeper. "I'll assist you when you need."

Absorbed in the ambiance, Carlee's parents moved deeper into the shop. Their shift in attention from watching their daughter to imagining the possibility of finding some sought-after treasure seemed to be a familiar habit, indulged in many times in the past, and Carlee wasn't expected to join in.

Carlee quickly returned to the newest game she had discovered. Hopscotch on old wood floors provided as much, if not more, entertainment than on the steps, especially when her small bare feet landed on a squeaky board. With her tattered pink tutu and a head full of

The Shopkeeper's Journal

auburn ringlets bouncing in time to her hops from one squeaky board to the next, the little girl made slow progress into the shop. After a few minutes of the self-devised game, Carlee stopped and threw her hands upward, then downward into the folds of her dress. Sighing, she looked up and into the face of the shopkeeper.

"Ummph," she uttered.

Leaning on his elbows across the counter, the smoke from his pipe rising in an intricate swirling ballet about his head, the shopkeeper lifted himself upright and nodded toward the newly placed stool.

"That stool there? It's magical," he said to the girl.

Without hesitation, Carlee edged toward the stool with a look of skeptical wonder. Reaching out, she placed one hand on the seat—which came just to the level of her nose—and another on the back. Then, with an expertly placed foot, she hoisted herself onto the stool, her tulle dress landing in a plop about her. Her bare feet dangling, Carlee leaned onto the counter, her face alight with expectation.

The enamored shopkeeper grinned broadly. "How do you suppose such a magical stool works?"

Pushing back some, but with her hands still gripping the counter, Carlee looked toward the ceiling. She gave the question a few seconds of thought before placing her feet on the face of the counter, twisting her body and the stool one direction and pulling the other, causing the stool to spin. As she spun, she raised her hands to drag them across the counter in a wide, full circle.

Dusting.

With another push, the momentum a little harder this time, she repeated the feat with apparent skill.

99

Troy W. Rasmussen

"If you can spin it all the way around in one push," she said simply, "that's what starts it—the magic." Then she stopped, facing the shopkeeper confidently.

"And how right you are," he responded. "What do you suppose happens if you spin around two whole times?"

Twisting back and forth, Carlee declared, "A wish. Two spins gets you a wish!"

The shopkeeper chuckled. He suspected Carlee was accustomed to getting her wishes.

"Then let's see, shall we? You give it a go, and if you make two spins, I'll grant you a wish."

With a push of her feet and arms lifted above her head, the girl shoved off and easily spun around two times, then came to a triumphant stop with her hands gripping the counter.

"Well, then," the shopkeeper said, "what shall it be? What sort of wish comes with a two-time spin?"

"A smoke ring," she replied. "A good one."

Leaning back from the counter, the shopkeeper raised his eyebrows, making Carlee laugh. Then, he took a pull on his pipe and, with expert flair, blew a thick, curling smoke ring into the air. Carlee's rapt gaze followed the floating ring of smoke as it rose up over her head.

She looked back at him coyly. "Two rings," she insisted. "Two spins, two rings!"

The shopkeeper looked at Carlee sideways with a cocked eyebrow once more, clearly letting her know he knew he'd just been swindled. Carlee simply shrugged, as if to ask, *whatcha gonna do?*

After a momentary pause, he took a deeper draw of his pipe and released a ring of smoke into the air. As Carlee watched it rise, the shopkeeper puckered his lips and blew a second ring behind it. This one, flying quicker

The Shopkeeper's Journal

than the first, caught up with its predecessor and floated easily through the now extended ring.

Carlee clapped her hands in delight. "My wish—my wish!"

Then, as the smoke slowly dissipated, she looked skeptical again. "You said this stool was magic."

"Indeed I did, Miss. But first, what shall I get you to drink?"

"Something that fizzes." She popped up, flinging her hands into the air. "And fizzes big. Lots and lots of fizzes!!"

"Then fizzes you shall have."

The shopkeeper reached into the cooler and pulled out a frosty bottle of sarsaparilla. Carlee's eyes followed the dark brown bottle as he set it on the counter. "Saaarrrrrsaypairila."

With a momentary pause for effect, the shopkeeper stooped again into the cold box to retrieve a thick chilled mug that he set in front of his guest with a *clunk*. Eager with anticipation, the girl twisted back and forth on the stool.

Sssssprittttt, came the sound of escaping gases as he popped open the elixir. At the sound, the girl's eyes grew wider and more excited. The shopkeeper poured the drink, very slowly and deliberately. As he leveled out the glass container, he raised the bottle slightly, causing the cold liquid to develop rich, bubbly foam that rose up the chilled sides of the mug. Once the liquid reached the mouth of the mug, he slowed the pouring to allow a few bubbles to ooze over the edge. With that, he handed Carlee an oversized straw and once again leaned onto the counter.

Carlee wasted no time inserting the straw into the cold brew. Reaching her chin upward, she drew the tip

101

Troy W. Rasmussen

into her mouth and promptly began to blow. The force of her action caused the thick, sweet mixture to bubble wildly. At that, she released the straw, clearly delighted. "More...more!" she cried happily.

Not one to deny either the child or himself the moment, the shopkeeper promptly lifted the bottle and filled the mug with the remainder of its contents. After a few more impromptu spins of the stool, Carlee leaned forward again and blew into the straw with even more gusto.

Hundreds of thick, sticky bubbles burbled up and over the edge, spilling onto the counter in a pool of dark brown liquid. Another deep breath sent more bubbles on the same path down the side of the mug, over the edge of the counter and onto the floor. The last few tiny bubbles popped as they collided with hundred-year-old wood flooring. Carlee's third approach to the straw resulted in a deep draw of the sweet drink, sliding down her throat in one massive gulp.

Magic.

Just as Carlee was finishing her drink, her parents approached the two. "We're interested in one of your grandfather clocks."

Carlee popped a large bubble.

"Carlee," her mother exclaimed. "Did you make that mess?"

"One person's mess is another's magic," the shopkeeper said. "Easily enough cleaned up. Which of the clocks can I help you with?" He spoke a few minutes with the couple and made arrangements for the purchase and shipping of the clock.

As the couple and Carlee went to leave the store, sarsaparilla still dripping to the floor, Carlee, her yards of pink tulle bouncing as she walked, gave the shopkeeper a

The Shopkeeper's Journal

bright smile and quick wave goodbye. Carlee bounded down the steps the same way she had bounded up.

The sarsaparilla stain on the floor remains to this day, as does a watercolor painting of Carlee and her magic spinning stool.

> *Wednesday*
> Old World charm and manners seem never to go out of style, although you don't see much of either these days. Not a fair statement, yet true when compared to Lady Worthingston. She'd scoff at the idea of being addressed as such. Odd how one is left with the feeling of having been in the company of royalty when graced by her presence—calm affability, born of a life of wealth.

The chords of Trudy's piano playing drifted through the shop as the shopkeeper busied himself sweeping and mopping the hardwood floors. He had to admit, a certain sarsaparilla spill received less attention than it should have, if he'd truly been earnest about removing it.

Grinning to himself, he gave it a light once-over before he was interrupted by the quiet ding of the brass bell. The shopkeeper noted with satisfaction that none other than the town's grand dame, Mrs. Worthingston, had arrived. Her stature left little question she had done so with purpose.

"Ahh, the keeper of the shop," she began. "How good to see you."

"Likewise, Lady Worthingston." At the reference to her as "Lady," Mrs. Worthingston gave the shopkeeper a sly grin and raise of an eyebrow. The gentle humor

Troy W. Rasmussen

between the two over his use of such formal salutations, and the insinuation that her status demanded it, had gone on for years. It was no secret she favored his shop, notably for his insistence on placing high-end, expensive antique pieces throughout.

"What a delight to browse," she had exclaimed during one of her first visits, and he never forgot it. Mrs. Worthingston's idea of a delightful browse ended with her purchase of an eighteenth-century French crystal chandelier spanning six feet across at the base. It took two crews of men to deal with it, in the end—one to dismantle and move the thing, and a second to hang it in the dining hall of Worthingston Manor, the three-story stone edifice in which she lived and entertained.

Mr. Worthingston had passed away some twelve years before and, upon doing so, left the lovely and elegant Mrs. Worthingston his entire estate valued at more than a hundred million dollars.

"Have you noticed the art of writing—letters, I mean—has all but died away? Gone are the days when one expressed oneself through the elegant marks of well-rehearsed penmanship," she continued.

"Mmmm."

"I do so miss it, and so I decided to give your shop a visit."

The shopkeeper frowned, not sure how those two things were connected.

"Well, you see," she finished, with a touch of impatience, "I'm of a mind to continue that grand tradition of writing, and thus have need of a table befitting the task."

With broom and mop in hand, the shopkeeper moved past his distinguished guest—giving her a slight bow as he did so—to his spot behind the counter. After wiping his hands on his trousers (a gesture not missed by Mrs.

The Shopkeeper's Journal

Worthingston), the shopkeeper proceeded to a small enclosure—an alcove, mounted in the wall—and gently pulled the glass door open to retrieve an exquisite porcelain teacup and saucer adorned with gold trim and enameled filigree. The cup and saucer had been purchased by Mrs. Worthingston on a previous visit and left on the counter; since then, it had been kept in its case for use only when its owner visited.

"Tea first, I presume," he said, setting the cup on the counter.

"Always a delight." Placing her Chanel bag on the counter and wiping her hands as if only moments ago she had removed gloves, Mrs. Worthingston relaxed to await the arrival of her afternoon tea. "But, tell me. Have you anything resembling a writing table?"

"Just the table, or do you require a seat to go with it?"

"Just the table, my good man. Just the table."

A visit with Mrs. Worthingston, the shopkeeper mused with no small enjoyment, was a visit with the eccentric, and therefore never a bother—even when conducted in the formal manner she so enjoyed.

After pouring the tea through a silver tea strainer, the shopkeeper gently placed the cup in front of his guest. He stood back a bit as she delicately sipped, closing her eyes in pleasure. She raised her head, nodding, then set the cup onto its saucer with a barely audible *clink*.

"A few more sips, my good man, and I shall be ready to view the piece."

While Mrs. Worthingston sipped her tea, the shopkeeper moved from behind the counter and into the shop. Although she could hear the sounds of furniture being moved this way and that, Mrs. Worthingston's

105

Troy W. Rasmussen

gaze remained forward, her only movement being her hands lifting the teacup and setting it back down.

With the help of a rolling dolly, the shopkeeper soon appeared a few steps away from his guest, writing table in tow. He brought it to a slow halt, then cleared his throat in a subtle bid for her attention.

Turning slightly, Mrs. Worthingston gazed upon a Louis XV writing table, masterfully carved and inlaid with rare imported woods. Caught by the grandeur of the piece, she spent a few moments in private reflection, then smiled.

"Isn't it wonderful?" she exclaimed.

With that, she stepped forward and began running her fingers across the tapered lid.

Dusting.

With her hand paused midway across the face of the piece, Mrs. Worthingston turned her gaze toward the lines and carvings adorning the elaborate table.

"Once again, dear sir, your selection of artifacts has brought a light into the world of an aging woman," she said quietly. The shopkeeper merely half-smiled and nodded.

"I'll make the arrangements for the desk to be delivered to the manor," he said.

"My thanks to you," she concluded.

With a tap of her walking stick to close the transaction, Mrs. Worthingston proceeded to leave. After gently cleaning and drying her teacup, the shopkeeper placed it back into its niche and, with the slight click of the latch on the glass door, he was back to work sweeping the floor.

Thursday
The jar containing Chester's wages in lollipops is nearly empty. Surprising,

The Shopkeeper's Journal

really, how long they lasted. Seeing the
lad without the paper stick protruding
from the side of his mouth has become a
rarity. Lollipops—the sugary companion
to boys and their imagination.
Sugar…sugar and chocolate…chocolate
tortes…someone once said to never write
down that which you don't want another
to know. Sometimes a memory needs to
stay just that—a deeply held, fond
memory.

Chester arrived in his usual way. His routine of
popping in, then disappearing, was interrupted only by
his casual stop at the lollipop jar on the edge of the
counter. He paused at the newly placed stool at the end of
the counter and concluded it made access to the jar
easier. Hopping onto the seat of the stool, he gave it a
push to start it spinning.

"Nice stool." He brought it to a halt, then reached his
arm into the depths of the jar holding his hard-earned
wages, unwrapped the hard candy globe, paused
momentarily, then continued. "How was your trip? Get
anything good?"

Having him ask about the shopkeeper's recent
auction trip wasn't a surprise. Chester was well-informed
about the activities of the shop.

"Mmmm. Overall, it was a success."

Chester wadded the paper wrapper into a ball and,
sticking it in his pocket, answered the shopkeeper with
his own "Mmmm." Then, with a final spin of the stool,
he hopped down to disappear into the back of the shop.
With a grin, the shopkeeper replaced the lid of the jar to
the sound of a secret door being opened, then closed.

Troy W. Rasmussen

Chester no longer paused when entering the space he now considered his own. So often did he come and go that the new had become the common, a familiar step in a rehearsed process that took him deeper inside.

A few days prior he had discovered a space he could squeeze into, just between the thickly cut wood columns supporting the building's structure. It was big enough for a boy his size, although nothing more than a small closet's worth of space. Large, by his definition, meant another world entirely. A place where anything was possible for Fagan, Chester's imaginary counterpart.

Ding-a-ling-ding! went the bell above the shop door, faithfully announcing the next visitor. Looking up from the jar with Chester's remaining lollipops, the shopkeeper was pleasantly surprised to see Natalia holding a small white cardboard box.

"Hello," she greeted the shopkeeper.

"Hello, my dear Natalia. How are you?"

"Busy," she replied. "In a good way, though."

Approaching the counter, she set the box down and slid it a few inches toward him. "I wanted to thank you, well, for all you did for me that first day here in the shop." Taking a deep breath and glancing back toward the place they sat that day at the window, she went on, "I'll never forget it—ever."

She hadn't expected to become this emotional; she'd rehearsed this speech several times. With her eyes tearing up, she leaned over the counter and kissed him on the cheek.

"Mmmm. The doing was yours, Ms. Natalia." He smiled. "As for the small part I played, though, you are welcome."

At this, he opened the box and gazed in at four carefully placed confections.

108

The Shopkeeper's Journal

"They're a new recipe, chocolate cherry tortes. I'm adding them to this month's menu, but you're the first to try them."

The shopkeeper reached in for one, then handed a second to Natalia.

"A toast," he said. "A toast to this month's treat and the beautiful woman responsible for its creation."

They grinned, tapped their tortes together, and proceeded to take oversized bites. Natalia giggled a bit at the crumbs falling from her mouth, and at the sight of the shopkeeper having the same thing happen. After swallowing, both stood quietly listening to the music playing in the shop, soft sounds of rain and mellow notes.

As Natalia gently wiped her lower lip of the last crumb, one stray tear escaped.

Looking up, she whispered again, "Thank you."

Friday

The popularity of Friday night has grown to such an extent that some people arrive early just to have a place to sit. It seems the five-o'clock bell has barely sounded before the place begins to fill.

At least two seats always have the same people in them, though, regardless of the time or crowd. Word has it our musician and Melanie have been spending time at Natalia's.

Progress.

It also seems our young entrepreneur Maarten has been making progress of his own. He's made more than a few trips to Matfield Greene, in an effort to better

Troy W. Rasmussen

> acclimate himself to the artistry of his
> commission. We'll see.

As the shopkeeper made drinks, he noticed the guitar player strumming his chords with a bit more flair than on previous evenings. In the few seconds it took the coffee machine to fill a small cup with espresso, the shopkeeper glanced over at Melanie's usual spot by the window, wondering what she thought of this new rhythm.

To his surprise, Melanie wasn't there. Instead, she was curled up next to the guitar player, an unopened book lying in her lap. Uttering his customary "Mmmm," the shopkeeper continued the task at hand.

After preparing the espresso for the couple in the corner, he shifted his attention to Maarten coming in the door. Maarten arrived at the counter with the air of someone who'd just met a goal—and started talking even before he got there.

"You were right," he said to the shopkeeper. "Spending time in the buildings at the Greene has yielded a far better understanding of what it will take to design the interiors. The idea of bringing two different eras together in the same place is more of a challenge than I realized. There's no way I would have been prepared to do it justice. You know, there was such a grace to that time period, a certain refinement you just don't understand unless you've been in its presence—such as it is."

"And now you're prepared?" the shopkeeper asked.

"More prepared than a few days ago."

"Mmmm. So the time to design is at hand?"

"Time to begin." Maarten slapped the counter, grinning, then turned around and disappeared into the crowd.

The Shopkeeper's Journal

As he watched Maarten become part of the crowd of people, the shopkeeper also caught a glimpse of Parker speaking with a group of young up-and-comers. The noise level in the shop didn't allow him to hear the conversations, but judging by the periodic nod or head tilt of his listeners, it was evident people were buying what Parker was selling.

> *Saturday*
> Big plans and big business. And it all seems to center around the revitalization of Matfield Greene. Maarten, our ever-enthusiastic designer, has become a regular to the shop—good for business. Backed by his father's connections, McAlister has secured his first tenant— good for Matfield Greene.

The shopkeeper stood at the door, gently stretching his back. The steady flow of weekend tourists reminded him of a slow-moving river in no hurry to get where it was going. He took an easy breath and then turned back inside to check on his customers, most notably McAlister and a very distinguished-looking man named Vatori.

The shopkeeper had seen them before, touring the town—McAlister motioning here and there, as he recited the community's history and the importance of various buildings. Today's tour, which apparently had included a drive-through of Matfield, had culminated with the two arriving at the shop half an hour earlier. McAlister shared with the shopkeeper that he thought Vatori would be more prone to closing the deal while sitting at ease in an overstuffed leather chair, nursing a drink and smoking Gurkha cigars.

111

Troy W. Rasmussen

Vatori Mastroberardino was the descendant of a wealthy Italian family. From what the shopkeeper gathered, the family, with Vatori as the newly crowned prince, made and continued to build its fortune in shipping. Vatori, looking to increase his overstuffed real estate portfolio, was attracted to Matfield Greene for its removed location and privacy; a kind of getaway in the Americas, if a seven-acre rundown stone estate built in the early 1800s —the largest at Matfield—could be described as a "getaway."

Watching the two as they discussed the future of what might become some of the most expensive real estate in the area, the shopkeeper grinned at the mental picture of the young Vatori pulling into the large circular drive, casually exiting his Maybach Exelero. The shopkeeper noticed Vatori carried with him the stature and dignity of a man accustomed to family wealth, who knew what it took to obtain and keep it; flaunting was not the Mastroberardino way.

"Gentlemen," the shopkeeper said, "I trust your afternoon is going well." Facing Vatori, he extended his hand by way of greeting.

McAlister performed the requisite introductions, adding, "Vatori is our newest resident. He's closing on the old Baker Mansion today."

"Mmmm. The Baker Mansion," said the shopkeeper. He wondered if McAlister had shared the local legend about the famed cloister with his new client.

"The location is perfect for what I have in mind," said Vatori with the lilt of an Italian accent. "The area, the hills—*bella,* beautiful. I am honored to be part of this project."

"The honor is ours, Mr. Vatori," the shopkeeper said.

"Please, Vatori is what I prefer. 'Mister' is for business. When I am here, I am among friends."

112

The Shopkeeper's Journal

"Maarten and Olivia will be joining us," McAlister said.

The shopkeeper bowed slightly before turning to leave the men to their discussions.

A few minutes later, Olivia stepped into the shop, with Maarten close behind.

"Good afternoon, sir," she called to the shopkeeper, winking.

"And to you, Ms. Olivia. Maarten."

Before Maarten could respond, the shopkeeper lifted his arm in the direction of McAlister and Vatori. "I believe you are expected."

"Ah. You've met Vatori, then," Olivia noted.

"Only just. It appears the formalities are all that's left and you are undoubtedly the one to manage the group through the mire."

Addressing Maarten, he said, "And you…"

Maarten spoke up excitedly. "I'll be decorating the place." Then, catching himself, he looked sheepish for a moment. "I mean, designing the interior of the location."

"Mmmm."

"I'm thinking to run the purchase of the antiques through your shop. You have several pieces already that would work beautifully—all high-end, of course."

"Of course," the shopkeeper replied, casting a knowing glance at Olivia.

Olivia and Maarten took their leave to join McAlister and his guest at their table. As he turned to go back to the counter, the shopkeeper glanced across the street. There, Natalia was in conversation with a ragged, hulking creature of a man.

"And what shall I call you?" Natalia asked him.

"Rugger, ma'am. I tell people it's Rugger."

113

Troy W. Rasmussen

"All right, then, Rugger. When was the last time you had a meal?"

"Kind of you, miss, but imposin' I don't mean to do."

"I know." Natalia put a hand on his shoulder. "It feels that way, and it can be tough to see otherwise, but it isn't so. Please, come with me."

With a barely audible sigh, Rugger followed her into the eatery.

The shopkeeper remained a few seconds more to see Natalia guide her weary guest to a certain reserved table.

The watercolor painter also watched the event in progress, following Natalia's movements as she eased Rugger into his seat. Just before turning to prepare the man his meal, Natalia paused. She placed one hand on his hunched shoulders and the other in the crook of his arm, bent to support his head, and gently hugged him.

As she returned to her easel, the watercolor painter lifted the heavy page of her current project to start another, depicting a young woman fulfilling her life's work.

The Shopkeeper's Journal

Chapter 12

Monday

Time has not so long passed as to wilt the memories of an old man, memories of times when the "otherworld" was as real to him as it is to Chester. The gateway, the secret passage, and all the mysteries it holds may change some, but the destination remains the same magical place, made all the more so by the belief of a young boy. It existed—exists still— and will again, to the next intrepid explorer ready to experience the magic and wonder.

Chester nestled into his newly discovered cove within the building's support structure, then flipped the switch on the side of a small mechanical light he had stashed a few days before. Resting the light into the joint of two beams, he leaned his head back against the rough-hewn six-by-six post and took in the quiet of the place. The thought of getting into trouble for wandering so far back didn't worry him.

No one knows. Nothin' wrong with just sittin' here, he thought.

Breathing easily, Chester took in the smells of ancient wood and dust, prompting his mind to relax and wander to a place of mystery…

115

Troy W. Rasmussen

A few moments passed before Fagan's eyes slowly opened and looked from side to side, his eyebrows knitted together in an attempt to decipher the sound in his ears. Sounds like water, lots of water. Except for the slight movement of his head, tilting forward in an attempt to hear better, Fagan remained still. Lots of water, like a waterfall...but can't be. As the sound grew louder, he sat up, went to his hands and knees, his head still cocked to the side.

Then he saw it. A few feet away, a heavy metal ring coated in rust lay against the floor. He'd seen such rings before in the movies, rings characters used to lift a door in the floor that led to a cellar or basement.

Not wanting to waste any time, Fagan quickly turned on his knees and reached back to retrieve the mechanical light, then moved back toward the ring. It appeared to be embedded into a wooden plank, with worn scuff marks around its base from being pulled upright.

Fagan reached forward, took hold of the ring, and pulled up on it—but nothing happened.

It's stuck.

Fagan slid his body forward to a kneeling position over the ring. Swiftly, he put his light on the floor so it shone directly on the ring. Then, using his back and legs for extra support, he grabbed hold again and pulled as hard as he could.

Sssuuffft...

With a sound like air rushing into a vacuum, the door heaved open.

The young explorer had done it! After months of following hidden clues, he'd finally found the secret entrance to the fabled Otherworld. Peering down the dark hole, he could hardly believe a place of wealth and magic, of disparity and the common, was to be found

116

The Shopkeeper's Journal

through such a dreary portal. Young explorers don't long concern themselves with such machinations, however, but rather bravely step forward. Anything else meant you were a scaredy-cat, not an explorer.

With a deep breath, and feigning more courage than he actually had, Fagan took the first step down. A second step, then a third, and all seemed well.

No rotting boards that break just when you trust them, throwing you into the abyss. Could still be other traps here, though. If so, Fagan was prepared.

Five steps, then six. Fagan continued down into the dark, his head slipping through the square hole in the ground. One last bit of light made a ring about his head; the next step brought him completely underground.

Fagan paused a few seconds for his eyes to adjust to the darkness. The air had changed—it was thicker, wetter than the air above. Looking upward through the square hole of light, he wondered briefly if he would ever breathe the air from above again. But he didn't stop.

Eight steps now, nine. The air, still thick, seemed to lighten, swirling about his face. And then there was the sound. What was that noise? He hadn't heard it from above.

Making the last step, Fagan released his grip on the steep stairs to stand upright. Just as he was becoming more comfortable with his surroundings, he heard a loud pop, then a scratching—the gritty sound of someone, or something, striking a flint to set a flame.

Pop—pop! Sparks flew, burning his eyes with their brightness.

Pop! Again, then—pufffdt, as the sparks ignited the flammable substance.

Fagan stood motionless in the realization that he was not alone.

117

Troy W. Rasmussen

The light from the bursting flame dwindled into a calm flicker, sitting in a clay container the size of a woman's makeup compact. Fagan's eyes widened and his pulse raced when he realized the container holding the flame was sitting in the palm of a hand, thick gnarled fingers extending out from the dish.

"State why you've come," said a voice. To Fagan's ears, it was as if those were the first words it had uttered in very long time.

"The Otherworld. I want to see it."

"Aye. And do you think you've found it?"

"I believe so." Looking around, Fagan wondered if he had made a great discovery or simply fallen prey to the first trap the entrance to the magical land was rumored to have.

"You don't seem afraid, boy," croaked the faceless voice.

"Have I something to fear?"

At that, Fagan heard a heavy, sliding sound of the feet of whatever creature was holding the flame, moving out from the shadows. He saw wrinkled, discolored skin, and wondered if he'd fallen into the lair of a human-sized Komodo dragon. He squinted his eyes for a better focus and realized he was staring at a troll.

"I have nothing to fear," Fagan responded.

The troll jabbed the flame forward. "Why not, boy?"

"'Cuz where there are trolls, there are gateways. I found one, didn't I?"

"How do you know I won't kill you?"

"If that were your purpose, you would have done it by now." Fagan looked the troll over more closely. "My guess is you're more of a guardian than an assassin. You're here to keep the gateway safe, not take the lives of the unsuspecting." Fagan moved about the space

The Shopkeeper's Journal

searching for something—a lever, a hole, anything that would trigger the exposure of the Otherworld.

"What you lookin' for, boy?"

"The way into the Otherworld. If you know it, show me."

The troll blinked. "Follow me."

As they entered a maze of tunnels, Fagan noticed the movement of the air getting stronger. The stone walls were slick and shiny with moisture. The musty smell of damp earth seemed to circle his head and fill his nostrils.

"Why is the air so damp?" he said. "Are we near a waterfall?"

At this, the troll stopped, stamped his foot, and shook his fist into the air.

"Yes. Just around the next corner is a waterfall, a big one. And yes, it is the gateway you seek, but you'll never get through."

"Why not?"

"Takes more than being clever to get through the gateway, boy. Clever boy, you've found it. Passing through it...." The troll turned to face him. "...is quite another matter."

At this point, the roar of the waterfall had made them shout, and Fagan saw the fall at last. Not as tall as its noise made him imagine, its waters were illuminated, but he couldn't tell how. There seemed to be a soft glow coming from behind them—maybe light from the Otherworld.

The troll noticed the direction of Fagan's gaze and said, "The Otherworld isn't what people think. What is can be something different, and something different can change. It all starts with a riddle."

Then, as if he'd shocked himself, the troll stomped both feet and clamped his free hand over his mouth.

119

Troy W. Rasmussen

"A riddle?" Looking at the falls, Fagan calculated his ability to solve the riddle versus taking a more direct route. "Why not just run through to the other side?"

"Only the riddle works. You either solve it or you don't. Trying to run through will get you a knot on the head." At this, the troll threw his head back in laughter.

"What do you mean, a 'knot'?"

Leaning forward, the troll lowered his voice. "Just a wall behind those falls, boy, just a wall." With the gleam of a challenge, the troll added, "Solve the riddle and go through. Fail and it remains a wall."

Fagan smiled to himself. He was up to the challenge. "State your riddle, troll."

The troll grinned at the boy's youthful arrogance. "Certainly. You can try, and fail, just like all the others." He paused, then went on. "This old one runs forever, but never moves at all. It has neither lungs nor throat, but still a mighty roaring call. What is it?"

Fagan barely flinched. "A waterfall."

The troll's dejected face made Fagan laugh.

"Some guardian! If the key to the gateway is a riddle, you'd better come up with a harder one than that."

Fagan had no sooner taunted the troll than the room was suddenly filled with light. The roar of the waterfall remained but, rather than being hard on his ears, it became a pleasing sound. Fagan turned his attention toward the falls and realized the wall had been replaced by a strong light originating behind them. It took a moment or two for him to realize the light filled the room and seemed to be coming from all directions. Snapping his head toward the troll, Fagan gasped to discover the troll had disappeared; in its place stood a beautiful young woman.

The Shopkeeper's Journal

The shopkeeper had just completed polishing a silver tea service back to luster when he heard the unmistakable sound of the door to the secret passageway open, then shut —*click*. Chester's time in the wall was done for the day. As the boy approached the counter, the shopkeeper, polishing rag still in hand, paused for a moment. "All is well in the secret places?"

"Yep." Chester's response was offhand, his attention riveted on the empty jar on the counter.

"Say," the shopkeeper went on, "just how is it nowadays a guy gets into a secret place?"

"Has to know the way…and the code."

The shopkeeper chuckled. *Always a code —it's written somewhere there has to be a code and only the chosen one, or at times the few, get to be privy to it. No girls allowed unless you know the code.*

"What's so funny, Mister?"

"A code, is it? What about a riddle?"

Chester's gaze snapped sideways and locked on that of the shopkeeper, peering over the rims of his glasses.

Slowly, Chester replied, "A riddle's just a trick, words that say one thing but mean another."

"Mmmm."

> *Tuesday*
> Young love—nothing compares. How glad we all are to see it blooming. Parker and the ever-lovely Natalia have been spotted, most often in front of her eatery, in proximity too close for anything other than a budding relationship. This one needs to last, to be strong.

Troy W. Rasmussen

"It would appear that Parker, there, has set his sights on more than public office," Bacardi said.

Having just delivered Bacardi's drink to the edge of the flowerbed, the shopkeeper raised his head and took in what the gardener saw.

Parker and Natalia walked out of the eatery deep in conversation, their heads bent in toward each other. Parker placed his arm around Natalie's waist as the two moved further down the walkway. He said something and both of them laughed. Natalia playfully punched him in the chest.

"That it would," replied the shopkeeper. "And by all accounts, he's hit the mark. Not the first time I've seen them together."

"Young buck seems pretty unaware of what he's taking on: new post with the city, lass like that one— where's that coffee?" From his position at the front of the flowerbed, Bacardi hadn't seen his drink sitting on the bricks, but when he bent forward, he found it and took a large swallow. "Pretty unaware, I'd say. The young ones think they can do it all and all at the same time. Ummmpfff." Bacardi returned to tilling, his coffee set to one side.

"Does seem a bit much. But, then, what is youth for, if not to take on too much?" the shopkeeper replied.

Bacardi slowly turned his head, eyebrows raised to a questioning point in the center of his brow. The shopkeeper merely smiled and shrugged.

Across the street, Parker lightly kissed the top of Natalia's head before lifting his hand and gazing toward the shopkeeper. With a brief word, he left Natalia and sprinted across to the shop.

"Glad I caught you," he said, a touch out of breath. "I have news." Looking back toward Natalia, picking up stray dishes from the sidewalk tables, Parker nodded.

122

The Shopkeeper's Journal

"Talia and I were just discussing the upcoming art festival. I'm on the committee responsible for signing on the artists. I wondered if the woman who does the watercolor paintings might be interested in a spotlight of sorts, in the brochure."

"You should ask her yourself," the shopkeeper replied. "I just display her work and sell a piece now and again."

"I will." Parker paused for a moment. "We're adding something new this season. With college costing so much nowadays, we thought it would be good to have a contest to help out."

Bacardi stuck his trowel into the soft dirt and sat up straight. "What do you mean, a contest?"

"Air bands. We'll have an air band contest, with the best of show winning a full scholarship to one of the state schools."

"Air band, huh? Not sure I follow."

"People sign up to do miniature shows—three or four of their favorite songs."

"What's that got to do with air?"

"People don't have to actually play the instruments. They pretend."

"Uh huh." Bacardi just shook his head, still clearly in the dark, and went back to his work.

Parker smiled and turned his attention back to the shopkeeper. "Since this intersection is the biggest on the street, the committee thinks it best to have the event here. There will be a few stands over there, and the stage on this side, in front of the sitting park. That should be enough room." He smiled. "The flyers for the event should be ready in a couple of days. I'll swing by to post one."

123

Troy W. Rasmussen

"Mmmm." From a young man plodding through a life of boredom to an energetic *Council hopeful.* The shopkeeper peered across the street once more, in time to see Natalia disappear into her eatery, and smiled to himself.

> *Wednesday*
> Our wanderer has returned. He was missed. Although his excursion was more work than esoteric exploration, he doesn't seem any worse for the wear. It's a small divide that separates helping others and learning about oneself.

Sweeping the walkways on days like today was more a pleasure, a brief reprieve, than actual work. Except for when Bacardi was busy at the flowerbed, there really wasn't much to sweep.

The shopkeeper started at the steps and began the methodical back-and-forth drag of the broom, moving dirt slowly to the curb. Sweeping the area just in front of the flowerbed, the shopkeeper pushed his broom into Bacardi's feet to get him to move, something Bacardi did only after shooting him an impatient look.

Once the shopkeeper moved further up the walkway, Bacardi took his shovel and with a secretive grin lightly tapped the soil stuck to its edge off onto the walkway.

"If you think he doesn't know what you just did, I'd wager you're mistaken."

Gordo's comment took Bacardi by surprise, but it didn't change his attitude. "Don't know it needed announcin'," he said slyly.

Both men grinned at one another. Then, slapping the old man on the shoulder, Gordo looked up to see the

124

The Shopkeeper's Journal

shopkeeper standing with his elbow on the tip of the broom handle.

"Got a cup of mud, Keep?"

"That I do."

Satisfied, Gordo gave a final pat to Bacardi's shoulder and stepped into the shop.

The shopkeeper followed—but not before gently tilting his broom handle against the pot of a new plant, spilling its contents. Bacardi caught the glint in the shopkeeper's eyes and held back on retaliation, instead mumbling something about picking his battles.

Gordo leaned forward on his elbows, watching the shopkeeper prepare his drink. "How's business?"

"No complaints. How was Africa?"

"No complaints. Good to go, and good to be back."

The shopkeeper slid the cocoa toward his guest. "Thick as it comes, hold the cinnamon."

Gordo's white teeth shown through sunburnt lips, and he wasted no time drinking it.

"Aaahh," he murmured, in pure pleasure. "Now there's something you don't find on the plains. Can't tell ya how many times I thought about this moment. It tastes as good as I remember."

"The palate never forgets," said the shopkeeper.

"No, I suppose not." Gordo set down the cup, still grinning, then reached into his backpack and pulled out something wrapped in burlap and bound by twine. Laying it on the counter, he looked at the shopkeeper. "For you, Keep. Right up your alley, if I don't miss my guess."

The shopkeeper took hold of the object, untied the twine and fabric, and rolled a pipe onto the palm of his hand.

Troy W. Rasmussen

"Hand carved," Gordo said, pointing at the gift. "Old man that makes those sits for hours in the heat of the day, carving away. Sometimes toys for the kids and sometimes, well, things like that pipe. It's made from snakewood. Never been smoked, so you'll have to break it in."

The shopkeeper turned the pipe back and forth, raising his eyebrows in approval of the workmanship. Carving a pipe by hand was no easy feat. He could tell a considerable amount of time had been spent polishing it.

Gordo went on. "Uses stones to get that polish. Scoops them up in his hand and rubs for hours—hands as bony as a skeleton. I sat with him the afternoon he hollowed the neck. A work of art in its own right— thought you would enjoy it."

Continuing his inspection of the piece, the shopkeeper fingered the cap over the bowl and gently pushed against the edge. The cap swiveled open, which would allow the user to pack the bowl and, when finished with his smoke, to push it closed again to extinguish the embers.

The shopkeeper inserted the pipe into his lips, sucked air in, then blew out to test the flow. Once that was done, he reached over, pulled out a drawer behind the counter and, taking out his pouch of tobacco, began packing the pipe. He lit it with a match—lighting a pipe with butane affected the flavor—and set the shredded leaves on fire as he pulled smoke through the stem. He repeated the process several times, causing the area around the two to fill with the fragrant smoke.

Without being asked, he turned and poured Gordo seconds on his "mud." Then, the two men spent the next few minutes in silence—one gulping chocolate, the other smoking his pipe, and both smiling. Only Bacardi's voice interrupted the spell.

126

The Shopkeeper's Journal

"If the two of you are done," he rasped, "maybe a guy could get a refill of his coffee."

With his new pipe locked between his teeth, the shopkeeper obligingly filled Bacardi's mug. Once completed, he returned to the counter.

"So tell me about the details of your trip," he prompted Gordo.

"Africa was great. Did some work in a small village helping the natives dig a freshwater well."

"By hand?"

"One of those charities raised the funds to pay for it, but then they ran into some problems with the government. Seems they wanted a bit of a kickback before allowing the equipment to be moved through. Problem was the charity doesn't operate that way. So there we were, equipment held up and the people without water."

"Damned bureaucrats," Bacardi put in. "Just as soon people die of thirst than to give up the lining of their pockets." He turned sharply and left the shop.

The shopkeeper puffed more smoke into the air. "What happened?"

"Meetings—four of them. The chief of the village was frustrated, but seemed to accept it all as 'the way it is.' I asked if it would make a difference if the politicians got the credit." Gordo shook his head. "The chief looked at me like I was crazy."

"Compromise—good approach."

"Yeah, well, the government's been crooked for so long that people prefer to go without than give them credit."

"What happened to the equipment?"

"Who knows? The charity representatives did their best to get it through, but those in charge just sat there

127

with big grins on their faces. Then one afternoon, while me and some of the elders were sitting in the shade looking out over the area where the well was to be, it occurred to me—people have been digging wells for centuries and none of them with heavy equipment. The locals had plenty of strong men, and women, that could dig and haul.

"So you know, that's just what we did, dug that well by hand. Seemed like we'd never reach the water, but then one day the men in the hole started trilling their tongues as loud as they could, the women and children joining them as everyone went running. At first I thought something bad had happened, maybe someone fell in. When I got to the edge, though, I realized they were trilling in celebration. Those in the hole were ankle-deep in mud."

Gordo paused a moment. "What a feeling. Mud on their feet meant the water was coming through. All that was left was to dig a bit more and line the thing with stone." He shrugged, but his face still held awe. "Pretty cool to see it all play out."

> *Thursday*
> The town's astir with the weekend's art festival. And, not surprising, it's the air band contest drawing the most chatter. All sorts of schemes developing from minor to extravagant. At the center are fathers doing what they can, in some cases more than they should, for their children to have a shot at a fully funded education. That I was approached by one of the participants to assist was a bit of a shock. If it all comes off how he has planned, it should

The Shopkeeper's Journal

be a fair show. What a father won't do for his child.

As one of the local business owners, Rodney was fairly well known in town. He and his wife of twenty-one years had lived in the area since their marriage. The family-run motel, one of the nicer in town, was busy nine months out of the year, but not so much that a chance to have his oldest daughter's education paid for wasn't appealing.

Rodney's daughter, Avery, turned eighteen in the fall and would start college in a couple of weeks. She was the oldest of four children and, along with her two brothers and younger sister, spent most of her summers helping their parents run the business. Since there was a four-year gap between Avery and her first brother, she carried most of the responsibility and was often both mother and sister to her siblings. She didn't mind; the family was close-knit and doing what you could to help made sense. Avery approached most things in life in the same practical manner, which was why she hadn't looked at any of the state schools but, rather, focused on local junior colleges instead.

A few days after the local paper ran the details of the festival's programming, Rodney secretly decided to enter the contest. Even if winning didn't happen, he and his family would have a great memory and probably a good laugh. If it did work, he and his family would have a great memory, an even better laugh, and a fully funded education for Avery. But to pull it off, he needed to enlist the help of a local merchant.

The shopkeeper was coming from the back of the shop with an armful of handmade coasters and glanced sideways at Rodney as he passed by.

Troy W. Rasmussen

"Be with you in a moment," he said. "What brings a busy man to this area of town?"

Instead of waiting, Rodney followed him. "A favor, actually. I need a favor."

The shopkeeper stopped short and turned toward his guest. "A favor? Can't say I deal in favors. What do you need, and how can I help?"

"You know this contest coming up? Well, I'm planning to enter. Avery is graduating this year. They've limited the participants to just dads. Guess the council thought they'd be more likely or willing to participate in such a thing—probably right. Anyway, we're supposed to come up with two or three songs and make a show out of it."

"Mmmm," noted the shopkeeper, nodding.

"The whole premise is basically faking it, acting like you're performing the music yourself. They've altered the rules a bit to allow actual playing or singing if one's of such a mind. It occurred to me, if someone decided *not* to fake it for one of the songs, say the last one, like a finale, he may put himself closer to winning the thing."

"I see." The shopkeeper still wasn't sure how this involved him.

Nodding his head, Rodney said, "I need to borrow your piano."

> *Friday*
> With the art festival barely a day away, it seems the entire town is bristling with anticipation. Can't say I blame them. Bacardi's grumbling about the noise and racket of preparation is entertainment in itself. The flower beds have never looked better, and not just the one outside the shop. I'm convinced he spends so much

The Shopkeeper's Journal

time there as much for the sake of
tormenting the proprietor as for the
flowers.

Rugger keeps busy and to himself, his
devotion to Natalia understandable.

Bacardi, sitting on the steps sipping his drink, was
startled out of his reverie when the crew building the
stage for the air band contest dropped one of the metal
girders. That he jumped wasn't so much his concern as
was the prospect that someone may have seen him.

"Damned bunch of racket," he mumbled.

Having finished sweeping, the shopkeeper
approached the door, banging the dust from the dustpan
with a quick, exaggerated slap of the broom. Bacardi
jumped to his feet, spilling his drink down the front of his
pants, and glared at the shopkeeper.

"It does seem a bit more 'rackety' lately, doesn't it?"
The shopkeeper went back inside with a satisfied grin.

"Drinks been weak lately anyway," Bacardi replied.
"Day's a-comin'...day's a-comin'."

Although he couldn't hear what was said, Rugger
found himself grinning at the tussle between Bacardi and
the shopkeeper. The brief interlude was a nice reason to
rest from his work, installing outdoor cone-shaped flower
holders on each side of the windows of Natalia's eatery.

Rugger wasn't a daily presence at the café, but he
was around often enough that most people figured he
was. He didn't care; he was determined to repay Natalia
for her generosity. If anyone asked—and, sometimes,
busybodies did—Rugger would simply reply, "A man
doesn't always know when he's needed. Best he's
prepared."

131

Troy W. Rasmussen

Saturday

There is no other way to put it: the day was a success. More than likely makes our local boy a shoo-in for the Council seat. Oh, there were plenty who helped in all areas of putting on an event of this nature and size, but the driving force came from Parker. The air band contest was a fitting highlight. Quite the show, really. Some of the acts were more a production. Some should have stayed home. It all made for good entertainment. Natalia's near miss gave us all a scare.

Tourists and locals alike spent the day wandering the streets watching, admiring, and buying the work of the artists randomly stationed the length of Tourist Lane. The setup of the artists was Parker's idea.

"Place the artists everywhere—anywhere," he said. "Some on the sidewalks, some in the street, some inside a shop. Put them on the roof, if they want. Get the people mingling, moving, and bumping into one another. The idea isn't just showing off the works of art and those with the talent to create them, but getting the people involved and engaged."

By late afternoon, the crowds began to move toward the intersection where the air band contest was to be held. Although the event had been months in the planning, it was obvious no one expected the numbers that were gathering. Only families and friends of the participants had reserved seats. Everyone else was left to his or her own devices.

Gordo, with Chester on his shoulders, stood on the shop steps. Although Gordo couldn't ever really replace the boy's father, Sheila was glad for the relationship and
132

The Shopkeeper's Journal

enjoyed watching the two of them interact, especially at events like this. Their personalities were seemingly cut from the same cloth.

Her mind drifted back to the last time she'd seen the two of them together like this, at the Splash Festival—her son lifted high with his arms up, the sun and water cascading around his head. It was one of her favorite memories.

Bacardi, with Natalia standing beside him, was firmly ensconced on the stones of the flowerbed, his clay mug in hand. People passing by saw the two of them exchanging pleasantries as they waited for the show to start, although Natalia anxiously stood on tiptoe every now and then in an attempt to locate Parker.

The shopkeeper finished a sale then—as promised—closed the store in anticipation of the show and moved to the doorway. Natalia gave him a big wave and smile—while Bacardi growled at spectators who were unaware they were blocking his view.

Parker took the stage to announce the start of the show, and the crowd cheered. As he walked to center stage, he caught sight of Natalia, which brought an even broader smile to his face as his eyes widened in mock imitation of nervousness.

"Greetings—and welcome to this year's Art Festival finale."

At this, the cheers and whistles rang out afresh.

"I want to thank each of you for coming," Parker continued, "and especially those who helped in setting things up. The events of the past few days wouldn't have been possible without your support." He glanced again at Natalia and felt emboldened by her smile. "Before the show starts, I want to remind everyone to fulfill your

Troy W. Rasmussen

civic duty by voting in the upcoming election for the Town Council."

The crowd broke out in laughter, as most understood Parker's winning the open seat was a foregone conclusion.

Parker grinned, and Natalia shook her head. "Please, enjoy the final event of the festival. Judging by the getups of some of the contestants, you'll be hard-pressed to do otherwise."

At that, Parker gave the microphone to the guitar player, the emcee for the event, before slipping through the crowd to join Natalia.

The opening acts proved to be little more than grown men bouncing around in striped spandex and wigs doing their best to imitate the "hair" bands of their generation. The efforts of the Welded Roses, who provided the music tracks, had little effect on improving the performances.

One participant took the time to choreograph his set. And, having a song that appealed to more than one generation, he was able to get the crowd dancing, their heads held high as they sang along. At the close of his song, the forty-something man walked into the stands to fist-bump his son, who seemed proud of his dad.

Shortly afterward, the lights dimmed, fog began to roll from center stage, and the next contestant walked slowly toward the oozing mass of mist, its tentacles crawling toward the edge of the stage. Looking into the eyes of his second child and only daughter, he lip-synced a ballad of a father's love. The song took the listener from the time she was a small child to a grown woman on her wedding day.

A few seconds of silence followed, and then the cheers started, mingled with not a few tears and hugs in the crowd. For a final curtain call, the man met his

The Shopkeeper's Journal

daughter as she came onto the stage to hug and kiss his neck.

The next acts of the show continued in the tradition of the first few—more clowning around than serious performances. Rodney hadn't performed yet, and the shopkeeper suspected he'd planned it that way; he adjusted his position to get a better view of the stage, and Bacardi followed suit, curious to see what the shopkeeper was anticipating.

Then it happened.

Music seemed to come out of an ethereal place, slow and quiet at first, then building to a crescendo as the lights dimmed then grew in intensity with the pace and beat of the music. Suddenly, Rodney appeared, seated at Trudy's piano and being pushed in with the help of some of his daughter's classmates. Spotlights followed him, highlighting his entrance. Unlike most of the other contestants, Rodney was performing his set for real. Wide eyes and dropped jaws met the spectacle, as very few knew he had at one time been an accomplished pianist.

The first few bars of the song featured low background sounds and a few deliberate chords of the piano, gradually joined by the full sounds of electric drums, a cello, and the unmistakable addition of the guitar player. The heavy beats of percussion joined in as Rodney's fingers began moving right and left across the keyboard sending the crowd into a frenzy of bouncing bodies. After first holding hands over open mouths in astonishment—the way teenage girls do when catching a glimpse of their favorite rock star or local hottie—Avery and her friends joined in.

As the music continued, the crew pushed the piano further into the center of the stage, pivoting it around in

Troy W. Rasmussen

sync with the lights. Midway through, a solo section began, and Rodney's fingers moved like rushing water across the keys, his head bobbing up and down in time. The guitar player added slides and electronic squeals into the air, punctuating the expert piano work.

As the rush of sound finally died down, Rodney played the last few chords with an *I know you didn't know, but now you do* look on his face for his daughter.

Amidst the undulating cheers of the crowd, Parker bounded onto the stage.

"How about some noise for our participants?" he enthused.

The crowd stood and cheered even louder. Some whistled, others jumped up and down. At last, the crowd settled down and looked toward Parker.

"Only one thing left to do—select a winner. You are the judges, so let's hear it for your favorite."

Parker called the name of each of the participants, some of which continued their antics of pretending to play guitar or raise their arms in an attempt to elicit a greater response from the crowd.

"And finally, Rod…"

The noise from the crowd was so loud that few heard Parker say Rodney's full name. Rodney moved to center stage, blew a kiss to Avery and bowed to the crowd. He left the stage the undisputed victor of the Art Festival Air Band Contest.

Bacardi gave the shopkeeper a thoughtful look. "Didn't know he had it in him."

"Mmmm."

With the festival over and the sun setting behind the hills, the city work crews and volunteers began the laborious task of tearing down the stage and cleaning the area. With a quick kiss for Natalia, Parker excused himself to go and assist where he could.

The Shopkeeper's Journal

Not quite ready to end her day, Natalia said her goodbyes to the shopkeeper and Bacardi and began walking to the other side of the street to wait for Parker. As she reached the back of the stands, litter in the street rustled around her feet and momentarily caught her attention at the same time an unobservant worker driving a front-end loader approached a section of stands in front of her.

Failing to realize the section was not centered on the loading fork, the worker started the lift—causing the metal stands to tip backward toward her.

Those witnessing the incident would later claim time moved in the slow motion of disbelief as they helplessly watched several hundred pounds of metal slip off the loader and crash to the ground, its sound muffling cries and shouts from spectators and drowning out Parker's wail of "Talia!"

The shopkeeper felt its reverb in the shop doorway and rushed toward where he had last seen Natalia playfully kicking pieces of garbage in the wind. Bacardi, numbed by the possibility of such a tragic end to the day, stood frozen, his clay mug falling from his hand to the walkway.

It took a few moments for the workers to remove the debris from what everyone expected to be Natalia's broken and bloodied body. But, as the dust and litter settled and the dying motor of the loader faded, those closest to the scene stood in amazement as Natalia shook her head a couple of times, then stood up, with nothing more than a few minor cuts and bruises. Moments later, Parker was at her side, scooping her into his arms and holding her close, thankful kisses smothering her face, grateful hands brushing the grime from her hair.

Troy W. Rasmussen

Stepping slowly through the twisted metal, the shopkeeper moved to the area where a few moments ago Natalia lay; in the melee, something had caught his eye.

It wasn't until then that most of the crowd, still in shock, saw Rugger lying under the heavy girders of the stands.

As he leaned in for a closer look, Natalia asked in a shaking voice, "Is he...okay?"

He wasn't.

No one, not even Natalia, could say where Rugger had come from, or even if he had attended the event. The only thing she remembered was that, just before hearing the crash of the stands, she'd felt someone tackle her to the ground.

Rugger, who'd been sitting under the stands to avoid the public, had rushed toward her much like he had in the countless scrums over his career as a professional rugby player. He placed himself between her and the tipping stand as it fell from the loader, absorbing the blow.

It rained the day of Rugger's funeral. Most of those who attended hadn't really known him, but they came anyway, to honor the man who'd heroically saved the young woman's life. Expressing her gratitude in the best way she knew, Natalia wore an oversized rugby shirt with colors like the one Rugger had often been seen in.

Honor given.

The Shopkeeper's Journal

Chapter 13

Tuesday

Election Day. Needless to say, our local boy is officially the newest member of the City Council. If for nothing else than the metamorphosis of his personality, he deserves it. Still reflecting on the weekend's events, Natalia was more reserved than usual. It's no small thing to accept such a selfless act, especially for those working through latent feelings of unworthiness.

To all things is the right time given.

Parker's celebration was held at Natalia's eatery, with well-wishers coming and going throughout the day. Most agreed it had been his enthusiasm in putting together the art festival, in particular, the air band contest, that had clinched his win.

Later that evening, after those wanting to congratulate Parker left and the doors to the eatery closed, Parker took Natalia aside. So much had happened in the past few days, and he knew that she was far from over it all. He did the only thing he knew to do—took her in his arms and kissed the bandage on her forehead.

"Sorry 'bout it," he whispered.

Natalia, her head against his chest, closed her eyes. A tear escaped, trickling down her cheek onto his shirt. Breathing in the scent of him somehow made it all less painful.

139

Troy W. Rasmussen

"Go ahead, Talia," he said. "I got all night."

Natalia folded her arms between their two bodies, buried her face deep into his chest, and wept. She cried for Rugger. She cried for the reality of coming so close to losing her life, the difficulty in accepting someone giving theirs, the gift of Parker and the relationship building between them. With the strength of Parker's arms around her, she had only one coherent thought: *Thank you, Rugger. Thank you. Thank you, thank you, thank you.*

> *Friday*
>
> The revitalization at Matfield Greene continues. Vatori's place is coming along rather spectacularly. He will spend a small fortune before it's complete, but I doubt that's an issue for the individual footing the bill.
>
> McAlister and Olivia are enjoying themselves, too; McAlister, with his never-ending delight in bringing life back to the old and decaying, and Olivia, doing what she does best, working with a steady stream of possible buyers. Today was a bit more special in that regard. Today, glamour came to town.

Redmond and McAlister were enjoying each other's company—as much as father and son do when discussing business—over a cup of Kopi. The two had been going over various documents pertaining to the development of Matfield, with McAlister highlighting the progress and providing details on various phases. Although not displeased, Redmond was concerned that other than Vatori, there were no buyers.

The Shopkeeper's Journal

"Olivia has several prospects. It may take some time, though," McAlister said. "The clientele base is fairly select. We set it up that way from the beginning."

Redmond nodded his head, but he still didn't look happy. Nevertheless, McAlister soldiered on.

"The challenge is not only finding people who are interested in purchasing property in the area, but who share the vision of what the estates will be. We're not building from the ground up with the latest modern design. The goal is refurbishment of dilapidated historic homes. Olivia will pull it off. She has a considerable network, and not just in the surrounding area. Landing Vatori was a coup that will pay considerable dividends."

Redmond sipped more coffee, then spoke.

"And where do we stand now with prospects?"

Just then, the bell on the shop door gave its familiar jingle to announce visitors. Smiling, McAlister rose to greet Olivia and her guest.

"The answer to that question has just arrived."

McAlister stood and slid his chair back with his leg. He met Olivia halfway, leaned toward her, and lightly kissed each cheek.

"Olivia, good to see you," Redmond put in. Olivia may have missed the lingering glance McAlister bestowed, but his father had not.

"And you," she said. "I believe you are familiar with the lovely Déjà."

As McAlister made the introduction, Olivia stepped aside and moved toward Redmond, who had come to his feet as well.

"And hello to the ever dashing Redmond," she said, winking. Redmond nodded hello, and shifted his attention to the glamorous creature standing beside his son.

141

Troy W. Rasmussen

McAlister raised his arm toward his father and did the honors. "Déjà, may I introduce my father, Redmond."

Redmond stepped forward and, taking her extended hand in his, bent slightly and brushed his lips across her slender fingers. He hardly needed an introduction; Déjà's gorgeous face had graced covers of high-end magazines everywhere.

"Accept my compliments on your brilliant career, Miss Déjà," he said with a smile. "We're honored you'll join us." He motioned toward an available chair. Déjà walked the few paces to the table and, with the coy shrug she'd developed as a child, sat down.

As the others took their seats, the shopkeeper approached the group. After McAlister introduced him to Déjà, the shopkeeper made recommendations on drinks and snacks he thought might interest her.

Crossing her arms in her lap, the oversized bangle bracelets jingling against each other, Déjà said, "Iced Italian Soda."

With a nod, the shopkeeper turned toward the counter to retrieve her request. Lemon water—rarely touched—was the unquestionable choice for Olivia and, as a regular, she enjoyed the convenience of not having to ask.

Vatori had met Déjà several months before, at a gala raising money to combat hunger in Third World nations, a cause she was particularly fond of. Using the clout her name carried, Déjà and others of her talent sponsored and participated in a fashion show benefit, at which no expense was spared to entice the wealthy guests to larger donations.

Nine designers, all volunteering their time, talent, and designs, were busy behind the scenes giving last-minute instructions. Each of them had, at some point,

The Shopkeeper's Journal

petitioned Déjà to wear one of their designs during the finale. To calm the persistent pleas, she agreed that at least one of each of their designs would close each session of the show. Déjà pointedly did not answer the inquiries as to whom she would be wearing for the finale.

The show began as most. A mist filtered across the front of the runway while mystical lighting moved from side-to-side in time with the latest pop culture beat. The guests began to settle into their seats. Those considering themselves privileged enough to be fashionably late continued their *"Enchantes!"* greetings with exaggerated air kisses.

With a bang of percussion and amplified synthesizers, the show began with the first of many models bursting through the mist in gowns and outfits costing thousands of dollars. Closing each set, and as promised, Déjà walked the runway in the couture of the sponsoring designer's choice. Such was the star power of Déjà that bids for the items she modeled would reach into six-figure amounts before her walk finished.

One particularly bold designer challenged Déjà that he would double the highest bid if she would agree to model a mystery piece of his work. Never one to shy from a challenge, Déjà agreed immediately, adding, "Make it spectacular, Franco, and we'll break the bank." Clapping his hands, Franco disappeared to collect the article of clothing.

Franco's challenge was nothing more than a nearly see-through black leotard accompanied by black patent leather stilettos and oversized metallic bracelets. Throwing open the sheer curtains, Déjà put the curves she was blessed with into motion. The five-foot-ten-inch frame, mostly leg, of the world's greatest supermodel,

Troy W. Rasmussen

powered her way through a wall of photoflashes, all assets in play.

Reaching the end of the runway, Déjà stopped and crossed one knee in front of the other, raised her right arm, and struck a classic picturesque Marilyn Monroe pose. Kicking off the stilettos, she gracefully turned around to continue her march back. As she approached her starting point, Déjà abruptly stopped, pivoted around, and bowed, arms behind her back.

Bids for the outfit reached $195,000 before the lights faded.

The pulse of the music quickened with all heads and attention turned toward the front of the stage. On queue with the beat, models sporting the latest evening gown couture began spilling from the head of the runway like bees fleeing a nest. Within seconds, more than twenty models walked the length of the runway taking various positions on the edge. Keeping pace with the music, the runway, lights at its base glowing hot, began to spread out in a hinged-at-the-middle motion, swinging each of models across the audience's visual plane. Then, each of the separate stage sections opened and, like a carnival ride, began to randomly lift each model a few feet into the air. The music slowed to an ethereal beat as bright lights surrounding the entryway burst into life.

A low bass hum reverberated through the stage, causing the area around Déjà to vibrate, and smoke and lights wound their way around her body like exotic snakes. As the stage began to move in rhythm with the music, Déjà, clothed in nothing more than diamonds arranged like vines on mesh winding their way around her body, began the deliberate march down the runway.

The stage began to close back up, with the models moving back towards the entryway. Déjà, still in command, followed suit. At her destination, she turned in

The Shopkeeper's Journal

a half-twist and simply stopped—as did the music, for a few seconds. Déjà, veiled again in smoke and light, disappeared—to a final explosion of sound.

The society pages reported the diamond spectacle worn by the incomparable Déjà during her annual fundraiser was purchased for $2.3 million by the son of a wealthy shipping magnate.

During a break from introductions and exchanging pleasantries, Vatori leaned into Déjà. "Would you care to join me on the balcony?"

Déjà placed her champagne glass on the tray of a passing waiter. "I'd love to."

As they stepped into the evening air, Vatori said, "Ahhh, how quiet it is."

Déjà sighed her agreement and stepped closer to the balcony rail, the metal caps on her stilettos clicking against the imported tile.

"I like it," she said. "The quiet. There isn't much of it anymore."

Vatori nodded. "Someone with your notoriety must find it difficult to get away."

Déjà's gaze at the changing colors of the sunset didn't move. "I've been fortunate and enjoy what I do. Especially when I can help with events like this." She turned to face her host. "There are times, though, when I think I would enjoy just escaping for a bit. A getaway without the lights and fanfare."

"You have a place?"

"Oh, there's the house in L.A., but that's more of a set for public relations showing off the life of a famous model. The flat in New York is sweet but expensive for the size."

Troy W. Rasmussen

Vatori nodded. He found it oddly touching that Déjà never seemed to forget her meager upbringing.

"It's not special, though," she went on, shaking her head. "Never mind me. How about you? Where does the head of a multi-billion-dollar enterprise go to get away from it all?"

Vatori smiled. "I've been made aware of an interesting project. The developer is the son of a business acquaintance of my father's. They've purchased a fair bit of property, Matfield Greene, that's being developed into an exclusive 'getaway,' if you will."

Her brow rose. "Tell me more."

"The area was built in the mid-to-late 1800s for local captains of industry, but the estates have long since been abandoned. McAlister, the developer, has made it his passion to bring the area back to grandeur, and I've recently purchased one of the properties." He paused. "I must admit there is a certain satisfaction being involved with the project—more than I expected. If you would like, I can arrange a tour for you."

"I'd like that."

A few days after Déjà purchased one of the properties down the road from Vatori, he extended another offer, this time for dinner.

> *Saturday*
> Teenagers. The time in life when the world's calamities revolve around outfits that don't match—or do, but someone else is wearing the same thing—stolen boyfriends, bad hair days, and too little sleep. According to Tatum, one notorious invader trumped it all. Napoleon.

The Shopkeeper's Journal

Tatum gave an exasperated sigh that caught the shopkeeper's attention. Setting aside his task of oiling the counter—a process he faithfully completed each year—he set the can of tung oil and rag aside and waited patiently for what was sure to follow.

"Do teachers have any idea what they put us through? I mean, really, when will I ever use history?"

There it was. The age-old complaint of students across the land: the perils of history and the unexplainable idea that learning it would improve anything. Tatum, a sophomore attending the local high school, was at odds with her history assignment—and, apparently, the instructor who assigned it.

The shopkeeper replied, "Without a doubt, it is the secret mission of educators to purposefully drive their students to madness."

With another sigh, Tatum shook her head and rolled her eyes. She clearly "got" the joke, but it didn't solve anything.

"Tell me," he continued. "What exactly is the cause of your dilemma, and how may I assist?"

"History, that's my dilemma. As part of our midyear grade, we have to write this however-many-page thing…"

"Essay?"

"Essay, whatever, on some famous person I don't even know and why they're famous. Who cares?"

"You do."

Tatum only blinked at him.

"You may not think you care about the individual you'll be studying," the shopkeeper went on, "but you care deeply about meeting the expectation of your instructor. What you struggle with has little to do with

147

Troy W. Rasmussen

the assignment and more with a lack of understanding how you will go about accomplishing it."

"They don't tell us how to do this. They just hand out assignments and give due dates."

"Mmmm."

"You know, it would help if they'd take the time to explain things." At this, Tatum shrugged off her pack and set it heavily onto the stool. Momentarily, the shopkeeper paused to reflect on another young girl using it to spin out magic, then resumed the conversation.

"Tell me what the assignment is."

More sighing. Tatum lifted her head, her shoulders sagged in exasperation, and said, "Napoleon. All I know about Napoleon is he was some sort of short dictator that eventually ended up on some island."

"Mmmm. You are correct, he wasn't a man of large physical stature. However, he was a man who cared deeply for his country and its people. He possessed an extraordinary strategic intellect that liberated a nation and conquered multiple kingdoms. But he also lost the woman he loved."

"The woman he loved?"

"Passionately." At this, the shopkeeper began a slow stroll to the bookshelves lining the walls at the back of the shop. Curious, Tatum followed.

"France, the nation Napoleon liberated, was in the throes of revolution, rebelling against aristocratic society." Raising his finger, he added, "Very large affair."

"France? The whole thing?"

Smiling the shopkeeper confirmed, "Yes, the whole thing. Somewhere in the midst of conquering the whole thing…"

Tatum cocked her head.

148

The Shopkeeper's Journal

"He fell in love with a woman by the name of Josephine. It wasn't meant to be, though. Josephine was a widow with two children, and many of his family and closest confidants did not approve of the relationship."

"Wasn't he, like, emperor or something? Why didn't he just tell them all where to go and hang with who he wanted?"

"I suppose he could have, and yes, he was emperor." Reaching the heavily carved circular staircase leading to the upper decks of books, the shopkeeper motioned for Tatum to come along.

"Wait," she said from behind him. "You mean he spends all that time liberating a nation, falls in love, becomes an emperor, then...loses it all?"

He stepped onto the landing and waited for her to do the same. "It's not all that uncommon. The scale is different, but what happened to Napoleon can happen to almost anyone." Seeing the girl's confused look, he explained further. "Many times people take note of an injustice and decide to do something about it. All too soon, ambition turns blind, and the lure of power takes hold. It isn't long before they become that which they so ardently fought against." Handing her a leather-bound book on the life of Napoleon, he said, "Such was the case of the illustrious Napoleon."

Tatum ran her hand across the old book. "And Josephine?"

Tapping the volume, he said, "She didn't end up on an island. Probably felt like it, though."

Troy W. Rasmussen

Chapter 14

Monday
Jack's hands still shake.

The first time Jack came to the shop, he did so in a stupor.

Darkness had fallen, and the shopkeeper was preparing to close for the day. But as he went to close the door, he caught a glimpse of a man standing to one side, staring at the opening as if transfixed.

The shopkeeper paused, then stepped out to the walkway and placed his hand on the man's shoulder. After seemingly a long time, the man blinked heavily and turned to look into the eyes of the shopkeeper.

"Who are you?" the stranger asked in a shaky voice.

"The proprietor of this shop."

"I walk sometimes," he said, turning his gaze back toward the stone wall. "Sometimes I don't..." The words trailed off.

"Come inside for a bit," the shopkeeper offered, and guided him through the doorway.

Reaching one of the tables in front of the window, the shopkeeper stood to the side as his impromptu guest eased into the seat, still looking confused. The man kept his hands clasped together and buried in his lap.

The shopkeeper sat down and spoke very quietly.

"A load as heavy as the one you carry must surely be set aside."

The Shopkeeper's Journal

Lifting his head, the man rubbed his hands together, then placed them, palms up, on the table. The shopkeeper was not unaware that the man's hands were shaking.

"Tell me your name, sir."

"Jack." Even saying the word seemed to exact a price from the man. His gaze never left those shaking hands. "They didn't always do this," he went on, nodding toward the tabletop. "I've tried before to make them stop, but…"

"They may not ever stop," the shopkeeper said calmly. "The larger issue is why. Why do your hands shake, Jack?"

Jack's stare was vacant. "I killed a man. Years ago, I killed a young man. He took my Alice and Stephanie Marie."

The shopkeeper sensed the delicacy of the situation. "How, Jack?" he asked gently.

"He didn't mean to, I don't think. He wasn't drinking or anything. We were outside in the yard, it was warm, and Stephanie Marie was running back and forth between Alice and me. The phone rang, and I went inside to answer it. I don't remember who it was." Jack paused, cringing. "I remember the scream. The scream of tires on pavement just before the world slowed down. I dropped the phone and ran outside and there were my Alice and Stephanie Marie all laid out limp and bloody. One on the hood of the car, the other underneath." Jack's gaze dropped to his hands again. "Her little feet just sticking out…she wasn't wearing any shoes…it was summer. The pounding in my head was so loud, and I felt hot all over, angry hot.

"That young man was just falling back against the seat when I reached the car. His head was cut, and bad, but it didn't matter. I grabbed him by the neck and

151

Troy W. Rasmussen

yanked him out of the window. I don't think he was wearing a seatbelt." Jack turned toward the window, his eyes far away. "People told me later they couldn't get my hands from around his neck. His head was flopping back and forth and I was screaming something about was he drinking. He wasn't drinking. He wasn't doing anything but driving along. He shouldn't have been, though."

"Why not, Jack? Why shouldn't he have been driving?"

"Narcolepsy," Jack said wearily. "His name was Jason and he had narcolepsy. He had a cataplexic attack, ran over my Alice and Stephanie Marie, and I killed him for it."

Silently, the shopkeeper stood up, walked behind the counter, and got a towel to soak in warm water. He returned to the table and gently wrapped Jack's hands in the warm cloth.

"Jack? How is it that you are here and not incarcerated?"

Jack's hands began to shake more violently.

"Jason's alive. Isn't he, Jack?"

The tremors in his hands seemed to radiate through Jack's body. "Yes."

"Mmmm."

Jack took a deep breath, his gaze shifting once more from his hands to the dark street outside the window. "When it came down to it, pressing charges and all, I just couldn't do it."

The shopkeeper waited.

"Still remember the day the judge asked if I wanted to say anything before he moved forward with the proceedings. Kept thinking about Alice…what she would do…and tiny bare feet." His body twitched as he uttered a low, sharp gasp. "They were so young."

152

The Shopkeeper's Journal

Jack slumped forward, his head falling into his hands, and wept.

The shopkeeper had no interest in subjecting Jack to curious stares from any potential passersby. Without comment, he locked the door and turned out the lights. He ran a glass of cool water and handed it to his guest.

"What then, Jack?"

Gradually, Jack collected himself, wiping the tears from his eyes with the back of his hand. "I stood up. No idea why I did it, but I stood up, walked over to that boy, and stood there looking at him. Put my hand on his shoulder. He was shaking…about to come apart. He looked at me—so did the bailiff." He grunted, his mouth twitching in a half-smile. "We stayed like that for a bit before I turned to the judge. Told him, 'This situation is over. What's done can't be made otherwise, and there's little sense in ruining another life.' I looked at that young kid again, then back at the judge. 'Sir,' I said, 'I leave it to you to decide.'"

The shopkeeper reached across the table and removed the towel from Jack's hands. "Life happens, Jack. The struggle comes in accepting how it defines you."

Jack continues to stop by the shop, always at night. His hands still shake from time to time, though not as much.

Tuesday
Children and rain. Even on gloomy days, the two combined can bring a smile, even laughter. Although I doubt Bacardi would agree.

Troy W. Rasmussen

Clark stomped his shoeless feet in the puddles on his trek down the gutter. The rain had been falling for most of the afternoon, providing ample opportunities for a young boy to soak himself in a myriad of ways. With a hop in the air geared to cause the biggest splash possible, he landed in a pothole, the spray of water drenching his legs. Before long, Clark had attracted a handful of other kids equally in the mood for water play.

The squeals of delight and excited chatter drew the attention of the shopkeeper, who found himself very much in the mood for a break. Stepping to the top of the entryway steps, he leaned out far enough to see the group moving slowly down Tourist Lane, kicking the running water as they went.

Someone got the bright idea to race makeshift boats in the gutter. Scattering, the children scampered to find a fallen leaf, twig, or small piece of paper trash. Some of the more industrious ones quickly made their boats, to gain a head start on the others.

"No fair," called one.

"That's cheating," wailed another.

Clark ignored them all, merely set his curved leaf afloat in the rushing water and began following it down the road. Soon, the others gave up their quarreling and joined in.

The shop, apparently, was the designated finish line. However, Bacardi, scowling under his breath about the miserable weather, didn't know this as he approached from the other direction. The shopkeeper, sensing what was about to happen, took a couple of discreet steps back, just in time to see the bustling, screaming group of children come splashing around the corner.

To the kids, it didn't matter who won. What mattered was the boats all made the trek, a feat that caused the group to jump up and down, cheering. Three of the

The Shopkeeper's Journal

children, their arms wrapped around each other, jumped in unison into a small pool that formed at the corner where the concrete had eroded away—and sent a large, heavy splash of water into the air and onto Bacardi.

Bacardi, a perturbed look on his face, turned and looked at the shopkeeper. "All fun and games."

"For some," the shopkeeper replied. "For others, it's just fun."

> *Wednesday*
> Chester was in today, ready to take on the world. Whatever the reason, his spirits were high. Add to those high spirits the confident walk of a boy enjoying the day and his life in it, and there's a recipe guaranteeing something will happen. And it did.

The shopkeeper was behind the counter as Chester strolled in, his satchel hanging across his chest. Peering over the top of his glasses, the shopkeeper thought, *mischief in a pair of cutoffs,* and decided to ride this one out to see what the next few minutes held. Chester lifted his arm to wave and merely said, "What's up?" as he proceeded to the recesses of the shop.

The shopkeeper merely continued his task of drying coffee mugs.

A short time later, Chester reappeared, this time with his satchel noticeably full. To the shopkeeper's inquiring glance he said only, "Supplies."

"Mmmm."

The shopkeeper noticed something else—a fair-sized cut above Chester's right eye. The bruising around it, faded and yellow, told him the injury was a few days old.

155

Troy W. Rasmussen

He didn't comment on it, only handed his young friend a lollipop.

"That jar of yours has been empty for some time," he said.

"Yep."

The shopkeeper pushed himself up from leaning across the counter, retrieved a white confectioner's box, and slid it toward the boy. "Mrs. Worthingston's waiting on these."

Chester took the box and placed it under his arm. "No problem."

The shopkeeper nodded toward the boy's forehead. "Run into something bigger than you?"

Chester just grinned. "The few. The proud."

"Mmmm."

> *Friday*
> Poise and talent combined this evening, as the private interplay between Melanie and the guitar player continues. Watching the two is akin to the quiet awe one feels at the sighting of a rare bird— intrusive, yet one can't seem to help staring.

The Friday night regulars had already drifted in, and the sounds of the guitar player's music filled the room. When Melanie arrived, book in hand, she paused momentarily at the counter as her drink was prepared, and couldn't help grinning at the sight of Gordo stretched out on a couch, one leg draping over the edge, apparently asleep. She moved quietly through the group to settle in next to the guitar player.

The Shopkeeper's Journal

Lighting a bentwood pipe, the shopkeeper sent a puff of fragrant smoke into the air and filled the lull between customers watching the two.

"I saw you walk in," said the guitar player, his fingers continuing their dance across the strings.

"I heard you before I reached the door," she replied.

"You must have very good hearing."

"You refer to your music," she teased.

"I do."

"Oh, well, I've listened for a different kind of music for years." She took a sip of her drink.

The guitar player grinned. "You've affected the tone."

"It didn't need to be."

"I don't mind."

He played the final few chords of the song, then set the instrument on the floor and leaned it against the couch, allowing him to turn toward Melanie and slide closer. As he placed his arm on the back of the cushion, Melanie moved in nearer to him. He reached forward to help, his fingers brushing hers.

"And what are you doing now?" she whispered.

"Enjoying the tone."

Saturday

If Maarten makes it through the challenge of Matfield without spontaneously combusting, it'll be a wonder. The refurbishment of Vatori's place is complete, and our young designer is nearly beside himself with the excitement that his turn at bat has finally arrived.

Troy W. Rasmussen

It was one of the shopkeeper's favorite kinds of days—lazy and laid-back. People came and went, meandering, ordering cool drinks, sitting, chatting, accepting the urge to slow down and enjoy. Even Bacardi seemed more at leisure; he leaned against the stone wall, one leg stretched out to the step below, sipping his rum and coffee. Tameril played the harp for a while, after which light jazz filtered through the air from the shop's sound system. The shopkeeper kicked the volume up a touch, catching Bacardi's attention for just a moment before the other man leaned back once more, eyes closed.

The ambiance didn't last long, however; no sooner had Bacardi's eyes closed than up the walkway and into the shop came Maarten, in high gear.

"My time has come!" he proclaimed, arms flung wide.

Bacardi opened one eye. "And aren't we all glad to hear of it."

Undeterred, Maarten sauntered to the counter. "The renovations of the interior of the mansion are complete," he told the shopkeeper. "Vatori's given the go-ahead to begin the interior design. I'm so excited."

"Mmmm," murmured the shopkeeper. Dare he ask what came next?

Maarten didn't wait for the question. "The next step" he went on, "is to begin perusing the grandest of furnishings to fill the place. I mentioned this to you some time ago."

The shopkeeper nodded. "The Baker Mansion is a sizeable edifice. Surely there are many places to obtain the artifacts you have in mind."

"A sizeable edifice" was an understatement. Easily the largest property at Matfield Greene, the Baker Mansion boasted seventeen bedrooms, two master suites, a large main library and a smaller private one, a conservatory, the grand ballroom, and four parlors. Although he wasn't particularly religious, Vatori had also respected his Italian heritage and his mother's influences enough to make sure that the small chapel, extending from the east side of the building onto a grassy knoll, was restored to its original grandeur, including its crowning adornment—a Bernini Madonna and Child.

"Of course, we won't be splurging on the entire home. No, Vatori was very clear about his wishes. 'The finest available for the two front parlors, entryway and the north side master suite,' But after seeing the sculpture he placed in the Chapel—my God, the Bernini!—there can be no doubt the caliber of furnishings he expects."

"Mmmm."

"I envision numerous meetings with you to consult on furnishing those areas he specifically noted. When shall we begin?"

The shopkeeper merely smiled. "The shop doesn't close until everyone has left."

Troy W. Rasmussen

Chapter 15

Monday

Our newest council member is at it again. The annual athletic event for students with disabilities is coming up, and solicitations for support from local businesses have started. All of us will ensure we do our part.

Parker entered the shop, bursting with enthusiasm, and placed the advertisement of the upcoming athletic event in the glass case just inside the door.

"That time again," he said, smiling at the shopkeeper.

"Mmmm. Hold there a minute, Parker." The shopkeeper vanished into the back of the shop briefly, then returned with two large boxes.

"These should do the trick," he said.

The shopkeeper set the boxes on the counter, then lifted the fitted lid off one to expose fifty white T-shirts of various sizes. Parker waited patiently as the shopkeeper lifted one of the shirts out and, with a flip, unfolded it to lay on the counter. Parker ran his hand over the shirt's black lettering, a single word: STRENGTH.

"Fantastic," he said. "What a cool thing for the participants."

"There are a hundred of these in these boxes," the shopkeeper said. "Each one has a different word on it."

Parker reached into the box and began unfolding the T-shirts, one by one, reading the word printed on each

160

The Shopkeeper's Journal

aloud. "RENEW, THRIVE, GROW, IMAGINE, FOCUS, UNLIMITED, POWERFUL, CONQUER... I can't wait to see everyone on the field with such powerful messages displayed."

"Give each of the athletes one. No need to be concerned with who gets what. The words apply to them all."

"I will. Thank you." Parker packed the shirts back into the box, nodded his thanks, and took off out of the store as fast as he'd come in. The shopkeeper followed his path as he crossed the street, nearly at a run, to Natalia's place.

> *Wednesday*
> A man's effect on the life of someone who needs him cannot be measured. The changes this world would see, the things that could be accomplished, if only more men understood this! By all appearances, one does.

The shopkeeper was kneeling in front of his wine cabinet, methodically placing each of the new selections into its slot, when he heard the unmistakable sound of Bacardi tapping his gardening tool on the frame of the door. Standing, he turned his gaze to where Bacardi indicated.

Grant, a fourth-year college student, was sitting on the bench. The scene was unremarkable; what drew the shopkeeper's further attention was the young boy with whom Grant spoke.

Pete attended the local grammar school with curriculum geared toward individuals with disabilities; judging by his posture, Pete wasn't having a good day.

Troy W. Rasmussen

"Going to the field event isn't a bad thing, Pete. Why not give it a try?" Grant was saying.

Breathing heavily, Pete replied, "I have before. I don't win."

"And winning is important."

"Yes, sometimes." Pete's body jerked.

"Sure, it is. As long as you understand what winning means."

Pete's attempt to sit up straight was interrupted by another muscle spasm, causing him to slump forward.

"Winning," he said with another deep breath, "is being first. But they tell us in school it's about part-" another spasm caught Pete mid-word, "—participating."

"Oh, it's more, Pete. You're right about that."

"I am?"

"Winning has to do with doing your best, meeting the challenge of what's before you, and not giving up. It's tough, though."

"It is. My mom says I do it all the time, but she's my mom."

Smiling at his comment, Grant replied, "And moms don't count."

"They have to say things like that."

"I suppose you're right. Doesn't mean they aren't serious, though."

Pete seemed to accept the logic, but his countenance didn't change.

"What would I do, if I went?" he persisted.

"You could throw the discus or propel yourself over the high-jump bar."

Pete laughed loud at Grant's joke.

"Or walk a tightrope high up," he joked back, trying to control the spasms raising his shoulders.

"Maybe just run, Pete. Have you done that?"

"When no one is looking."

The Shopkeeper's Journal

"And how does it go?"

"Not good. I jerk too much, and my feet get caught on each other."

Grant nodded calmly. "That happens sometimes, Pete. But different people run in different ways."

"Not…" Pete sighed as another spasm ripped through his body. "Not like me. I fall a lot."

"Other people fall, Pete. And other people see it. Is that the problem? You don't want people to see?"

Pete did his best to nod his head.

"So you don't run because you don't want people to see you fall."

Pete shook his head yes before the weak muscles rebelled again.

"I've fallen before," Grant said.

Pete turned his head. It didn't jerk.

"At school, in front of a bunch of people," Grant said, shrugging. "I run the hurdles. Do you know what those are?"

Pete tilted his head forward without jerking.

"A hundred meters of 'em. I was plowing along, neck-and-neck with the guy next to me. On the second to last hurdle, I didn't lift my leg high enough and fell head-first into the ground. Broke my nose—blood everywhere." Grant paused. "I got back up, Pete. Oh, it wasn't easy. Everyone stared and wondered what would happen. I stumbled over the last hurdle as well, but I finished. The way I figure it, a guy's better off falling and finishing than not running at all 'cuz he doesn't want anyone to see."

The shopkeeper glanced at Bacardi who, raising his eyebrow, tilted his head in affirmation.

163

Troy W. Rasmussen

Thursday
Few things can rouse people like a
good story. Even better is the wonder and
intrigue of a legend, the inevitable stares
of those hearing the tale as their
imaginations race through the possibilities
and what-ifs. A mental lottery.

Chester sat idly at the counter indulging in a lollipop, one of many stuffed in his jar as payment for making his latest delivery. The shopkeeper, accepting the boy's reflective mood, left him to his thoughts as he prepared drinks for McAlister and Maarten, who were discussing the progress of the interior design of Vatori's place. The shopkeeper found himself grinning at the antics of Maarten describing his latest find.

"It will hang in the entryway," the shopkeeper heard Maarten enthusing. "One hundred-light chandelier dripping with Baccarat crystal. It's truly a spectacular find." Maarten sat back, giving the shopkeeper a smile.

"You're just in time. I was telling McAlister of the chandelier we've procured."

"Mmmm."

"It's scheduled to arrive any moment. A grand piece for a grand building." Looking toward the shopkeeper, he continued, "What is the name you use when referring to Vatori's place?"

"The Baker Mansion."

"That's it. Has a dignified sound to it. You mentioned before something about a legend?"

The shopkeeper was hesitant to occupy his guests' time and made an expression to indicate such.

"A legend?" McAlister prompted.

With nothing else pressing, the shopkeeper decided to tell the tale.

The Shopkeeper's Journal

"Thomas Baker was the son of an affluent family from the Eastern seaboard. Anxious to make his own way, he left the halls of the family estate shortly after his education was complete and purchased more than a few pieces of property, which he developed into habitation for the working class. Far from the typical cheaply-built shacks that dotted the area, the places Thomas built were of strong construction and offered at affordable prices.

"Having earned a reputation for fairness and honesty, Thomas soon expanded into larger commercial endeavors. After five years, with his financial worth anything but meager, he took a trip to Africa, where he discovered the means to create a truly impressive fortune—diamonds.

"Thomas wasted no time selling his holdings in the States to finance a mining operation in the Sierra Leone region. He insisted on heading the operation himself but, after a few years, moved back to America, where he systematically morphed his fortune from impressive to outlandish.

"At age thirty-seven, he married the lovely Fey Dupree, who within two years gave birth to their first child, Robert. Other children would follow, but it was Robert who displayed the drive and talents to one day take the reins of the family business.

"Desiring to spend more time with his family, Thomas purchased a hundred acres of remote land, named it Matfield Greene, and built a lavish estate on the hill in the middle. His obligations as the country's foremost diamond broker were stealing too much time away from his beloved Fey and their children, however, so Thomas took Winston Carlyle, a friend from his

Troy W. Rasmussen

school days, on as a partner. It turned out to be a fatal mistake.

"The first few years of the partnership went well enough, and both men's fortunes grew. In appreciation for Winston's part of the work, Thomas deeded ten acres of Matfield Greene to his friend and financed the construction of a sizeable, if smaller, estate for him to live in. Shortly after the completion of the Carlyle Estate, Thomas convinced Fey to allow him to take Robert on a trip to Sierra Leone. This provided the lad a firsthand look at the operation that formed the financial foundation of the family fortune. It was during this trip that Thomas discovered the fabled Monarch Diamond, a 157-karat uncut rock, valued in the millions. He named it after Fey's favorite butterfly, the Monarch.

"It's said that Thomas showed the marvel only to Fey and his partner Winston before locking it away. He was well aware the impact such a discovery could have on the diamond market.

"As time passed, Winston made several risky investments in foreign shipping. The sea is a tough bet; after a series of misfortunes, Winston Carlyle found himself near financial ruin. Of course, he assumed the benevolence of his friend would again pay off, and so approached Thomas for help.

"However, with his own assets tied up in a slowing market, Thomas declined to help directly, sending Winston into a rage. He claimed Thomas was being selfish in his refusal to sell the Monarch—a move that, to his limited understanding, would solve his looming financial demise. Unable to calm his friend, Thomas asked Winston to leave and take some time to settle himself down. He promised that, together, they would work the following day to find a solution.

The Shopkeeper's Journal

"But Winston was too desperate to wait. Instead, fueled by desperation, he lunged at Thomas, sending him backward through the second-story windows to his death on the cut stone veranda below. The following day, Winston Carlyle shot himself in the head.

"Fey never recovered from the loss of her beloved Thomas and spent the remainder of her life in seclusion, while Robert assumed the responsibilities of the family business and relocated everything to Antwerp, Belgium. He would return to the United States only one time: to handle the burial of his mother. Matfield Greene and the Baker Mansion held memories he preferred to forget, and Robert sold both to a business acquaintance."

"Utterly tragic," Maarten whispered.

"Quite the tale, that one," said McAlister. "What became of the diamond?"

"Mmmm. Therein the legend stands. It's said the diamond was never found. After showing his find to Fey and Winston, Thomas hid the gem somewhere on the property."

"My God—you mean the thing could still be somewhere at Matfield Greene?"

Smiling at Maarten's reaction, the shopkeeper replied, "Mmmm. Legend also has it that shortly after they married, Fey gave a gold medallion to Thomas to remind him of how priceless their relationship was. Supposedly, the medallion is the key to finding the diamond."

With this, the shopkeeper excused himself, leaving his guests to their own thoughts and speculations. He didn't fail to catch the amazed stare on Chester's face, his lollipop hanging loosely from his mouth, as his fingers slowly played with a certain gold medallion he'd found in a wall.

Troy W. Rasmussen

Saturday
The world, or our little corner of it, was witness to the capacity of the human spirit today. The triumph of Pete as he conquered his mountain—and the miracle at 50 meters—were wonders to behold.

The day of the competition arrived. Athletes rushed from buses and vans and were directed to various stations for processing. Each, in turn, approached the table to announce his or her name, and everyone proudly wore a bright white T-shirt with a descriptive word printed in black letters across the front.

Throughout the day, Grant caught glimpses of Pete as he wandered from one area to the next, stopping to watch and wonder. He seemed not so much to be gauging his ability against those participating, but rather convincing himself that participating was worth it.

Pete stood to the side where the others had gathered in preparation to run, his internal torment of deciding to join not yet complete. Something was wrong. Something deep inside Pete kept him from committing. Several of the volunteers approached Pete, doing their best to encourage him to join, but to no avail.

Seeing Pete's inner turmoil, Grant stepped closer and quietly stood beside him as he watched the others prepare for the race. As Pete's agitation increased, he began to make small guttural sounds and pace clumsily back and forth in the grass. Turning at last to face Grant, he stopped and with jerking movements of his head looked into Grant's eyes.

The Shopkeeper's Journal

Taking a deep breath, Grant reached for the plain white T-shirt hanging from his back pocket and held it out to Pete. The two stood in this manner for a few seconds. Pete lowered his head, focused on the muscles in his arms, and began to remove his shirt. Once that was done, he stood to face the resolute look of the only person who seemed to understand.

Accepting the commitment of what was to come, Pete reached out a skinny arm and took hold of the T-shirt. *Where's the word? All the other shirts have a word.* Pete looked to Grant for his answer and received none. Pete's mind was occupied with this singular question as he struggled to put the shirt on and step from the grass onto the asphalt pavement. *Where's my word?*

Twelve athletes had signed up for the 100-meter run, yet thirteen stood ready at the start line.

"On your mark…" Pete turned his head to see Grant standing solidly.

"Get set…" His eyes searched for a sign, a nod, some affirmation—his word—but Grant remained still. At the sound of "Go," the other participants began running. Pete, every nerve of his body startled by the volume, jumped uncontrollably, faltering his start.

With a supreme effort, Pete began to run. It was a spectacle, he knew. Running required greater balance and in order to keep it, his arms and legs flailed in awkward, jerking motions as his head bobbed from side to side. With his eyes wide in concentration, Pete's progress was slower than the other runners. The exertion of his efforts caused him to breathe clumsily through his nose.

Pete's mother, watching, clasped her hands tight, praying with every fiber of her being. *Please, please let this go okay.*

Troy W. Rasmussen

Pete's progress down the track was slow; frustration at his ill-coordinated body—and its inability to perform the tasks he wanted it to—built with each step. Worse, his concentration on any one particular thing could only be held for so long. When he dared look up to see where the other runners were and saw they were halfway to the finish, and he was not, his balance faltered, his foot clumsily dragged on the track, and his body slammed in a heap onto the asphalt.

Pete's mother rose to her feet. *Oh, no,* she groaned inwardly. *Someone help him...pick him up.*

Pete was accustomed to falling. He had done so many times throughout his life. The pain of injury was not foreign to him. He instinctively knew that in a few minutes, he or someone else would be checking his body for the latest scrape, cut, or bruise. He hated that part. Hated that it happened so much. Hated that it mattered.

And, sure enough, several volunteers and onlookers raced toward his crumpled mass—only to stop, bewildered, when Grant waved them back.

What's he doing? Peter's mother thought angrily. *Help him...I can't get there before you...do something!*

With concentrated effort, Pete rolled himself to a sitting position, then leaned forward onto skinned, bleeding palms to push himself upright. He gave one sideways glance at Grant, nodded, and resumed running the race.

Oh, thank God.

The level of concentration and physical exertion required to continue was already taking its toll on Pete; his hair was matted with sweat and loose chunks of asphalt. He wasn't wearing a headband, either, and he could feel the all-too-familiar burn of salty sweat in his eyes. What could he do? If he tried to wipe it away, he

The Shopkeeper's Journal

could lose his balance again. If he didn't, it'd look like he was crying. And he didn't want that either.

Something's not right. His mother's thoughts buzzed in her head, insistent. *He only gets that look when something's not right. What's wrong, Pete? What's wrong?* With one hand on her mouth and the other on her chest, she watched her son stumble on to the inevitable. She knew it would come—it always did.

Pete could no longer endure the possibility that others might think he was crying. Not because he felt sorry for himself, but that in spite of his efforts to achieve something as simple as running, his frustration that his body would not allow it to happen the same as the other kids—kids with better bodies.

Pete reached up to wipe the sweat out of his eyes. *Oh, Pete…*

The falls didn't typically register with Pete. Usually, his vision went dark and sound stopped. When it was over both, along with the searing pain of the newest injury, came screaming back into his consciousness. This time was no different.

Those watching saw Pete's body fall forward, wildly out of balance, and land in a gangly mass. With his arms unable to respond fast enough to catch him, his face bore the brunt of the impact. As the blood flowed and his body rolled like a rag doll thrown in anger, a collective gasp rose from the spectators. Some once again went running toward him; others watched in shock, unable to move.

Why can't I move? Pete! You're hurt. Someone start the world again so I can get to him…someone please start the world again…

Grant walked toward the fallen boy, the force of his presence stopping those on their way to aid him.

"Pete," he said quietly. "Get up."

Troy W. Rasmussen

Pushing to an upright position, blood and gravel smearing the side of his face, Pete released a heavy sigh and slowly shook his head no.

Grant waited. The world waited. And tears slid down the cheek of Pete's mother.

Grant stood by, waiting. And then, like a marionette with broken and tangled strings, Pete once more unfolded his limbs to stand up. His knee, popping with the strain, caused him to falter and fall unsteadily into Grant, but Grant didn't move.

Help him. Please, help him. Lift him. Carry him. Someone move. Why can't I move? He's so tired and hurt. Someone start the world again.

The other athletes crossed the finish line as the miracle at 50 meters stood up and started again. Pete fell two more times before reaching his destination. Until he did, Grant remained at the place where the world started back up.

When Pete crossed the finish line, the spectators and fellow runners burst out in unison screams of excitement and congratulations that rang in his ears. He hurt. He hurt bad. But he was glad, too. Glad he made it.

But still, something was missing. Just then Pete felt a poke in his chest, steadied himself, and looked up to see Grant holding a thick black marker.

Without a word, Grant popped the cap from the marker, bent down, and in broad strokes, wrote one word on Pete's blood and sweat-stained T-shirt.

CHAMP.

To all things is the right time given.

172

The Shopkeeper's Journal

Chapter 16

Monday

There are countless firsts: first kiss,
first car, first job, first love, first child.
How endless is the list! For Dexter, the list
narrowed to just one—his first-year
anniversary. Can perplexity be any better
defined than a young man searching out
the ideal gift for his mate?

The shopkeeper had been watching the young man
for nearly twenty minutes. With his hands in his pocket
or supporting his chin, Dexter meandered through the
shop, stopping here and there, assessing the item before
him. Finally, as Dexter sighed for the twentieth-or-so
time, the shopkeeper figured a helping hand might be in
order.

"That's a shiny ring you have there," he said quietly,
coming up next to the young man. "Judging by how
much you've been fingering it, I'd wager it's new."

Holding out his left hand to view his wedding ring,
Dexter smiled. "It is. Our one-year anniversary is coming
up, and I don't have a clue what to get."

"Mmmm."

"Isn't there some list a guy can follow?"

"There is. Traditionally, paper is given on the first
anniversary. However, I understand the modern gift for
such an occasion is a clock."

Troy W. Rasmussen

Motioning around the room, Dexter nodded. "I've seen a couple grandfather clocks, but that really isn't her style."

"Style is important. What would you say your wife's style is?"

"Well…" Dexter scratched the back of his head. "Sort of Victorian, but with a lot of rustic, metal old things thrown in."

With a slight chuckle, the shopkeeper turned to walk toward the middle of the shop, Dexter in tow. The pair proceeded to the end of one aisle facing an oversized cabinet with five long drawers. Bending over to pull out the second from the bottom, the shopkeeper said, "I believe what you've attempted to describe is Steampunk."

He slid the drawer open and stepped back for Dexter to take a closer look. Lying in the drawer was a piece of art, approximately two feet by four feet. Jagged pieces of metal extended to either side in mock formation of cloth, surrounding a Romanesque clock with a section of its side eroded away, leaving small extended shards in the center. Other metal pieces were welded onto the sides in the form of letters so cleverly designed that the word *moment* was barely distinguishable. The hands of the clock were exaggeratedly thin metal, extending from the center like the legs of an enormous spider.

Whoa!" Dexter said in awe. "That's some clock. She'll love it."

"Now as to the paper, I think you'll find what you are looking for over here."

At this, the shopkeeper proceeded to another cabinet an aisle over. He slid one of the twelve thin drawers open and stepped to the side, allowing Dexter a closer inspection of the handmade paper.

The Shopkeeper's Journal

"A note from the heart," finished the shopkeeper, "written on one of these, should do the trick."

Dexter turned toward the shopkeeper, seemingly puzzled. "Do what?"

"There's nothing to it. Jot down a few words of how you feel, or how she makes you feel, add 'I love you,' and sign your name. Guaranteed to do the trick."

Dexter didn't seem convinced, so the shopkeeper clapped his hand on the young man's shoulder bracingly. "Follow me."

As the two reached the counter, the shopkeeper opened a small door under the counter and retrieved a bottle of twenty-one-year-aged Chivas Regal Royal Salute Scotch and two small cut-crystal rocks glasses. Removing the stopper from the already opened bottle, he poured two fingers of the elixir into each glass, then slid one of the glasses toward Dexter. "To firsts," he said, lifting his own glass. With a slight hesitation, Dexter followed suit, and both men smiled as they set their glasses down.

"That," the shopkeeper finished, "should help with the note part."

> *Wednesday*
> What would an adventure be without the risk?
>
> How many times have we heard those words? They're almost a byline for Gordo. But his excursion to South America nearly changed all that; in fact, it nearly changed whether he would ever go on another.

As far as Gordo was concerned, South America was no more than a simple excursion. He had no mission, no

Troy W. Rasmussen

plans to better the world. Just time spent in a remote jungle for nothing more than the experience—his favorite type of adventure.

However, barely a week into his trek through the remote, mosquito-ridden Suriname Rainforest, Gordo developed the early signs of Dengue, or Breakbone Fever, so called due to the severe joint and muscle pain it brought with it.

Since there is no cure for the disease, the victim has little choice but to suffer through. Their only reward is that they will be immune to one of the four sub-types contracted…although that's little consolation to the infected.

Reg and Lodi, locals from a not-too-distant village, came across a mildly delirious Gordo late one afternoon while returning from trading handmade goods across the river. The characteristic red rash with islands or blotches of white throughout covered most of his lithe body like an uneven sunburn. Well-versed in the signs of the fever, the two did their best to explain, in a combination of broken English and their native tongue, his condition and guide Gordo inside to begin administering what comfort they could while his body fought the virus.

The sun moving across a thick canopy of trees caused shadows to drift across the deteriorating adobe walls of Reg and Lodi's hut. Shadows slipped across Gordo's heaving and sweat soaked chest, his pack crumpled on the floor at the foot of the bed. The heat and humidity added to the difficulty of breathing and fighting the fever. Gordo's physical condition was relatively good; however, this would have little effect on the fever.

In the days he lay groaning on a makeshift cot, Gordo occasionally called out—sometimes screamed— for no apparent reason, causing his throbbing head to pound more severely. The pain behind his eyes had

The Shopkeeper's Journal

progressed to the point that to move them, even when they were closed, sent waves of electric pain radiating through his skull. Lodi did what she could, but outside of a cold rag and what fluids she could get him to drink there wasn't much to do except wait.

"Will he make it, Lodi?" Reg asked, standing over the pain-ridden young man.

"Can't tell. He seems strong, but Dengue don't always care about that."

Just then Gordo threw himself upright, vomiting the pale yellow bile churning in his gut. Lodi could only shake her head at that.

"Poor soul," she said sadly. "Barely has strength as it is…now, this."

Reg could tell by the look in Lodi's eyes they shared the same concern: bleeding. Their limited knowledge of the illness, combined with superstition and stories, told them that once the victim began to bleed, there was little else to do but wait for the inevitable. There wasn't a hospital nearby, and neither Reg nor Lodi possessed the physical strength to carry Gordo the long distance to the limited medical facility of the region.

Late the following evening, as shadows of the firelight danced across their faces, Reg and Lodi stared helplessly, fearfully, as a stream of blood oozed from Gordo's nostril. Reaching to wipe it clear Lodi said, "It ain't much, but blood is blood."

Reg lowered his head and moved a few steps to the fire to add another piece of damp wood. Grasping his hands behind his back, he stood for several minutes contemplating the potentially dire fate of their guest. *Why does it have to be? He's so young. Why does it have to be?*

177

Troy W. Rasmussen

"The young are strong, Lodi, the young are strong." Leaning in closer, Reg added, "Give 'em more broth, Lodi. See if he keeps it down. Gotta keep it down. Young ones are strong." Reg chanted this phrase many times over the next few hours. "Young ones are strong. Young ones are strong."

Lodi, lending what support she could to her mate, simply reached up from time to time, patting his arm in silent support of his desire for Gordo to recover.

And he did.

Young ones are strong.

> *Thursday*
> My sentiments about auctions haven't changed—they're dismal affairs. Attending them with Maarten has done little to change that. In all fairness, though, there is a certain added enjoyment watching someone of such fervor bounce up and down in the seat waving his paddle. Watching him was an event in itself, and I fear too many of the stoic bidders opted out of the proverbial race for little reason other than seeing Maarten time and again come unglued at winning the selected prize.

"The time has arrived. The hunt is on," Maarten set the empty espresso cup solidly down on the counter.

The shopkeeper, far less passionate about the hunt than his compatriot, pointedly removed the cup, then tapped out the charred tobacco remains from his pipe and placed it in his pocket. "Enthusiasm at the level you're accustomed to needs no further fuel."

The Shopkeeper's Journal

Waving his hand in the air, Maarten continued, "Any auction advice for the novice set?"

"Wave your hands like that and you'll end up carting back a 100-year-old piece of shit."

Startled by the response, Maarten started, then turned to see Bacardi standing just outside the door. Lifting his cup toward the shopkeeper, he added, "Fill this up before you and Mr. Excitement head out?"

The auction house, specializing in high-end antiques, was located a couple of hours from the shop. Maarten's three espressos kicked in shortly after departure, solidifying the shopkeeper's earlier impression that it would be a long day.

Shortly after they were in their seats, the house auctioneer took the podium welcoming bidders, those present and those on the phone lines, to the auction. A small painting by an artist of some note opened the auction, followed by a few incidental pieces ranging from blown glass to highly ornate pieces of silver. Although those first offerings provided Maarten a fair example of the proceedings, it did little to quell his anxiety and excitement at participating.

The auction was in full swing and had been for under an hour before the first of several items Maarten wanted for Vatori's estate came up for bid. As the turnstile pivoted around, displaying the next item, the auctioneer announced, "Coming up for bid, a carved walnut cabinet in neo-Renaissance style, late nineteenth century, circa 1884, the bidding to start at $50,000."

The speed at which Maarten's arm raised his paddle caught more than just the shopkeeper's attention—as did the fact that after being acknowledged as the opening bidder, Maarten failed to lower his arm.

Troy W. Rasmussen

The shopkeeper leaned in and tapped him lightly. "You can put your arm down now."

Embarrassed, but not detoured, Maarten did so, but never took his eyes off the podium.

"Do I have $55,000?" the auctioneer continued. And he did.

"Oh, I bid more," Maarten enthusiastically said.

"That may be, sir," replied the auctioneer. "And when the time comes, if you'll raise your paddle…"

Maarten's arm, paddle firmly gripped in hand, shot straight up. Shaking his head, the shopkeeper sent a silent message to the auctioneer.

"I haven't announced the bid, sir."

"Oh. Well, when you do, I'm ready."

"There can be no doubt, I'm sure," came the auctioneer's droll response as he adjusted his glasses.

Some considered it bad form to excuse oneself from an active bid; so, for propriety's sake, the shopkeeper remained in his seat—a feat taking more control than anyone present would ever be aware of.

"Do I have $60,000?"

Maarten's paddle once again made its meteoric rise.

"Sixty thousand to the gentleman…" The auctioneer paused a moment, gazing steadily at Maarten. "Do I have $65,000?"

Unable to control himself Maarten said all too loudly, "I'll top it if you do."

"Of course you will. Do I have $65,000 then?"

"Yes!"

"Sir, you have the bid at $60,000." With his exasperation beginning to show more clearly, the auctioneer added, "Decorum."

Realizing his error, Maarten noticeably slumped in his seat like a schoolboy after a reprimand.

The Shopkeeper's Journal

"Do I have $65,000? Going once…going twice." At this, Maarten's posture straightened in anticipation, his paddle thumping excitedly on his leg.

"Sold. To number…" The remainder of the auctioneer's words fell on mute ears as Maarten bounced uncontrollably up and down in his seat.

By day's end, Maarten successfully bid on and won seven items destined to grace the halls of his benefactor's estate. To the shopkeeper's chagrin, there would be several more auctions before the intrepid designer was satisfied with his selection of artifacts.

> *Friday*
> Love blooms eternal. Fitting, I suppose, for those in its grip. That it does so amidst the tone-deaf squalling of the love-struck is another matter entirely. In all fairness, it did us all good to see it play out—Parker giving it his all, and Natalia's response. It was truly a beautiful close to the day. Chester has found a new venue for his energy. "Let no stone go unturned" is surely the motto befitting his endeavors to find the Monarch Diamond.

It was early morning and, to the shopkeeper's surprise, Olivia was his first guest.

"It's not often I see you so early, Miss Olivia. What does our consummate professional desire to start the day off right?" said the shopkeeper.

Rolling her eyes at his flowery language, Olivia responded, "Oh, all right. Something light, I suppose, to go."

"To go?"

Troy W. Rasmussen

"Yes, I've agreed to chauffeur Chester to Matfield today. Little scamp worked me over good, claiming he doesn't collect full payment for his deliveries and I, therefore owe him. I've agreed to pay off 'my bill,'" Olivia tilted her head sardonically, "by providing transportation so he can continue to scavenge for that rock he heard you talking about."

"Mmmm. If there's a deal to be made, he'll come out on top. Of that, you can be sure."

"No harm done. I rarely see him. Seems the moment the car's in Park, he's out the door for the next 'sector' to be checked. He's mapped out the entire area of Vatori's place."

"I can only imagine," the shopkeeper said with a grin.

"It doesn't help that the landscaping crews feed into it. One brought an old mining pick the other day. Said it was for 'that kid hunting fortune and fame'."

"I am," said Chester, strolling to the counter. He slid his jar of lollipops closer, selecting one like a connoisseur of fine wine would a bottle for his table. Once this was done, he went on with the next order of business as if he was glad everyone necessary was present. "Say, Mister, how 'bout I trade some of these in for a bottle of pop. One for the road."

"One for the road?" the shopkeeper repeated skeptically.

"Yep. Gotta watch dehydration."

Olivia and the shopkeeper exchanged a comical glance.

"Two bottles," the shopkeeper countered, "and you sweep the shop."

Tilting his head in contemplation, Chester agreed.

"We're off, then," Olivia said. Tapping her designer watch, she continued, "I'm meeting new clients."

182

The Shopkeeper's Journal

The shopkeeper reached into the cooler and retrieved the ice-cold bottles of soda, which he handed to Chester.

"Off with you, then," he said.

With his fists around the bottles and a lollipop stick protruding from his mouth, Chester turned to go. "Later."

Shrugging her shoulders in a 'what are you going to do' motion, Olivia added, "A bottle of Perrier, if you please."

Arriving at Matfield, Olivia was relieved to note that her clients hadn't yet arrived; it was important to her that she was already on location when they did. It added a level of professionalism. True to fashion, Chester hopped out of the Mercedes just as it rolled to a stop.

"Thanks for the lift." With a shove of the door, he disappeared up the lane toward Vatori's place, a rumpled notepad and pen sticking out of his back pocket.

Olivia watched Chester's trek for a few moments before stepping from the vehicle, her Louboutin heels sinking into the soil. Unlike her passenger, she gently eased the door of her coupe shut just as a fresh-from-the-lot Lincoln Continental, high-gloss black paint gleaming in the morning light, eased to a silent halt. Olivia noticed the gentleman leaning forward for a better view while pointing toward the estate. *Usually, a good sign when the discussions start before the tour begins,* she thought.

Olivia had contacted the Albrights—Stefan and Elizabeth (Liz)—about the Matfield development after learning from an associate they were in the market for a Victorian-style home in a remote location, but still with close access to quaint shops and friendly townspeople. Stefan, a retired executive from an aircraft manufacturing conglomerate, had only one stipulation: "It needs to have a yard big enough to entertain in."

Troy W. Rasmussen

Olivia gave them a brief description of the property, the history of the location, and the condition of the estates. At this Liz had chimed in, "Oh, honey, it's got to have charm. It doesn't really matter what it looks like now, but when all is said and done, it's got to have charm."

Stepping toward the two as they exited the vehicle, Olivia introduced herself, shaking each of their hands in turn.

"Welcome to Matfield Greene. How was the drive?"

"Beautiful," Stefan replied. "The countryside is just beautiful."

"And peaceful," Liz added. "I said to Stefan on the way, just imagine living in an area like this."

"I'm glad." Stepping to the side and gesturing toward the place, Olivia continued, "This is the estate I spoke with you about on the phone. Two of the twenty-five have already sold. One is nearly ready for occupancy. If this particular location doesn't suit, there are twenty-two others we can tour."

Stefan kicked at a rotting tree limb. "Two? Who are the early birds?"

"The largest estate is owned by a Vatori Mastroberardino. He's—"

"The shipping magnate," Stefan interrupted. "I've heard of the family."

"The other was recently purchased by a model named Déjà," Olivia continued.

"Oh, Stefan, she's the model doing so much for underprivileged children. How exciting."

Moving toward the house, Olivia began, "This particular location was completed in 1863. The industrialist who originally occupied the home built it with a family in mind. But, as fate would have it, he and

184

The Shopkeeper's Journal

his wife were unable to have children. The home was used as a weekend retreat and for overnight entertaining."

Although the house was three stories high, its compact design gave the impression it was smaller. It was constructed of limestone from local quarries, with copper overlay on the peaks. The most notable architectural point of the place was the circular tower rising four stories, each level adorned with a different-shaped window.

"The doorway is far too small," Stefan pointed out.

"It is," Olivia agreed. "The couple built it with children in mind and wanted it to look like a castle. The arched door you're referring to was made smaller for the children." She pointed to her right. "The formal entryway and portico were used as the primary entrance."

"What a splendid idea for the children," Liz said. "We have six grandchildren. Oh, Stefan, can't you just see them coming and going? What an imaginative place for young minds."

The remainder of the tour was a mere formality, as the prospective buyers were already thoroughly sold on the possibilities of the location. After a short drive-through of the surrounding area, the Baker Mansion included, Olivia closed her third sale in Matfield Greene. Giving the Albrights directions and the general layout of the town, she agreed to meet them for lunch at Natalia's place. The only order of business before she could leave, then, was locating Chester.

This, as it turned out, wasn't as difficult as she'd thought it might be. As she pulled into the wide circle drive of Vatori's estate, Olivia spotted the boy sitting on the carved stone steps writing in his notepad.

"Any luck?" she called.

Chester finished his writing before responding.

185

Troy W. Rasmussen

"Nah. Big place." Then the boy stood, stuffed his pad and pen in his pocket, and bounded down the steps to where Olivia was parked. Getting in, he added, "There's time."

Later that evening, the shop was nearly packed with patrons. The guitar player had sent word out that he and the Welded Roses would be playing for a karaoke event. Arriving hand-in-hand, Parker and Natalia were given a prime location near the front.

The event was in full swing with one brave soul after the other getting up, giving their request to the band, and then doing their best to belt out the words. More than a few had the pipes to pull it off. It was the remaining many who didn't that brought wide-eyed stares and jeers from the audience. Those that came with a group found themselves heckled and booed as they muddled through a familiar tune. Karaoke isn't as easy as it may seem; therein lies the fun.

Just before the guitar player and the band were to break for a few minutes, Parker stood and approached the area where previous participants stood to sing (or wail) into the microphone. The cheers from the crowd escalated at the sight of a council member about to take part. Natalia was so surprised at the move she failed to notice Parker didn't make any request to the band.

The guitar player raised his hands for attention, simmering the crowd noise down. He then nodded to the band to begin playing.

Parker fidgeted from one foot to the other, cleared his throat, and then bent toward the mike. Natalia recognized the tune from the first note and brought her hands to her mouth in surprise as Parker did his best to sing "their" song. As the song continued, Parker's courage seemed to grow, and he slowly lifted his gaze from the floor to the eyes of the girl he'd fallen in love

The Shopkeeper's Journal

with. Parker was no pro, yet the love and sincerity flowing from the young man as he sang about an uncommon love and what it meant touched the crowd.

Lifting the microphone from its stand, Parker made his way toward Natalia, who began to tremble when he knelt to the floor on the song's final few words. Retrieving a diamond ring from his pocket, Parker finished with, "Talia, will you marry me?"

With tears streaming down her cheeks, Natalia leaned in, kissed his forehead, and whispered, "Yes."

The celebration of Parker and Natalia's engagement began seconds later, with cheers of the crowd ringing through the rafters. Parker stood and took Natalia in his arms, then kissed the tears from her cheeks.

To all things is the right time given.

Chapter 17

Monday

Parenthood. Is anyone ever prepared
for the barrage of raising children?
Probably not. The effort and energy spent
just getting a child through the toddler and
grammar school years are immeasurable.
As exhausting as this can be, it's worth the
effort—or so I'm told.

The morning came with a welcome peace and quiet. The shopkeeper, having completed the mundane task of sweeping the floor, was of a mind to spend a few serene moments sipping coffee. Easing himself onto the stool, tapping his pipe clear of remaining soot, he slid an open book within reading range, packed and lit his pipe, and leaned forward on his elbow to read.

"BAM! You're dead."

"Am not. Was inside before you shot me."

Jolted from his reverie, the shopkeeper lifted his head to see two young boys running into the depths of the shop, with a third a few steps behind them, doing his best to keep up.

"Wait for me!" demanded the third.

"Mom told you not to run in stores," admonished what appeared to be the oldest child—a daughter—as she grabbed the back of the small one's overalls. Not that it did much good. Although smaller, the young boy, apparently in possession of superhuman strength,

The Shopkeeper's Journal

continued his forward motion, pulling his older sister along, her shoes slipping on the hardwood floors.

Bemused, the shopkeeper marveled at the spectacle before he heard the commanding voice of an exasperated parent.

"Children, please." Looking toward the shopkeeper, the mother of the brood, fatigue written across her face, gave a nod his way. "I'm so sorry. Their father is at another store, and I'm afraid they are out of the mood to listen to me."

"Mmmm."

"I hope nothing gets broken. If it does, I'll gladly pay for it," she went on.

Closing his book, the shopkeeper said, "Before we concern ourselves with things that haven't happened, can I offer you a drink? A cup of tea, perhaps?"

The woman still looked sheepish. "I…I guess so."

Meanwhile, the girl gave a sharp jerk to the straps of her young brother's overalls. "That's enough. Mom's had it, and so have I. Now straighten up."

She said it with enough authority that it stopped him, at least for a few moments.

Looking toward the two, the shopkeeper asked, "Now, what's all the fuss about?"

The smallest lad pointed toward the back of the shop. "They ran ahead. Told 'em not to. Told 'em to wait, but they don't, never do." He threw an elbow at his sister. "Let go."

"Only if you promise to calm down and stay by me," she said, pulling harder.

"What about them?" the boy said.

"What about them?" asked the shopkeeper as he placed a cup of chamomile tea in front of the mother.

189

Troy W. Rasmussen

"That's a good question. What do you suppose there's to do about them? About you?"

"They always have all the fun."

"And you, of course, have been denied any fun at all."

"But—"

A nudge from his sister cut the boy's comeback short.

Peering over his glasses, the shopkeeper continued, "Having fun can sometimes only be part of the experience."

The boy's eyebrows did their best to cross in the center of his forehead.

"How many points would you score if you were the one to announce some fun?" the shopkeeper continued.

The boy's eyebrows flew up as quickly as they had down. "Lots."

"Well, then, how about you go and find your brothers and tell them you have super awesome news about something that's more fun than you've had all day, that your parents would never let you do in a store."

Like a racing hound from the gate, the boy took off at full speed to deliver the message and even the score with his brothers. His sister slapped her leg in frustration.

Reaching into the drawer, the shopkeeper took out a piece of paper and, with a large black marker, wrote seven words. He tore off a piece of tape, attached it to the top of the sheet, then turned to the woman. "If you will allow, I can guarantee you'll have at least twenty minutes to enjoy your tea."

With a grateful nod of her head, she agreed.

The shopkeeper disappeared into the back of the store, emerging as the two boys, their younger brother in tow, arrived at the counter.

190

The Shopkeeper's Journal

"He says he knows something fun," demanded one of the older boys.

"Did not." Pointing to the shopkeeper, the boy added, "He told me." All four heads turned toward the shopkeeper, while Mom took a sip of tea.

"Follow me," the shopkeeper instructed.

He led the band of four to a small room in the back of the shop. As they entered, the children were dumbfounded to see the only item present was an oversized bed with rusted-out head and footboards, the lumpy mattress and springs showing years of wear. The piece of paper taped to the wall read, NO LYING ON THE BED—JUMPING ONLY.

To all things is the right time given.

Tuesday

The revitalization of the Baker Mansion is complete. With all the Italian flair he can muster, Vatori has announced a gala, an open invitation extended to the entire town, in celebration.

Word has it that invitations to a smaller private affair will be delivered sometime in the near future. I suspect this has more to do with Déjà being out of town with overseas commitments. The speculation surrounding their relationship has kept most of the gossip rags in business. Who knows what will become of it all? And, if nothing does, more's the pity to living vicariously through this generation's jet set.

I doubt there's too much concern. The benefits the town will enjoy having

191

Troy W. Rasmussen

> Matfield Greene thriving again are not lost
> on those currently in residence. The only
> one less than enthusiastic is Chester. Once
> the owner takes residency, the lad's
> excursions of the property in the hunt for
> the Monarch Diamond will diminish
> considerably. That being said, though, I'd
> wager Vatori is about to meet his match.

Olivia was busy putting the finishing touches to the table arrangement when Redmond and McAlister arrived at the shop. Vatori was due to join them any moment. Ever the gentleman, Redmond, housewarming gift tucked under his arm, greeted Olivia warmly.

"Miss Olivia. It's good to see you again and under such circumstances. Please accept my sincere appreciation for your work with this project."

"Completely my pleasure," she replied, leaning forward to kiss his cheek. Extending her toned arm toward the other man in the party of two, she said, "McAlister." McAlister took her hand in his. Olivia watched as he struggled with the disappointment that the kiss on the cheek went to his father.

"Ciao. My good friends in the Americas, *ciao,"* said Vatori as he approached. He turned to the shopkeeper and extended one hand to the counter. "And to the keeper of the shop, *ciao* as well."

"Mmmm," responded the shopkeeper, placing the last of four rocks glasses on a tray. Those assembled took their seats at the table as he approached, setting the glasses in the center.

"Vatori," said Redmond, "allow me to be the first to formally welcome you to our community." With this, he slid his gift toward its recipient.

192

The Shopkeeper's Journal

"Grazie." Vatori unwrapped the package and, with a raised eyebrow, nodded his appreciation of the hundred-year-old Louis XIII Remy Martin Cognac. *"Grazie. Grazie Mille."*

Vatori filled all the glasses, then raised his own toward his hosts. *"Salute! Cento di questi giorni.* May you live a hundred years."

As the drinks were downed—Olivia opted to sip—the shopkeeper quietly turned to leave them to their discussions and found himself standing toe-to-toe with a determined-looking Chester. Stepping to the side, the shopkeeper lifted his arm in signal for the boy to proceed.

Chester didn't hesitate. Marching up to the table, he cleared his throat and put his hands on his hips.

"It appears we have another guest," Olivia said, with a small smile.

Chester pulled up a stool next to Vatori and climbed onto it, taking his pad and pen from his pocket as he did.

"You are Mr. Vatori? I'm Chester," he said.

With a slight chuckle, Vatori turned toward the boy. "I am. Very nice to meet you."

"Right." Chester adjusted his position on the stool to face Vatori directly. "Ever heard of the Monarch Diamond?"

Vatori shot a quick glance at his companions. "No. What is this diamond?"

"Long story. What it comes down to is, it's lost." Chester pointed to himself. "And I'm looking for it." Pointing to Vatori he said, "On your property. Get where I'm going?"

It didn't take long for Vatori to catch on.

"I see." Pointing to the notepad, Vatori added, "And your search is not finished. Do I have it correct?"

193

Troy W. Rasmussen

Chester's fingers curled into the pretend shape of a gun. With a *click* from one cheek, he indicated the point was made and understood.

Resting his chin in his hand, forefinger extended up to the side of his eye, Vatori the negotiator peered intently into the eyes of his counterpart. "What do you propose?"

"I need access."

"Access?"

Shaking his head, McAlister slowly turned his glass. Redmond, on the other hand, appeared to be impressed with the boy's fortitude and followed the conversation, his gaze volleying from one to the other.

"To the backyard and chapel. The house is a dry bone, and I checked the drive before they put in the stone. My money's on the chapel."

"You think this diamond is in my chapel?" He looked to McAlister. "I think this story is one I need to hear. Maybe I should go looking, no?"

"It's a one-man job. Got it covered. What's it gonna take?"

"For this...access?"

Chester remained as he was.

The discussion between the two continued for some time, one countering the other. In the end, Chester was granted access to the chapel as long as the Bernini was not disturbed. The yard was taken off the table, as neither party felt there was a serious chance the diamond was buried.

Hopping off the stool, Chester grinned. "Pleasure doin' business with ya. It's a nice place."

He turned to go before Vatori had a chance to respond. As he passed by the counter, the shopkeeper, a lollipop sticking out of his extended hand, said, "Played it like a pro."

The Shopkeeper's Journal

Wednesday
Finding one's niche, such a road.
How much easier it would be if the
journey were mapped out, clear signs
pointing the way toward what one is to do
or be in life. For those in the throes of the
dilemma, what to do tends to override
who they are—especially the young.

A fresh bouquet of azaleas sat on the piano's edge as
Trudy played. Gone were the heavy chords that had so
often sounded from the instrument. Taking note of the
change, the shopkeeper, a haze of pipe smoke hanging
about his head, sat idly listening to the new song.

The bell announced visitors to the shop, and he
placed the pipe in its holder. The first visitor he saw was
a teenaged girl in blue jeans and T-shirt, her hair pulled
back in a loose ponytail, an irritated look on her face. A
few steps behind her came the watercolor painter, a long-
strapped bag slung across her shoulder, who waved as
she closed the door. The shopkeeper didn't miss a brief
look of concern on the painter's face as the girl
approached the counter.

"The day is far too young for troubles the size you're
carrying," the shopkeeper said.

Other than shrugging her shoulders, the girl
remained still, her chin resting in one hand while the
other traced the grain in the counter.

Dusting.

"How about something to drink? My guess is you've
outgrown hot chocolate. Maybe that's part of the
problem."

Raising her head toward the ceiling, the girl wiped
her face with long capable fingers. The grease embedded

195

Troy W. Rasmussen

under her short nails seemed a contradiction to the grace of the movement.

"What do you say to an iced café au lait?"

The girl took a deep breath and shook her head *yes.*

The shopkeeper placed the drink in front of his guest and waited patiently for the story.

"I don't understand why it's such a big deal," she started. "Where's it written you have to know what you want to do with your life before you graduate?"

"Mmmm." The shopkeeper raised his eyebrows at how quickly, and with such force, the issue presented itself.

"It's not that...I just don't..."

"Let's leave all that for now and start with a name."

"Jonesie," she said, shrugging again.

"Well, Jonesie, I understand why school administrators push the issue. My guess is this isn't what you struggle with."

"Oh, it is. The problem...I don't know."

"Maybe the problem is you're attempting to identify who you are with what you do?" The shopkeeper's statement was met with a blank but thoughtful stare. Pointing to the grease embedded in her fingers, he said, "How does this happen?"

Jonesie glanced at her fingers.

"Oh, that. I like to work on cars. Well, I thought it would come in handy someday, so I'm taking a course on it at school. I don't mind it, but..."

The shopkeeper waited.

"I'm not sure...I guess...I thought there would be more to it," she said at last.

"Mmmm."

"It's more the same old thing. Like I said, I don't mind it, it's just..." Looking at her fingers again, she

The Shopkeeper's Journal

trailed off. Then, abruptly, she looked the shopkeeper squarely in the eye. "It's not who I am."

"And since you thought it was, you felt it may be a good vocation."

Jonesie confirmed the statement with a tilt of her head and an *I guess so* look in her eyes.

"Come with me," he said.

The shopkeeper led Jonesie outside. Bacardi, already at his flowerbed, tapped his mug on the steps, signaling it was empty. Pointedly ignoring the gesture, the two continued down the walk, the late morning sun bouncing rays of warmth off the stone wall. Turning into the alleyway, the shopkeeper took out a key, fitted it into the lock, and opened the door. Its rusted hinges creaked in rebellion from lack of use.

The shopkeeper moved further inside while Jonesie, her eyes adjusting to the dim light, stood in the doorway correcting the tension in her ponytail. Soon enough, she moved forward to stand next to the shopkeeper in front of a tarp-covered vehicle. Motioning for her to grasp the corner, the shopkeeper did the same on the opposite side, and they pulled the tarp up and over the length of the car.

At the sight, Jonesie stood wide-eyed, the tarp falling haphazardly from her hand.

"It's a Talbot Lago T23 Teardrop Coupe," he said. "Mr. Joseph Figoni designed and built only a few."

Jonesie clearly didn't recognize the significance of the automobile she was staring at, but this didn't stop her eyes from widening as they followed the sleek lines.

"Holy crap!" she whispered.

"Automobile enthusiasts around the world share your sentiment. Mr. Figoni would no doubt be complimented."

Troy W. Rasmussen

Stepping forward to run her hand along the curve of the roof, Jonesie said, "It's beautiful. How long have you had this?"

"No matter. What does matter is your appreciation and understanding of the skill it took to create it."

"What are you going to do with it?"

"More important is what *you're* going to do with it."

Jonesie's head snapped toward the shopkeeper.

"It requires a fair amount of attention, and not just under the hood. Something for the hands to do while the mind works out a few of life's conundrums."

"But I…I don't know…don't have the…"

"Mmmm." Moving toward the door, the shopkeeper held out the key to the lock. "You'll need this."

Jonesie took a few moments to allow what had just happened to sink in, then quickly turned to catch up with the shopkeeper.

"Sir, you don't understand. I'm just now learning about working on cars." Throwing her arm backward, she continued, "How am I supposed to work on…*that?*"

"Fear, or laziness, is more often than not the culprit to not realizing one's dreams."

Jonesie stopped. "I'm not lazy. And yes, maybe I am afraid to work on your car, but it's because I don't know what I'm doing and I don't want to mess it up."

"Mmmm."

"So you're a-needin' some help with that project of yours, are ya?"

Caught off guard, Jonesie turned her astonished glare toward Bacardi. "What?"

"If ya need help, ya need look no further than the guy you're a starin' at. Tho' ya might want to ease off the crazy a bit."

"You? You know how to work on cars?"

"Didn't say that. I know someone who can."

The Shopkeeper's Journal

Jonesie's arm fell to her side. "Who? Who can help me?"

"Guy by the name of Rueben. If it comes with four wheels and an engine, he's your man."

"How do I get in touch with this Rueben?"

"He'll be here tomorrow 'bout the same time you were today," Bacardi said, then raised his mug to signal it was still empty.

> *Friday*
> Our newly engaged councilman is at it again. No one can say he's not living up to his campaign promise of bringing new life to the community. With the success of the splash festival, the art festival, and its impressive finale, people seem like moths to the flame whenever Parker walks around with flyers tucked under his arm.
>
> Everyone has a role in life, a part singular to the individual. There are no stand-ins, no backup, and no understudy. It's a one-time shot. Every so often, someone comes along with an uncommon grasp of what it means—or doesn't—to live. Gordo's returned.

The smooth chords of Tameril's harp playing were no match for the periodic outbursts emanating from Bacardi over his latest frustration at tourists using the flower bed as a trash receptacle.

"Damned if they can't walk three more steps to put their crap where it belongs," he muttered. Reaching into the flowerbed to retrieve a cellophane wrapper, he stopped short and slowly stood. Bacardi brought the

Troy W. Rasmussen

wrapper to his nose, his nostrils flaring with the scent. With a *you're-not-fooling-anyone* look, he slowly turned his head, leaning back a bit as he did, and glared at the shopkeeper.

For his part, the shopkeeper merely raised an eyebrow and took a puff of his pipe—with the newly opened bag of tobacco, the smell of which had just been recognized by a certain gardener, sitting on the counter.

"That's a double dose the next time you fill my cup, Keeper," Bacardi bellowed.

"Mmmm."

Parker stopped at the steps, his hand resting on Bacardi's shoulder, and asked, "What seems to be the problem?"

Bacardi shrugged Parker's hand off. "An old fart that don't know when to leave well enough alone is the problem."

With a chuckle, Parker stepped into the shop. "Good afternoon. Have a posting to place, if you don't mind."

"Not sure why you ask. What's the news?"

"Noise and mud."

"Noise and mud? Mmmm."

"Talia and I were upstate the other day and came across a small county fair—you know, the kind where people wander around licking flavored snow cones and try to win stuffed animals by knocking over old milk jars."

"Mmmm."

"About midday, nearly everyone starts moving toward this open field, so we follow them to see what's going on. All of a sudden there's this explosion of noise. Huge jacked-up trucks, jeeps, and jalopies of all sorts fire up their engines—it was amazing. Seems each year the highlight of the fair is this mud run—bogging, they call

200

The Shopkeeper's Journal

it—where anyone looking to get covered head to toe in mud can participate."

"And now you've got it that we should have a similar event here."

"Why not? We're posting it in the papers of the surrounding area. I think it's a great way to bring people from other communities together. Good for local business as well."

Tapping his empty mug on the doorframe, Bacardi said, "As long as they put their trash where it belongs." Raising the mug into the air, he gave the shopkeeper a pointed look. "'Bout time for that double dose, litterbug."

The shopkeeper nodded to Parker, then turned to prepare the cranky gardener's favorite. Tipping the bottle of rum twice, the shopkeeper stopped at what he heard next.

"Add a cup of mud to that order, Keep," came Gordo's voice. The shopkeeper let out a breath of relief.

"Look who's back." Bacardi wiped dirt-encrusted fingers across his mustache.

Raising his gaze, the shopkeeper stared at Gordo. Gone was his normal healthy glow, although the shopkeeper didn't doubt it would return in time. In its place, he saw a thinner young man, with a sickly gaunt look still hanging about his eyes.

"You've looked better," the shopkeeper said.

"Felt better," Gordo said with a grin.

Parker slapped Gordo on the back and left to finish putting up his flyers. Bacardi entered the shop, something rare for him, and joined Gordo at the counter. Taking his mug from the shopkeeper, he slurped audibly, then gave Gordo a once-over. "Damned close call."

Troy W. Rasmussen

"It was. If it hadn't have been for Reg and Lodi, the last time you saw me probably would have *been* the last time."

"It was good of you to send word," the shopkeeper said.

Once he'd reached stateside, Gordo convalesced at Bart and Julia's until he was able to travel further. While there, he'd managed to pen a letter giving details of his close call with Dengue fever. The shopkeeper would never say it out loud, but the scare had affected him deeply.

Without missing a beat, the shopkeeper slid Gordo's drink toward him. "On the house. That and as many as it takes."

As Gordo took a gulp of the thick cocoa, Bacardi noticed a welling-up in the shopkeeper's eyes.

To all things is the right time given.

Later that evening, as the regular crowd shuffled from one group to the next, the music stopped when the guitar player noticed Gordo walking into the shop. Setting his guitar aside, he bolted from the couch, his long legs covering the distance in a few steps, to wrap Gordo in his arms.

"It's awesome to see you," he murmured, all but smothering Gordo in his chest. "It's never the same without you." He flung an arm out, keeping a hold on Gordo with the other, and called the group to attention.

"Kilimanjaro tried and failed," he declared. "The Amazon gave a fair blow but came up empty. Who knows what other places on the planet have attempted to best him, yet here stands our traveler." Releasing his hold, he added, "He's missed when he goes, and we thrill at the stories when he's back. Always loved, and perpetually tan."

The Shopkeeper's Journal

A wave of laughter rippled through the room.

"Clear a path, make a space," the guitar player went on. "My friend's returned, and we all want to hear."

Just before Gordo went to sit down, the guitar player leaned closer and finished in a whisper.

"Don't ever do that again."

> *Saturday*
> Rueben and Jonesie. The effect of a mentor on the life of another is difficult to measure, yet there is no denying that for good or bad (most often good), there is a life-changing impact for both parties. Clanging and banging aside, the intermittent expletives—in response to knuckles taking the brunt of a slipped wrench—provide their own entertainment.

BAM!

"Sonofa—!" His knuckles bleeding, Rueben stopped short and glanced at Jonesie.

"I've heard people swear, ya know," she said with a grin.

"I bet you have."

"Maybe I should try to loosen it."

Shaking his fingers to ease the shock of the blow, Rueben replied, "Go right ahead. Damn thing's stuck and good. Just remember kid, if you get it, I loosened it some."

Kid. Jonesie still recalled the first time Rueben had used the term. It was the day they met. After introductions, the two walked silently to the back of the shop, Rueben having asked to "see just what it was

203

Troy W. Rasmussen

needin' fixin'." Standing at the front of the exotic car, Rueben gave a quick whistle.

"You sure know how to pick 'em." Looking Jonesie in the eye, he continued, "Feelin' a bit over your head, I 'spect? You'll get it, kid. Sure as I'm standin' here, you'll get it."

Jonesie stood still a moment, reveling in wonder at the confidence in his tone and the marvel of feeling tears falling on the inside.

Jonesie reached for a can of WD-40 and approached the motor. *Ssssst...sssst* came the sound of the lubricant escaping from the can to coat the rusted bolt. Setting the can aside, she retrieved the fallen wrench from the floor and stood, contemplating the bolt, as she waited for the spray to work.

After a couple of minutes, she bent over, applied the wrench and tugged. Nothing. Giving his sore knuckles another shake, Rueben grinned at her effort. Jonesie adjusted her legs to a wider stance, bent in again, and pulled on the wrench to the point where her arms shook and her face turned red. A second before she would have let go, she felt a slight give, and the frozen bolt began to turn.

Heart pounding, she released her grip some, repositioned the tool to compensate for the turn, and gave it another pull. After a few more twists, the only sound was the solid thud of the bolt hitting the cement as it fell off. Suppressing a grin, she picked up the bolt and placed it in Rueben's hand. "I know—you loosened it some."

The Shopkeeper's Journal

Chapter 18

Tuesday

Adventures. To a certain extent, we all have them. At some point, most realize it's not what you find at the end that matters, but the adventure itself. Chester is fully convinced this bit of wisdom does not apply to him.

Chester sat idly at the counter, pushing the stool back and forth with his feet and staring at his medallion.

"Didn't you say this was the key to finding the diamond?" he piped up.

"The legend says a gold medallion is the key," the shopkeeper said.

"I wonder how."

"My guess is you'll get the answer when the time comes." He paused for a moment. "Enjoying the adventure?"

"Sure. It's been fun and all, but I haven't found it. Not yet anyway."

"Mmmm. And that's the goal?"

Chester released the medallion, and it thumped against his chest, "Yep. Why else spend all the time?"

"So I suppose the enjoyment of the hunt hasn't crossed your mind."

"Nah. Why run the race if you don't get the prize?"

"One can win without getting a prize."

Chester's *you've-got-to-be-kidding* look brought a grin to the shopkeeper's face.

205

Troy W. Rasmussen

"A lesson for another time," he said.

Chester merely cocked his head, gave the stool a final spin, and hopped off, bound for the back of the shop.

Wednesday
Given time, answers come. With the arrival of one Edward Kent, the answer to the change in Trudy's playing is here. Decent Chap.

Trudy arrived just as the sun streaming in through the windows made its ritualistic path through the shop. The shopkeeper, setting a fresh pot of coffee onto the hot plate, instinctively reached under the counter to turn down the stereo volume. Leaning in a bit to catch the scent of the fresh azaleas, Trudy sat to play.

Shortly after she began, a distinguished-looking gentleman dressed in tweed entered and approached the counter.

"A cup of your darkest roast," he said to the shopkeeper.

Nodding to his guest, the shopkeeper poured it, then asked if there was anything else.

The man, already immersed in a book, looked up long enough to add, "Just the coffee and a couch will do." Then, as if suddenly remembering his manners, he gave a slight smile. "I'm Edward. Edward Kent. Professor of analytics at the university."

"Mmmm. And you've come all this way for a coffee?" The shopkeeper answered the man's slight smile with one of his own.

Edward chuckled. "I'm an acquaintance of Trudy's. She speaks often of your shop and the piano. Having an interest, I decided to take a drive."

206

The Shopkeeper's Journal

"Mmmm."

Trudy played through the hour while Edward sipped his coffee. In the same span of time, the watercolor painter completed her work of a woman playing the piano and a man reading—the essence of the two masterfully merging into a crystal vase of draping azaleas.

> *Thursday*
> Planned spontaneity—or as today's youth terms it, a flash mob. Like a contagion, given the right conditions, it grows to infect others around it. One hears of such goings-on and wonders at the point of it all—unless, of course, they engage a bit and experience a different sort of wonder.

Tourist Lane was nearly packed. With the season in full swing and the weekend approaching, people—locals and tourists alike—milled about from one shop to the next. Some moved faster, others more leisurely at this place, then that, stopping every so often to point at things catching their attention: a frock in a window, unique architecture, missing members of a group. The bumper-to-bumper traffic crawled like a snake that, having spent too much time in a cool place, was heading into the sun to warm itself.

Midway through sweeping the walk, the shopkeeper stopped a moment to take in the activity. Natalia, stepping outside to mingle with her guests, waved a quick hello before turning her attention to a family having just received their order. The shopkeeper lifted his chin in response, then bent back to his own task.

Troy W. Rasmussen

No sooner had his broom touched the stone, though, than a low thump of bass reverberated through the street. More than a few people, the shopkeeper, and Bacardi included, stopped to look for the source. When no explanation was forthcoming, people returned to their activities.

Thump. Thump.

This time, the sound made more than a few onlookers concerned. The shopkeeper noticed Natalia lifting her head and moving her attention from her guests to the street; unlike the crowd, she seemed to know and expect what was to come. Moments later, a large 4x4 truck pulled to the center of the street. Amid honking horns, two enormous speakers began to unfold out of the back of the truck like floating pontoons; four smaller speakers followed suit.

Thump!

The truck doors flew open, and six college-age riders jumped from the cab. Two bounded onto the hood of the truck, while the other four took positions in the front.

Thump!

One of the four up front hurled himself into the other three, who propelled him in a swooping flip over the hood and onto the roof.

Thump! Thump! Thump!

On cue, more young people sprang out of the truck's bed, and onlookers moved back and grabbed onto their children. Half a block away, one last motorist honked a horn…then gave up.

More than twenty dancers were already in action around the truck when more dancers emerged from the midst of the crowd itself, springing into action from prearranged places on the sidewalks. In time with a crescendo of music, four of them executed fully

The Shopkeeper's Journal

extended, slow-motion backflips into the crowd. Coming upright, they urged the onlookers to join in.

Unable to resist the invitation of the chorus saying something about people and the freedom to feel good, Natalia stepped from where she stood, threw her hands and body into the air, and did just that. By mid-song, over half of the crowd was dancing. Clapping, gyrating, doing their own versions of a jig, parents, and kids alike sang and cheered.

Watching them was its own entertainment. But what caught and held the shopkeeper's attention was Parker, leaning against a streetlamp also watching—but with a singular focus. Over a hundred people joined in the flash mob, but as far as Parker was concerned, only one was worth watching.

Grinning at the sight of the young man watching the love of his life, the shopkeeper turned back toward the shop to witness another spectacle that made his grin even wider. Caught up in the moment, Bacardi sat cross-legged on the steps, his foot keeping time with the beat.

"Seems that foot has a twitch," the shopkeeper teased as he passed by.

Embarrassed at being caught, Bacardi quickly wrinkled his brow and turned back to his work in the flowerbed.

Thump! Thump! Thump!

The music ended on a final, throbbing bass, a note that reverberated for long seconds as the crowd cheered.

One of the locals called out, "Awesome!" A small boy, hyped up from the energy around him, asked, "Mom, can we do that again?"

Parker chuckled at the boy's plea, then stole one last glance of Natalia.

Troy W. Rasmussen

Friday

With the gala at the Baker Mansion approaching, the entire town is buzzing with anticipation. All but one, that is. Seems our young explorer is more concerned with the diminishing prospect of his access to the property than celebrating its completion—the Albrights an unwitting solution to the problem.

The shopkeeper gave a satisfied sigh as he set his cup of tea down.

Strolling into the shop, hands in his pockets, Chester said, "'bout to get some visitors." He hopped onto one of the stools, landing his feet on the front of the counter to start his usual rounds back and forth.

The announcement of guests wasn't what caught the shopkeeper's attention, but rather, the look of accomplishment on Chester's face as a couple entered the shop.

"Good morning," the man called out, stepping through the door.

"And to you," replied the shopkeeper.

"If I may—I am Stefan Albright, and this is my wife, Elizabeth."

"Liz," she said with a polite nod.

"A pleasure to meet you," the shopkeeper said, enjoying their smiles. "How may I be of service?"

Liz clapped her hands together. "That lovely realtor, Olivia, recommended your shop for all kinds of good things." Pointing to Chester, she continued, "And this young man was just telling us of his adventures looking for a stone or something."

210

The Shopkeeper's Journal

The shopkeeper's eyes slid sideways toward the boy, who nonchalantly continued his twisting back and forth. *Stage set,* thought the shopkeeper.

"The Monarch Diamond," replied the shopkeeper.

"Yes, that's it," Liz replied.

"Seems Olivia is making fewer trips to the area," Stefan put in, with a glance at Chester. "Which leaves the lad without transportation. According to…Chester, is it?"

"Yep," the boy answered.

"Yes. According to Chester here, there is a more scenic route to the area, one he's willing to show us."

"I'm sure he is," the shopkeeper said. *Phase one complete.*

"Stefan has odd jobs around the grounds, and Chester's agreed to help with them, too," Liz said.

"How industrious," said the shopkeeper. *Phase two executed.* "Chester knows the Greenes well."

"The Greenes. Is that what the locals call it?" Liz reached up to pat her husband's shoulder. "The Greenes, Stefan, how exciting. Anyway," she said, turning back toward the shopkeeper, "I think he and Stefan will become fast friends. And, of course, we'll pay him for his time."

Chester pulled his jar of lollipops closer, selected one, then hopped off the stool.

Golden parachute deployed, the shopkeeper thought.

Liz smiled at the boy's smooth move. "Thank you so much for your help, young man."

"No problem, Liz," Chester said, giving a slight wave as he left.

Mission accomplished.

"We'll need to speak with the boy's parents, of course," Stefan said, with a tilt of his head.

211

Troy W. Rasmussen

"Sheila, his mother, lives in the area," the shopkeeper replied. "His father, a military man, was killed in action."

Liz's eyes filled. "Oh, my."

"If you'd like, I can make arrangements for you and Sheila to meet."

Stefan nodded in agreement.

"Well, now that you've met our local mover and shaker," the shopkeeper said with a slight grin, "how else can I help you feel more at home in the area?"

> *Saturday*
> Sometimes, the simplest ideas have
> the greatest impact. Not surprising, the
> one presented today came from a group of
> young people, completely unaware that
> their desire to meet an educational
> requirement had the potential to bring
> such enthusiasm and laughter.

The shopkeeper was finishing wiping down the third of a five-volume set of first-edition classics by James Fenimore Cooper when his reverie was interrupted by the jingle of the bell. Looking over the rims of his glasses he set the book down as four teenage girls approached the counter. *They really do travel in packs,* he thought with a touch of humor.

Looking from one to the other in unspoken communication, the girls silently elected a spokesperson. "Sir," she said, "we are from the local high school and members of the Build a Better Community Club."

"Mmmm. Good afternoon, members of the BBC Club."

Grinning, the leader of the group continued. "We've been tasked with the challenge of developing and

The Shopkeeper's Journal

implementing ways to increase community involvement."

"Part of which is a formal presentation of the whys and wherefores," the shopkeeper said, still gazing over his glasses. The speaker shuffled a bit as she struggled to keep her concentration.

"We...part of..."

"Yes?"

"The assignment is supposed to be something in the community that not only benefits people but also gets them involved."

"Involved," said the shopkeeper, prompting them further.

Another member of the group quickly spoke up. "Yeah. You know, like a swing in the park or something."

"Or something. I'm guessing you mean interactive."

The group chimed in as one. "Yeah, like that."

"I see. And how is it I can be of assistance with your project?"

"Well, what we came up with is a game," said another of the four.

"A game."

"Hopscotch! Who can resist hopscotch?" said another.

"Mmmm."

Sensing they were losing momentum, the leader hastily took over. "Our idea is to create a game of hopscotch in the sidewalk. Since your shop is on the busiest corner, we thought it would be the best place. The project requires tearing out a section of the sidewalk and pouring new cement. We've already met with the City Administrator's Office and have their approval." She

213

Troy W. Rasmussen

smiled. "Parker overheard us talking and told us you would help."

"Parker was correct." He nodded. "What do you need?"

The shopkeeper was not expecting the squeals of delight and hand clapping that followed his statement and waited patiently for the enthusiasm to pass.

"The city is donating the equipment and cement, plus a couple of the guys from the crew to do the tear-out and stuff. Once that's done, the hopscotch will be created from glass. Like a mosaic." She glanced at the others and bit her lip. "We don't have any colored glass, though. We were wondering if maybe you do."

"That I do, miss." The shopkeeper set the book and cheesecloth aside. "If you ladies will come with me?"

Like a school of fish, the four girls turned in unison to follow the shopkeeper to several stacked packing crates in the back of the shop. The shopkeeper moved aside two antique headboards leaning against one of the crates and lifted the heavy wooden lid, its rusted hinges popping in rebuke. With one hand holding the lid open, he motioned with the other toward its contents.

Leaning forward, their heads pressed together, the girls let out a collective gasp at the site of some fifty quarter-inch thick panes of colored glass.

"I purchased these years ago with the intent of adding them to the windows out front. Seems to me they'd be better suited for your project."

To all things is the right time given.

Sunday

How does the universe top the enchantment of a small child in the throes of wonder and discovery? Probably doesn't. Something as simple as a

The Shopkeeper's Journal

dripping hose is all it took to enthrall little Meridy. Big gifts in small packages.

The noise from the back had subsided enough to cause the shopkeeper to take a break from his duties and look in on the progress Jonesie and Rueben were making on the car. With the early afternoon sun starting to warm the day, it didn't take much to justify the walk outside and around back, versus going through the shop.

At the same time, Bacardi was just arriving to check the plants. Since the area had gone without rain for several days, he probably needed to water. As the shopkeeper stepped into the light, Bacardi reminded him his mug needed filling with the day's libations.

"Tank's on empty," he said.

"Mmmm."

Continuing to the back alley, the shopkeeper arrived just as Rueben and Jonesie were appraising the completion of the motor and chassis and laying out plans to set the body. Jonesie's choice in wheels—solid black rubber with wire spokes—gave a glimpse of the beauty and level of class its designer had created.

"Bet she purrs like a kitten," Rueben said.

"Only one way to find out," Jonesie added, the excitement in her voice betraying her attempt at a cool stance.

"Start her up, kid."

Approaching the steering column, Jonesie lifted the ignition mechanism hanging loosely by its wires and paused for a moment.

What if it doesn't start?

What if it does?

Not one to deliberate long on such things, Jonesie gave the key a turn and, in seconds taking too long to

215

Troy W. Rasmussen

pass, heard the motor come to life. The shopkeeper, Rueben, and Jonesie stood in silence listening to the soft hum. Placing his hand on the top of the engine, Rueben commented, "Like touching silk." A peaceful pride radiated in his eyes.

Jonesie stood silently listening, staring at the motor for the miracle it was.

"We did it," she said. With the ignition switch clasped in her hands, she looked up, wide-eyed, to the two men standing before her. "It works, it really works!"

Unable to control her enthusiasm, she dropped the ignition component with a clunk and all but ran to the shopkeeper, throwing her arms around his neck and kissing his cheek. "It works! It works!" Leaping over toward Rueben, she wrapped herself around her mentor like a child running to a long-absent father. Caught off guard, Rueben looked as wide-eyed as his protégé, then wrapped his arms instinctively around her waist. Both began to laugh.

Understanding this moment was theirs, the shopkeeper quietly left, a smile of knowing satisfaction on his face. The shopkeeper rounded the back of the building and came face-to-face with the second wonder of the day.

Bacardi's watering hose ran from the spigot the length of the walkway, up and over the top of the shop's steps, and provided Meridy a welcomed source of entertainment. With a light breeze catching her sundress, the child watched in fascination as small trickles of water ran down the underside of the hose to drip on the sidewalk where she stood. Her mother stood a few feet away catching up on the goings-on with a friend.

Drip.

The Shopkeeper's Journal

Meridy stood still in her observation. Another trickle ran its course and, reaching the same destination as its predecessor, released its hold to fall in like fashion.

Drip.

Tiny toes wiggled in the wetness and a head full of curls bent slightly, following the drops as they landed on her feet.

Drip.

Drip.

Looking back toward the source of the drip, Meridy held out her hand and, with pudgy fingers splayed wide, caught the next drop in the palm of her hand.

Drip.

The little girl leaned forward and watched the small bubble of liquid dissipate in her palm, filling the folds of skin. Squirming and bouncing, she watched the next drop move down the hose, slowly stretching into an elongated teardrop, before releasing to land with a splash in her hand.

Drip.

Meridy lifted her arm in an attempt to follow the drop as it ran the short distance to her elbow.

Drip.

With her elbow still up in the air, she focused on the hose—*drip*—in contemplation of the similarity. She stamped both feet in the small puddle; then, hands on her knees, leaned in for a closer inspection.

Drip.

Tiny feet shuffled forward.

Drip.

Drip.

Her curiosity left her only one choice: to lean forward until her face was under the hose.

Drip.

217

Troy W. Rasmussen

Drip.

Cool drops raced over her forehead, down the valley of her nose, around the corner of her mouth, and off the end of a tiny chin. Squealing in delight, she raised up, bounced around, and clapped her hands.

"Time to be off, Ms. M," her mother said, giving a nod to her friend. Meridy took her mother's hand and continued her bouncing a few more paces, dripping hose forgotten.

Drip.

Grinning at the scene, the shopkeeper completed his trek up the walk and into the shop, the flooded flowerbed catching his eye.

Bacardi cleared his throat. "Cup's still empty."

The shopkeeper feigned perplexity.

"Mmmm."

The Shopkeeper's Journal

Chapter 19

Tuesday

Hell on earth. To each is their own definition, as is the life experience that qualifies. Love gained and lost, a soul tortured. One story told, another lived, elegance and poise the result. It's late.

Melanie, a chilled drink sitting on the table beside her, sat curled up on the couch reading a first edition copy of *Effi Briest,* a book known for the writer's ability to bring its reader to tears. Melanie proved the point and, with a sigh, closed the book in her lap to wipe a tear from her cheek.

"It's a sad tale, my dear," came a voice near her. Melanie looked up to see an older woman half-smiling. "Not a grand one, but sad."

"You know Fontane?" Melanie asked, referring to the author.

"My dear, I know him well," the woman responded.

"Personally?" Melanie asked.

The woman chuckled.

"No, no. Only in that when I was younger, much younger, I read his *Effi Briest* many times. Such a story."

The woman slowly turned her nearly empty cup of tea in its saucer.

Melanie, intrigued, got up to sit closer. "My name is Melanie," she said to the older woman.

Troy W. Rasmussen

The woman brought her attention back to the conversation at hand. "And mine is Grace. How do you do?" They both laughed at the instinctive formality.

"It's my first time reading the book," Melanie said. "Silly, I guess, to get so emotional."

"No, my dear," Grace replied. "Great stories and the tragedy they sometimes are is not this silliness. It is but the way of life." Her teacup continued its circular motion. "I had a great love once," she said, closing her eyes for a moment. "Before hell came to town, I had a great love."

Melanie was startled at the comment. "Hell?"

"Such a story," Grace said.

"I'd like to hear if you don't mind."

"Oh, I was such a young girl then. Germany was alive and strong, getting stronger—but not so much in a good way, you know. I loved the stories and read many, but none captured my young heart as did this *Effi Briest.*" Grace gestured with her hand. "I read and read, always the same one, this *Effi Briest.* Got herself in such a mess. So young, she was."

Melanie hardly dared breathe. "Go on."

"The one thing worth it, worth it all, child—love. How I dreamed of the love and longing. The passion." Grace leaned forward. "The scandal." Then, unexpectedly, she smiled. "Such things a young woman should not desire, but I did. One day when my Rupert showed up—*ach*—I was helpless."

"Rupert was your husband?" Melanie asked.

"No, my dear. He was my love. A secret tryst to set the romantic heart of any young girl on fire." At this, Grace laughed again shaking her head. "He was married, you know...I knew. Everyone did. I knew this about him and didn't care." She sighed. "We loved. With passion, we did this. Meeting here, then there, in secret." Grace's countenance dropped. "It couldn't last."

220

The Shopkeeper's Journal

"Why?" Melanie put one hand over Grace's.

Raising her sad gaze, Grace said, "He was a wealthy man, everyone knew him…it couldn't continue."

Melanie lowered her eyes then, catching three tattooed numbers on the inside of Grace's forearm. Grace followed her gaze and nodded.

"I was a Jew. I am a Jew. My Rupert knew this, and one day he said goodbye. He held me tight, my Rupert, and as I cried he said goodbye."

"I'm so sorry," Melanie said sadly.

"*Ach*, those Germans." Taking a deep breath, Grace continued, "They came for us, you know. Jackboots, marching, fists banging on doors. How my heart pounded. It was no good, that time. Mama and Papa told us to be strong, but all I could think of was my Rupert. The day they came I was reading *Effi…* the noise downstairs was so loud. Mama and Papa saying, 'This isn't right, you have no right.' I held my book to my chest and, God forgive me, I longed for my Rupert."

Melanie sat motionless…waiting.

"I lost my *Effi* that day," Grace said, shaking her head. "And in return, they gave me this." Grace pulled her shawl back, exposing the remaining tattooed numbers. "Auschwitz, you know. Hell on this earth."

"Grace," Melanie whispered. "I don't know what to say."

"*Ach,* just a time, child. The worst of times, but it's done. Don't you worry none."

"Did you ever see Rupert again?"

"No, my dear. And until I was watching you there, I never saw *Effi,* either. Such memories."

The two women talked on, losing track of time, sharing memories. At last, Melanie caught hold of Grace's hand.

221

Troy W. Rasmussen

"I need to go," she said, "but I'm honored to have met you, Grace." She placed her copy of *Effi Briest* into the old woman's hand. "I want you to have this. Thank you for telling me the story, your story. I won't forget."

> *Wednesday*
> Is there no end to the machinations of those on the hunt? Where Chester is concerned, probably not. With Vatori's gala on the horizon, the lad seems to have worked a final deal with the magnate in his efforts to find the elusive Monarch Diamond.

The shopkeeper had just completed placing the last of six bottles of imported wine into the case when Chester, his mother in tow, strolled into the shop. Accustomed to the antics of the lad, the shopkeeper turned toward his visitors with no small expectation.

"How's it goin'?" Chester approached the counter.

"Going," Sheila corrected him with a touch of exasperation. "Hello."

The shopkeeper nodded. "Likewise." He stepped behind the counter, his gaze on Chester. "And what's on the agenda for today?"

"That dude Vatori's in town for his party, and I'm gonna help."

"Going to, Chester. Really," Sheila said.

"And just how is it you'll be helping?" the shopkeeper asked.

"Tour guide. Big guy needs someone to show people around. Told him I can help out, bein's I know the place."

"Bein's?" Sheila chimed in. "What kind of language is that?"

222

The Shopkeeper's Journal

Undeterred, Chester continued, "Told 'im I'd be willing to help," emphasizing the 'ing' for the benefit of his mother.

"And what's that going to cost him?" the shopkeeper asked.

"The statue."

"Vatori's giving you the Bernini for being a tour guide?"

"Nah. Told' 'im it's the only place I haven't checked. He's been hold'n out since our last agreement so I told 'im I'd help, but it'd cost him."

"The Bernini."

"Yep."

"Yes," his mother corrected.

Pulling a lollipop from the jar, Chester shook his head. "Yes. Says I can look around the chapel as long as he's there."

"Sounds like you have it all worked out."

"Yep." Looking sideways, he amended, "Yes. You goin'?"

Sheila rolled her eyes.

"I am," the shopkeeper said.

"Look me up. I'll show you around." Satisfied, he and his mother left the shop.

Thursday

The Talbot is nearly complete. In truth, it is. Once the body was set, Rueben and Jonesie were hard pressed to pull themselves away from completing a goal so visibly within reach. One would arrive early, only to find the other already there. One would stay into the early morning hours, only to wake at the sound of the

223

Troy W. Rasmussen

> other sanding or polishing or rubbing
> leather with yet another coat of
> specialized oil. All their efforts paid off,
> though, in more ways than one.

Jonesie couldn't remember a time when she felt so tired, yet so completely alive, as she did today. It was early morning and the time had come to take the Talbot for its first drive.

"Early morning quiet is the best time, kid. Ain't nothing like a drive in a machine like this with the sun peekin' over the hills."

Jonesie caught a vision of her mentor's experience.

"No breeze but the one you make, the soft purr of a motor tuned to perfection." Rueben stopped and took a satisfied breath. Extending his gaze toward a far horizon, he went on. "Then it hits." He moved his hand as if along a road. "That first beam of the day's sun strikes a paint job so smooth it can't grab hold. Just glides right off as you pass into the next one."

Jonesie smiled at the picture...and waited.

"Well," Rueben said, dusting off his jeans, "Best be gettin' her ready, don't ya 'spect?"

Jonesie nodded. "Open the door, kid, and let's do our best to meet the day how we've been dreamin' of."

Jonesie felt tears burning her eyes as she pulled the handle and slid the bay door open. Part of her was glad her back was turned so Rueben wouldn't see. Another part felt sure he would understand.

With a clap of his hands and a "whoop!" to punctuate the occasion, Rueben stepped outside into the predawn light. Confused, Jonesie gave him a questioning look.

"Moment's all yours, kid, don't be a-wastin' it." He placed both hands on her shoulders. "It's been a grand

The Shopkeeper's Journal

time bringin' that machine back to life with you. Now start her up and let the world see just what we've been hidin'." At this, he cupped her face in weathered hands and kissed her forehead.

Jonesie took hold of his wrists. "Rueben, I'm not going without you."

"Course not! But pullin' her out of her cage is all yours, kid. Now get to it."

The tears wouldn't stop this time, and in a quick movement, Rueben found himself the recipient of one of the most sincere hugs of his life. Hesitating a bit in his surprise, he wrapped his arms around the girl's waist and hoisted her into the air, turning in circles. Jonesie swore to herself she would never forget the sound of his laughter.

Click.

Hearing the slight but firm catch of the door, Jonesie recalled Rueben's words, "Doors on a machine like this need to have just the smallest click when they shut. You'll see, kid. First time you sit in her and pull the door shut, you'll see."

Jonesie smiled at the memory of Rueben tilting his head as he held his pinched fingers close to his ear…"You'll see, Kid." Turning the key, Jonesie sat a moment listening to the barely audible hum of the motor, her hands caressing the top of the steering column.

"That old thing's past savin'," she recalled him saying, shaking his head at the worn, split steering wheel. "Have to make a call on this one, kid."

"A call?"

"Yep. Gotta replace the thing. Do you want to go with tryin' to find a similar replacement?" Then his face lit up. "Or should we do our best to find one made of wood, and see what that does to spruce things up?"

225

Troy W. Rasmussen

Grinning, she replied, "Wood."

Jonesie's excitement reached such a level she wondered if she would be able to maneuver the car out and into the alley. With her arms stretched out, hands grasping the wheel, she slid back into the new leather seat, still savoring the sound of the engine. Taking a deep breath, she put the car in gear, *smooth engagement,* she thought, and slowly moved the vehicle outside.

Having walked a few paces past the corner of the shop to the opposite side of the street, Rueben raised his hands into the air and began to laugh again at the sight of the sleek machine easing out of the building to roll silently toward him. Giving her a thumbs-up of approval, he murmured, "Nice job, kid. She's a real beauty."

Jonesie rolled down the window and deadpanned, "Wrong side, Rueben." Realizing his error, Rueben jumped into action, rounded the rear of the vehicle, and got in.

Click.

"You'd think," she said, rolling her eyes, "that a guy with your knowhow would remember the passenger side of a foreign car is on the left."

"Now, just a minute," Rueben played along. "I know the steering's on the right. Thought I'd trip ya up some."

"Right."

The shopkeeper was just arriving at the shop when he noticed the Talbot moving toward the main street. Watching its progress, he found himself beaming as Jonesie brought the automobile to a stop.

"Well done, Jonesie," he said.

Lowering her head to better see, she raised one hand in a shaka sign. "Thank you. We're taking her for an inaugural ride through the hills. Rueben says that's the way to do it."

"Mmmm."

The Shopkeeper's Journal

"Kid did a right nice job," Rueben chimed in. "Sun's about to show her face—can't miss it."

The drive in the newly restored coupe was like something out of a commercial. The morning mist, yet to rise out of the small valleys, seemed to wrap the car in softness only to release it a few seconds later. Neither occupant spoke as the mechanical marvel wound its way through the hills, the vision of Rueben's description of the first rays of light striking the paint still fresh in Jonesie's mind.

She thought of their conversation about paint...

"What color do ya have in mind, kid?"

She'd stood to wipe her brow with the back of her hand. "Hadn't thought of it, really. Something rich, though, with a lot of shine and gloss."

"That's a wide open door."

"I know." She stood, hands on hips, contemplating the partially sanded body. "Not red or yellow or something plain like that. It's got to be...well, black looks nice in gloss."

No sooner had the words been spoken, though, than she thought better of them.

"No," she said, suddenly excited. "No. Not black. Ever seen one of those paint jobs where you think it's black, but then the light hits it just right and you realize it's another color?"

"Sure have."

"Something like that, only richer." Jonesie's hand lifted to punctuate the air.

"Richer."

"Yeah. A real deep..." Jonesie paused to think. "Deep...it's not red. What is that color?"

"Not red," Rueben said, giving her a sly look.

Troy W. Rasmussen

Returning the look, Jonesie continued, "No, it's like that but different. Deeper, maybe?"

"How deep do we go before we nail this thing?"

"Cute." Wrinkling her nose, Jonesie looked her mentor square in the eye and said, "What *is* that color?"

Rueben gave her a wry smile. "Don't know. It's deep and not red is all we got so far."

"Oh. This is ridiculous. It's right on the end of my tongue."

"Hate to say it, kid, but *that's* red." Rueben threw his head back and began to laugh.

"Impossible," she replied, rolling her eyes.

Half a mile away from where Jonesie knew they would be out from under the trees, she uttered, "Cherry. Black cherry."

"Yep, that's it, kid. 'Bout to see it, too."

Jonesie concentrated on her speed, hoping the timing worked. Adjusting in the seat to focus on the long slope of the car's hood and exaggerated curves of the fenders, she waited in anticipation. Waiting…the purr of the engine the only sound…waiting…her heart beating faster. Just a few more feet.

Waiting…waiting……

And then, magic.

The car left the canopy of trees just as the first light of day raced across the countryside, catching the black cherry paint of Jonesie's Talbot Coupe.

To all things is the right time given.

Vatori, the smoke from his Gurkha trailing behind, passed the massive window of his suite when something outside caught his attention. Following the source as it wound its way around the edge of Matfield, he wondered who was driving a vehicle of such caliber.

The Shopkeeper's Journal

Friday

The elite attending Vatori's gala have arrived, part of the allure adding to the excitement of it all, I suppose. Not that anyone minds. It's good for business and the town. With the open invitation, more than a few hearts have quickened at the possibility of running into someone famous—the chance encounter minor compared to the telling of it. Redmond is well pleased, in more ways than one. The day ended with an informative tour of Vatori's estate. Both the estate and Chester's knowledge of it were impressive. All things considered, the private meeting with Vatori amazed me most.

Redmond arrived at the shop and, seemingly, with an agenda. Choosing a favored table with an open view of the street, he sat all but motionless, smoke from his Ark Royal drifting about.

The shopkeeper sensed his guest's reflective mood when he approached the table, and so set Redmond's cup of Kopi down with barely a sound. As he turned to go, Redmond spoke.

"Street's quiet, for all the goings-on at Matfield."

"Mmmm," the shopkeeper responded.

Redmond watched Natalia arranging patio chairs on the sidewalk. "I understand business across the street is going well. And an engagement."

"Correct on both accounts," the shopkeeper replied.

"Good to see it." Redmond nodded. "McAlister will be joining me. A second cup of Kopi, if you would."

Troy W. Rasmussen

Excusing himself to the counter, the shopkeeper was midway through the brew when McAlister, manila folder in hand, entered. He gave the proprietor a quick wave and then walked to where his father sat. Redmond's expression left no doubt the meeting concerned business and McAlister's apparent reporting of it.

Redmond flipped the folder open and gave the contents a quick glance before closing and sliding it to the center of the table.

"Are there other prospects?" he asked.

"Olivia's lined up several. Things are progressing nicely."

"Olivia, sharp lady." Redmond finished his Royal as the shopkeeper set McAlister's cup down and, with a nod of his head, excused himself again.

McAlister finished his coffee in one gulp, slapped his father on the back, and left. Returning to the table with the intent of retrieving the cup and leaving his guest to his thoughts, the shopkeeper was mildly shocked that Redmond had other intentions.

"He's a bit more relaxed about business than I was— am," he said.

"Mmmm."

"Has things at Matfield well in hand. Maybe other areas are following suit."

"Suit?"

"Seems Vatori's upcoming ball was the final nudge."

"Nudge?"

Redmond turned toward the shopkeeper. "He's asked Olivia to accompany him to the ball."

"I see."

As a preparatory step to departing, Redmond stood and placed the pack of Royals in his pocket. "I don't plan on staying long myself, just long enough to deliver a housewarming gift, I suppose." Facing the shopkeeper,

The Shopkeeper's Journal

he added, "What might you have befitting the welcome of a less than middle-aged tycoon?"

Redmond left the shop with a Faberge enameled and gold-mounted cigar holder encased in an unpretentious wooden box.

The shopkeeper arrived at Vatori's estate as the sun was lowering itself behind the ridge. Pulling into the circle drive, the tires of his vehicle making a nostalgic padding sound on the imported stone, was an experience in and of itself.

Valets hired for the event met him at the door before the car came to a stop at the base of the enormous curving stone stairway leading up and into the main second-story entrance. Stepping from the vehicle, the shopkeeper was momentarily drawn into the splendor that had once been the Baker Mansion. The sinking sun cast a warm evening glow of gold across limestone walls, making them shimmer.

"Buona sera! Good evening," Vatori greeted the shopkeeper heartily. Opening his arms, Vatori descended the stairs to envelop the shopkeeper in a strong embrace.

"How glad I am you came, my friend. What do you think of all this?" he asked.

"Impressive," replied the shopkeeper.

"I hoped to bring some of the heritage of its builder back to life." Gesturing with his arm, Vatori added, "Come. I will show you the work of the craftsman, and you can tell me what you think."

"Judging by what I've seen so far, I'd wager it's a thing of beauty, Mr. Mastroberardino."

"And yet, with your assistance, this place is filled with things of beauty." Vatori placed his hands on the shopkeeper's shoulders and lowered his voice

231

Troy W. Rasmussen

conspiratorially. "No small feat, I know. And for you, it's Vatori, always Vatori. *Si?"*

"Mmmm."

Vatori stepped back and, with a swing of his arm, motioned for the shopkeeper to join him. As the two proceeded up the stairs and into the main foyer, the shopkeeper couldn't help but raise an eyebrow at the grandeur around him.

Two grand staircases rose from the drive to the second story on either side of the structure's center where enormous, intricately carved double-hung doors opened into the main level foyer. The polished black marble floor of the expanse rendered a feeling of walking on a calm midnight sea. Further into the rotunda, the shopkeeper had just looked up at the Baccarat Chandelier when Maarten came up to him, bursting with enthusiasm.

"A hundred lights! Isn't it grand?" With his hands clasped like a choirboy in prayer, Maarten approached Vatori and the shopkeeper in one fell swoop. "Thought it would never get hung. My God, the doing it took to get it there!" Placing his hands behind his back, he continued, "What do you think?"

"From what I've seen so far, you've done a fine job meeting the expectations of Mr.—Vatori."

"That he has," Vatori chimed in. "The selections are rare and well-placed." Bowing slightly, he added, "Please accept my appreciation for your part in bringing the estate back to life. And now, if you'll excuse me, I need to greet some more guests. Make yourselves at home."

"Glad to see ya made it!" The shopkeeper knew who was addressing him before he turned around. Maarten even more so.

"Ahh, and here's the event's designated tour guide," he said. "I'll leave you in his trusty care."

232

The Shopkeeper's Journal

With that, Maarten gave Chester a pat on the head—something the boy clearly disliked, if the *you've-got-to-be-kidding* look on his face was any indication.

"He's been doing that all day," the boy muttered.

"You don't appear any worse for the wear."

"Whatever that means. You want to see the place?"

"Guide away."

Put on his mettle, Chester did just that. His monologue about the history and renovation of the estate was well-polished and delivered with confidence. After a thirty-minute walk through of the main rooms, he led the shopkeeper onto the back patio and, without breaking stride, cut across the thick lawn headed directly toward what, in his opinion, was the "coolest" part of the estate: the helipad.

"It's an Augusta Westland," he said, in the manner boys do when pretending they understand. "AW109, Grand Versace VIP. Sweet ride, huh?"

"Sweet," the shopkeeper replied blandly.

"Big guy uses it to fly around on business and stuff."

"Mmmm."

"Told me I could have a ride in it sometime." The boy tilted his head, an effort to make the claim sound casual. The shopkeeper hid a smile.

"Where we're headed next," the boy said, turning, "has the Bernini thing in it. The chapel."

The shopkeeper grinned at the young boy's reference to a centuries-old sculpture as the "Bernini thing."

"Any luck with the diamond?" he said.

"Nope. Looked everywhere. Vatori even tried to move the statue to see if maybe it was underneath. Didn't budge."

"How unfortunate."

Troy W. Rasmussen

"Yeah. Not really sure where to look now." Chester absentmindedly fingered the medallion through his shirt. "Gotta be around here somewhere."

"Mmmm."

They finished the tour as evening set in, the lights of the estate casting a majestic glow across the compound. As the shopkeeper was about to leave, Vatori approached asking for a few minutes to meet privately. The host led his guest down a carpeted hallway to an imposing room the shopkeeper took for an office and shut the door behind them.

"I won't keep you long," Vatori said. "Did you enjoy the evening?"

"I did. You're to be commended for the results of your efforts here."

"It's nothing." Getting to the point, he continued, "What I wish to speak with you about concerns something I saw the other day. An automobile, a beautiful dark red automobile. Very classy."

Saturday
Day two of the gala and the one
individual most of the people are hoping
to meet has arrived: Déjà. The official
word from her agent is she's in town to
check on the progress of her new getaway.
Many of the locals suspect otherwise.

The gang's all here, the shopkeeper thought, looking at Olivia, McAlister, Vatori, and Déjà gathered around the table. Early birds out to get their coffee before word got out that the world's most glamorous woman was in town.

The Shopkeeper's Journal

Approaching the table with a tray full of drinks, he nodded a greeting to the group. "Miss Déjà, how good to have you in town again."

Smiling, she touched his forearm. "It's good to be here. It's so quiet and the people so friendly. I hope to visit with some today."

"No problem there," McAlister said. "Poke your head out that door for more than thirty seconds and you'll have all the conversation you could hope for."

The group chuckled at the comment.

Olivia spoke then, all-business. "First things first. We need to get you out to the Greene's. The renovations at your place are coming along nicely." Tilting her head, she added, "With the nearly completed construction awaiting your approval, all that's left is the decorating."

"The fun part," Déjà said, grinning at the group.

"A sentiment shared by our ever-diligent designer," McAlister added, then sipped his drink.

"Who—unless we get you on property in the very near future—I suspect is going to combust!" Olivia said with a laugh.

"I must admit," Vatori said, "his exuberance is a bit much at times, but if that's his secret to accomplishing what he does…"

"Well," Déjà broke in, "we'd best be on our way, then." She turned toward the shopkeeper again. "I understand you were instrumental in helping acquire some of the pieces for Vatori's place…truly wonderful. I hope Maarten can again rely on your expertise and guidance?"

"Mmmm."

Déjà took a deep breath. "Good. Then that's settled. Olivia, we'll leave these gentlemen to their discussions."

Troy W. Rasmussen

Chester entered the shop just as Déjà and Olivia were leaving, prompting him to do a double-take on his way to the counter.

"Who's the babe?" he asked.

"The babe?" The shopkeeper feigned innocence.

"Yeah, the chick with Olivia."

"The chick, as you put it, is the most famous model in the country, possibly the world." The shopkeeper lifted one brow in mild reproach. "Déjà. Her name is Déjà."

Chester nodded. "Heard of her."

As Chester reached for a lollipop, something moved at the top of his satchel. He twisted a bit, reached into the bag, and pulled out what appeared to be a lizard.

"This is Jax." Chester wrapped his hand around the lizard, the spikes of scales running across its back pricking his palm, to hold it up for a better look. "Cool, huh?"

"Mmmm. And how is it you came by such a creature?"

"A friend of Moms. They're moving or something and couldn't take him with. Said I'd watch him for awhile." Shrugging his shoulders, he added, "They told me I could keep him."

He set the animal on the counter, and then rested his chin on his arms to get up close. "Doesn't do much. Likes to ride on my shoulder, though. They told me what kind it is, but I forgot."

"My guess is a Bearded Dragon." The shopkeeper nodded his head and, tapping the air with his pipe, added, "Australia."

Privately, he wondered if dragon bum swishing from side to side counted as dusting.

The Shopkeeper's Journal

Sunday

All good things must come to an end,
and where one of the world's wealthiest
men is concerned, they do so with
considerable fanfare. Masquerade.

It was one of those events you see in a movie or read
about in a book: an enormous house full of famous
people, lights, laughter, and mystique. Beautiful women,
gowns slipping from across long legs, were assisted from
the seats of expensive automobiles by men with bank
accounts to support both. True, the red carpet laid out
across the stone driveway may have been a bit over the
top; if it hadn't been for the persistence of the event
planner, Vatori would have had it pulled.

"It's what the night is about, my dear," said the
planner, her arms arching through the air. "It's a
celebration, and the theme *demands* mystery and excess."
She reached out and patted his ascot. "Who hasn't
dreamed of arriving at an event like this and stepping
onto the carpet?" With a knowing look, she added, "My
guess is that even the likes of you had visions of doing
such a thing when you were younger."

Vatori couldn't help but respond to the jest. His
schoolboy grin, rarely seen, testified to the truth of the
remark. "You drive a hard bargain," he said simply, then
turned from the planner's side to greet a new arrival and
extend his arms in welcome.

Earlier, Vatori had sought to have Déjà host the
event with him. His offer was politely declined.

"Won't *that* cause a stir!" she'd said, with a laugh.
"But, no, darling. I'll arrive, just as the others, showing
my utter amazement at the grand accommodations of the

237

Troy W. Rasmussen

tycoon hosting the affair." She grinned, toying with him. "Maybe we'll stalk about, dodging cameras glued to the palms of eager paparazzi. Who knows, we just may reward one of those poor souls with something worth printing."

"And what would we offer that is worth printing?" Déjà leaned closer and whispered.

Each time he recalled her words, Vatori's grin returned...a smile that complemented the grand evening nicely.

Arriving guests moved like a river, with tributaries branching from red carpet to entryway to the depths of the estate, pausing here and there to "kiss" a cheek or send a shout of recognition through the air. Couture gowns, tailored tuxedos, and elaborate masks added to the exuberance of the spectacle. Vatori stood at the top of the stairs when the clamor below rose to fever pitch.

Déjà had arrived.

The crowd pressed forward, bending and straining for a better view, as a dark cherry-red Talbot Coupe came to a stop. Playing the scene as the expert she was, Déjà waited a moment before exiting the vehicle. Vatori began his descent.

Vatori had closed the $3.1 million deal to purchase the Talbot before leaving the shop the day before.

"Have the arrangements been made for the vehicle we spoke of?" he'd said to the shopkeeper.

"They have."

"I have confirmation the fund's transfer is complete. Is everything to your liking?"

The shopkeeper nodded. "It is."

"I would one day like to meet this 'Jonesie' you speak of."

238

The Shopkeeper's Journal

"I'm sure you will."

"How are you sure of this?"

"If you're in agreement," the shopkeeper explained, "I think it would be fitting for Jonesie to deliver the car to Miss Déjà. She would undoubtedly enjoy telling its new owner of the process to bring it 'back to life,' if you will."

"I see."

"That you intend her efforts to be a gift will mean a great deal."

"Then it's settled. Please tell this Jonesie I look forward to meeting her when she delivers the vehicle."

The shopkeeper gave Jonesie a sizeable share of the sale, which paid for her higher education at the state university. Rueben received just compensation—a heartfelt hug—when he indicated that his payment be given to Jonesie.

"You deserve it, kid," he said. "Workin' with you on that ride was one for the books. I'll never forget it."

The remaining funds from the sale of the Talbot were used to set up a trust to support young people in entrepreneurial and educational pursuits.

The flash from the cameras ignited like gunpowder as the valet opened the door. In a languid gesture, Déjà extended her hand in mock request for assistance. The valet stepped forward—only to find his path blocked by Vatori's forceful hand against his chest. Bowing, the young man stepped back, but not without a grin and respectful nod of acknowledgment.

Taking Déjà's hand, Vatori stood motionless as she lifted shapely legs and planted a stiletto-clad foot on the carpet. As Déjà stood, her form-fitting, midnight blue liquid lamé gown fell into place, causing an explosion of

Troy W. Rasmussen

camera flashes. Ever the trailblazer, Déjà wore a mask that was nothing more than a six—inch wide strip of oversized mesh metallic ribbon that twisted gracefully over one eye, past swept back brunette locks, before disappearing across her neck into the front of her gown.

"Bellissimo," Vatori said.

Déjà tilted her head back in a classic model pose, uttering a small laugh as her eyes caught the lenses of the cameras.

The two entered the estate arm-in-arm as the excited valet eased into the soft leather seat of an automobile the likes of which he would never drive again.

The event planner gave a discreet nod to the orchestra conductor, the prearranged signal to fade the music for the event's host to formally greet his guests. Reaching the second-story balcony overlooking a vast ballroom, Vatori, with Déjà standing a few feet behind, lifted both arms and called out, *"Benvenuto."*

To the event planner's chagrin, an attendant handed Vatori a basic black mask as he and Déjà descended the stairs. She'd tried, without effect, to urge Vatori to don a more extravagant mask, one that would give him the countenance of an exotic bird.

"Extravagance," he'd said gently, "is for the best food and drinks for my guests, not for personal embellishment for me. There will be enough peacocks as it is!"

What Vatori didn't say was that he considered his greatest adornment to be the woman who would be by his side. He left the event planner muttering to herself, "Impossible man."

240

The Shopkeeper's Journal

Chapter 20

Monday
The success and excess of the gala is behind us. When one is younger, staying late into the evening isn't the issue one finds oneself confronted with when one is not! The young. How strange for life to so often affect them in such immediate totality. There's time. Maybe not for everything, but time enough for that which is destined.

The shopkeeper noticed the woman's carriage and stance as he returned from arranging shelves in the back of the shop. Her quiet spirit of confidence and physical elegance led him to the thought, *Ballerina. Without question, a ballerina.*

As he approached, she turned her head—bringing to the shopkeeper's mind a rare bird, realizing it's been noticed and wondering what the fuss is about.

"Good afternoon," he said.

"Yes," she said.

"Of what service may I be to a lady such as yourself?"

The woman gave a small chuckle and tilted her head at the flowery speech. "Something cool and light, I think."

The shopkeeper was about to list several such drinks when she apparently changed her mind.

241

Troy W. Rasmussen

"Oh, what the hell," she cut in, seemingly irritated. "Keep the cool, but make it heavy."

"Keeping in mind the strict diet common to those in your field," the shopkeeper replied, "the heavy would be…?"

"I don't know, exactly, maybe something with cream. One of those salted caramel brulée lattes…huge."

The shopkeeper smiled at her attempt to size the forbidden fruit. "Let's start with a tall and see where it takes us. May I ask your name?"

She pooched her lips and turned toward the shop. The way she cast her gaze was more an appraisal than mere observation.

"Serena."

"Well, Serena, Feel free to look around," the shopkeeper said. "This *huge* drink will take a few minutes."

The dancer glared at him a second time. Her eyes wide, she scanned the shop from shelf to shelf.

"Your place has a magical feel about it," she said.

He set the painted mug on the table. "Now serving one huge brulée."

Serena stopped mid-turn as she caught the shopkeeper's knowing glance and nod of the head indicating for her to sit. Accustomed to obeying orders, she did so, then sat still for a few moments, gazing at the cup of steaming liquid.

"You're too disciplined to miss practice," the shopkeeper said. "And I wager your talent all but ensures offers to perform, probably many."

Other than the welling of a tear, little changed in Serena's posture. She hated that she showed even that much.

"If I may, it appears you have something on your mind? How can I help?"

242

The Shopkeeper' s Journal

"I'm not sure you can."

The shopkeeper waited.

Serena gave in. "Have you ever wanted something, and then, when the time comes for it to happen…"

"There's no shame in desire, my dear. Only in the failure to act on it according to the abilities in one's possession."

"You can't possibly know," she whispered.

"Mmmm. My guess is you have an opportunity before you and now you struggle with doubt."

Time slowed. Serena was sure of it, staring into the shopkeeper's eyes.

"Prima," she said.

"A saddened spirit is the companion of hidden desire. You reached Prima some time ago."

"There's nothing else," she said.

"Failure to act weakens the soul."

"It's arrogance," she uttered with more force than intended.

"Acceptance," he countered mildly.

Serena's bone-thin fingers played with the mug handle like a spider tacking in its web.

Pointing to the mug, he said, "Drink. You've earned it. Better yet, take a gulp and accept what's been placed before you."

With that, he moved into the back of the shop.

Serena placed her hands on either side of the mug, letting her gaze follow the slight movement of foam as it danced across the milky surface, and contemplated the implications of "gulping."

"This will help."

She started at the sound of the shopkeeper's voice. Watching him carefully, he approached the table and set down a glass box containing very old, worn pointe shoes.

243

Troy W. Rasmussen

"Whose—?" she whispered.

"Eva Evdokimova," he said.

A bolt of emotion shot through her.

"These, my dear," he went on, "were the pointe shoes of Eva Evdokimova, Prima Ballerina Assoluta to the Royal Danish and Berlin Operas, among other accomplishments. One of only fourteen ballerinas to receive the honor of 'Assoluta,'" he added. "There is no higher honor in the dance community."

She knew this, of course. Now, if she could only stop her mouth from hanging open…

"Acknowledging the desire of the heart," he said quietly, "and acting on it in the way only you can…is not arrogance."

Another tear, yet she remained motionless. "I couldn't possibly…"

"What? Hope? Dream? Tell me, if you knew this honor was yours at your birth, would you struggle so?"

She raised her eyes from the mug to meet his. "How could I know such a thing as a child?"

"How long have you been dancing?"

"Most of my life. I started when I was very young."

"How young?"

She felt her shoulders relax.

"What if, on some level, you did know this day would come, and you've been working toward it, consciously or otherwise, since you were a child?" he persisted. "Would that change your feelings about accepting it as reality?"

"Maybe." She felt like a child, waiting for the punch line of a joke.

"So what you struggle with is not knowing. If you knew for sure, accepting what you've worked nearly your entire life for wouldn't be such a cliff."

She swallowed emotion. "Ohhhhh….kay…."

244

The Shopkeeper's Journal

"Tell me, do you feel people only deserve what they get if it's something they've worked toward their entire life?"

"No. Many things come to people. Some happen quicker."

"So knowing isn't the sole catalyst, then."

"No."

"That leaves you with…?"

She sagged, slumping in a way her teachers would never have allowed. "Acceptance."

"Mmmm. Why struggle so accepting something to the magnitude of 'Assoluta' when you've put in the time, paid your dues, and sacrificed more than you probably should have to get there?"

"I shouldn't desire such things."

"Ah, desire. Better adjust to that one, my dear. You've been doing it for most of your life."

Catching herself, she pulled back up to better posture once more. Suddenly, she wanted to grin. AND gulp. She did both.

The day was not far away when Serena would enter a dressing room overstuffed with bouquets of congratulations for the honor of "Assoluta," and notice a watercolor painting resting against the wall, depicting a prima ballerina gazing into a cup of *huge*. Her squeal of delight would come from the sight of the caramel-colored mustache on the dancer's lip.

To all things is the right time given.

> *Tuesday*
> Where young boys are concerned,
> patience is given only so much time to
> produce results; then, virtue be damned.
> Given the time and effort he's put into

Troy W. Rasmussen

> finding the Monarch Diamond, Chester
> deserves credit for handling his
> disappointment as well as he has. Often
> nothing more than a bit of encouragement
> is all that's necessary to turn brooding into
> celebration.

The shopkeeper returned from the back to find Chester, chin resting in one hand, deep in thought, the other toying with Jax's tail.

"The day hasn't turned out as planned?" the shopkeeper asked.

"Not really. Not that it matters." Chester moved Jax's tail from the side of his nose.

"That bad."

Chester shook his head as he lifted the lizard from his shoulder onto the counter. "Just don't get it. I've looked everywhere. Even marked the places down and still nothing."

"Mmmm."

"Rock probably isn't even real."

"I see. So because you haven't found it, it's not real. Doesn't sound like the young man I know."

Chester turned the stool to face the door, and Jax lifted his head in the same direction. The shopkeeper couldn't help but notice what a pair the two of them made.

"So you've looked everywhere, have you?"

"Well, not everywhere, but a lot of places. Not even a clue."

"A clue's all it would take?"

Chester turned back toward the shopkeeper, and Jax did likewise.

"Maybe…?" Chester said tentatively. Jax's wet tongue flicked out and back.

The Shopkeeper's Journal

"It's been said the best place to hide something is in plain sight, or where least expected."

"That's not a clue."

Jax made a croaking sound the shopkeeper took as the reptile's attempt at a growl.

"How about this: why don't you try going back to the beginning?"

"The beginning?" Chester asked as Jax tilted his head.

"The beginning. Where the magic first happened."

Chester dropped his gaze. "I got nothin'."

Jax scurried up Chester's shoulder and, with front feet resting on the boy's head, directed his gaze toward the shopkeeper.

"Mmmm. The sale of the Baker Mansion by Thomas's son Robert included everything in it. As fate would have it, a couple living in the area purchased the wardrobe from Fey's bedroom. Several years later, when it became necessary for them to move out of the area, the couple sold the wardrobe to an antique dealer. It's been in his shop ever…"

The shopkeeper let his words trail off deliberately, to watch Chester do a slow turn toward the back of the shop. Jax scurried forward over the boy's head, stopping with his body pointed like a hunting dog.

Chester slid off the stool and began walking toward the back of the shop, Jax did a quick figure-eight, returning to Chester's shoulder. The shopkeeper grinned. As the two disappeared into the back of the shop, he dialed a phone number written on the back of a business card.

Chester stood mesmerized in front of the wardrobe where so many adventures had taken place. Staring up at

247

Troy W. Rasmussen

the ornate wooden piece, he reached his hand forward to turn the key.

Jax's tail swayed back and forth.

Click.

The back of Chester's neck prickled in gooseflesh.

Raising his hand to the piece of wood protruding from the action, he gave it a quick turn one way, then the other.

Click.

Jax adjusted his stance to lean forward in earnest. With the release of pressure from the locks, the doors eased open. Holding them in his outstretched hands, Chester peered into the recesses of the wardrobe.

Nothing.

It's the same, he thought. Sliding his hands down and releasing the doors, he stepped up to his box resting on the pillar. His thoughts drifted to the dagger of the prince, broken pieces of a clay mug, and the shards of spent fireworks. The sadness still came whenever he thought of his father, but mostly the memories were good.

Running his hand across the top of the box, Chester glanced around the inside of the wardrobe, intent on discerning the diamond's location. The only thing that stuck out was the floor. He didn't know what to call it, but instead of just a couple of planks, the bottom of the wardrobe was inlaid with parquet flooring.

Fancy. Probably did it 'cuz that Fey wanted it fancy.

Shrugging his shoulders, he moved around the box and pillar and felt along the walls. *Maybe there's another secret lock?* He bent over, feeling along the wall to the base, and accidentally bumped the pillar, causing it to topple.

He ignored Jax's claws digging into his shirt, focused instead on what had just happened.

248

The Shopkeeper's Journal

The pillar base was sunk into the floor a bit, giving the object the appearance of being stationary.
Thoughtfully he lifted the pillar to the side, exposing four of the parquet sections laid together in a herringbone pattern.

"Interesting pattern," the shopkeeper said.

Chester and Jax tilted their heads toward his voice.

"Not all that unique," the shopkeeper went on, "yet you don't see it so much in wardrobes."

"It has something to do with the diamond, doesn't it?"

"Mmmm."

Taking the response as favorable, Chester squatted down to inspect the area more closely. Running his fingers over the wood, he noticed each of the four-by-one-inch pieces of wood had a separate texture, yet fit together as one piece.

He felt something. A space?

Leaning in closer, he moved his finger more slowly, back and forth, over the area and noticed a gap between two of the thin pieces of wood that comprised the center of the square.

"I think there's a gap," he said.

"There is," the shopkeeper replied.

Chester dug his fingernail into the area in an attempt to pry the section up.

Nothing.

Jax's eyes rolled towards the shopkeeper.

"It's almost like there's a key," the shopkeeper said.

Chester paused, then reached into the top of his shirt and slowly pulled out the gold medallion. Catching the glint of light from the shiny object, Jax snapped his head around toward it.

Troy W. Rasmussen

Without looking up, Chester pulled the medallion over his head and contemplated it.

Doesn't look like a key.

After a few seconds, a sudden impulse occurred to him. Shifting his body to balance his weight, he undid the clasp and pulled the chain through the hole in the top. Holding the medallion as if he were putting a quarter into a vending machine, Chester inserted the edge of the medallion into the gap.

Nothing.

Not to be deterred, he adjusted his position and applied more pressure—the universal course of action for boys in the throes of discovery. The medallion slid halfway into the gap before the carvings in the middle caught on something inside.

Click.

A heart-stopping moment. A heart-stopping sound. Chester looked back toward the shopkeeper.

The shopkeeper came closer and squatted down. "Give it a turn."

Chester grabbed onto either side of the protruding medallion with his fingers and rotated it, causing the section to pop loose and slide down and into the false floor. Reaching into the space, he pulled the Monarch Diamond loose from where it had remained hidden since Thomas Baker first placed it there many years before.

To all things is the right time given.

Chester's gaze remained on the diamond, clasping it in both his hands as he and the shopkeeper walked to the front of the shop.

There, Sheila waited anxiously, not sure what to make of the cryptic call from the shopkeeper. Mothers of young boys do not relish such calls. Seeing Chester was all right, she took a deep breath and gave the shopkeeper a warning look.

250

The Shopkeeper's Journal

"I found it, Mom." Chester held the diamond up for her to see.

"It?" she asked, shaking her head.

"The diamond, Mom. The one that guy hid. The one I've been looking for!"

"What?"

"It's real," he said, "and I found it."

"Chester—?" she stammered. "I don't—where did it come from?"

"The wardrobe. From the hidden place in the bottom."

"The wardrobe?"

"Yeah. I had the key the whole time. It's the medallion, Mom!"

The shopkeeper remained by Chester's side as the boy regaled his mother with the details.

"Who does it belong to?" she asked.

"A man that finds a thing in a place he calls his own," said the shopkeeper, "is the owner of the thing."

Sheila's slow turn of the head matched her son's, both incredulous and marveling at once.

After numerous conversations and meetings—some with an attorney and a diamond broker—Chester and his mother decided not to sell the diamond but to use it as collateral for a trust to benefit the families of veterans killed in action. Chester renamed the diamond "National Hero" and, by way of a final statement, informed the shopkeeper that since he was now "loaded," the candy jar should always be full of lollipops.

> *Thursday*
> In and of itself, wealth is not a bad thing. How one uses it is the key. One man flaunts prosperity, another does not.

Troy W. Rasmussen

> Who is right? Who is greater? Neither.
> Both possess an equal right to spend that
> which they have earned how they see fit.
> The greatness lies in the man, not his
> pocketbook.

"Those are some fine-looking flowers," The man said.

Bacardi gazed up, his brow furrowed when he saw the speaker's false jovial grin and gaudy suit.

"Nature does the work," Bacardi replied.

"How true," the man said. "Judging by the grime on your hands, though, she gets some help." The man turned up his nose and smacked his lips in disgust.

Bacardi brushed his hands together, sending a spray of encrusted dirt across the man's patent leather shoes.

"Might you be the proprietor of this establishment?"

"I might be a lot of things," Bacardi retorted.

The man grinned again and gave a half-hearted snort before proceeding up the steps into the shop. As he did, Bacardi announced, "Man in the fancy pants wants somethin,' and it ain't no good."

Having heard the exchange, the shopkeeper waited behind the counter to greet his guest. "Good afternoon."

"And to you, my fine sir. You then are just the person I wish to speak with."

"Mmmm."

"Name's Jenner, Carl Jenner." The man said extending his hand, diamond rings on every finger.

"Mr. Jenner."

"I see you're a busy man, but if I may have a few minutes of your time, I have a proposition for you."

"Mmmm."

"I'm a businessman, you see. High-end jewelry." Carl waved his diamond-encrusted fingers for effect.

The Shopkeeper' s Journal

"I'm in the area scouting locations for the newest store in a chain of many. My surveillance team tells me yours sits in a prime location. I'd like to talk with you about that."

The shopkeeper took a puff from his pipe. "Nothing wrong with talking. Especially when it benefits the speaker and listener alike."

The man seemed taken aback for a moment, then regained himself. "Yes, of course. After hearing what I have to say, I believe you'll find the benefit clear."

"A man believes what he wants, Mr. Jenner. I find no amount of talking changes that until he's of mind for it to."

Carl chuckled. "Getting to the point."

"Yes, the point. That's what you're here for, correct?"

"I am. You see, I deal in the finest of jewels, handcrafted designs, and aim to set up business in your quaint little town."

"Mmmm," the shopkeeper uttered noting the condescension in Carl's tone.

"Seeing this location is the best, I'd like to make you an offer to purchase your little shop. A mighty fine offer, if I do say so myself."

"You have said so yourself. Mr. Jenner, that you esteem this shop worthy of being one of yours is, to some degree, flattering. It's your premise I call into question."

Bacardi snorted.

Carl stood blinking. "My premise?"

"Mmmm. You are operating on two mistaken presumptions."

"Two?"

"One, that this shop may be for sale. Two, that this conversation, should it continue on its current course, is beneficial to both parties involved."

Troy W. Rasmussen

The shopkeeper slid a dirt-encrusted clay mug toward his guest who promptly leaned back as if the object would come to life.

"As you've noticed, Mr. Jenner, I am a busy man. Would you do me the favor of delivering this to the gentleman by the flowerbed on your way out?"

After watching Carl leave in a pompous huff, Bacardi turned toward the shopkeeper and raised his drink—both men benefiting from the conversation.

"What beautiful flowers," the woman said. "John, look at these flowers."

Moving his attention from the store window to the object of his wife's focus, her husband nodded his agreement, as did their two teenage daughters. "Are you the gardener who manages such blooms?" the woman went on, speaking to Bacardi.

"Nature does most the work, ma'am."

Noticing his callused and dirt-encrusted hands, she said, "But not without your help. What a gift. John?"

"Yes," said John, "A gift. Are you the owner of this shop?"

"That would be the feller inside."

Commenting again on his work, the family proceeded up the steps into the shop. Having heard the conversation, the shopkeeper came from behind the counter to greet his guests, as was his fashion.

"Good afternoon."

"And to you," John responded.

"What an amazing shop you have," the woman said. "And those flowers! What a blessing, the man who tends them."

Bacardi peered through the door, waiting to see how the shopkeeper would answer.

"Oh, he's blessed, all right. How may I help you?"

254

The Shopkeeper's Journal

John placed one arm around their twin daughters and the other around his wife. "Do you carry bracelets? We're looking for two of the same style for the girls." He gave his daughters a squeeze.

The shopkeeper led the family to the row of drawers at the end of the counter. "You'll find what you're looking for in either of these two drawers."

With that, the girls and their mother began the serious business of shopping. Seeing that it would probably be some time before a decision was reached, the shopkeeper asked if John would care for a drink.

As he sipped, he told the shopkeeper the family was on vacation with a purpose.

"And the purpose would be?"

"We're driving this time, off the beaten path, with the point of enjoying lesser-known places and the people living in them. Your town is the seventh one we've been to so far."

"Mmmm."

"We want to provide the girls the experience of different cultures if you will. Seems each place we've been to has its own soul. It's been very educational."

The shopkeeper noticed that while John was speaking, his attention drifted several times to the small jar on the end of the counter with a picture of a boy, roughly fourteen years old, taped to the front.

"His name is Daniel," the shopkeeper explained. "He's a young man dealing with the regrettable effects of brain damage after a fall from a ladder. The family is unable to pay for the medical expenses."

"Dreadful," John said, shaking his head, then turned toward his family. His daughters, catching they were again the center of their father's attention, smiled and approached, their selections already gracing their wrists.

255

Troy W. Rasmussen

"What do you think, Daddy?" the girls asked almost in chorus.

"Beautiful."

"Mom thinks so, too. We've decided on these. They match!"

John smiled. "Looks like the decision's been made."

The shopkeeper smiled in agreement and, with a nod of his head, began to ring up the cost of the bracelets.

"Double that, if you will," John said. "And put the other half in the jar."

"John?" said his wife.

The man looked to his wife, then back to the shopkeeper.

"The purpose I mentioned earlier is that at some point during our travels, each of us is to support a cause of our choice as it arises." He nodded toward the jar. "I'm choosing Daniel."

The shopkeeper smiled as he rang up double the cost of the bracelets.

The man and his family left the shop in high spirits—but not before Bacardi held out a flower in full bloom to the woman so complimentary of his work.

Both parties benefited, again, from the conversation.

Friday
From start to finish, the day was a success. Parker's acumen for events that can bring a new level of enthusiasm to the town is paying off. The long-awaited mud run started at first light with what seemed an endless parade of oversized, jacked-up trucks and jeeps roaming the town. For some, the antics of the men and boys, as each participant drove by, were as much if

The Shopkeeper's Journal

not more entertainment than the actual event.

It was midafternoon when Chester and Gordo walked into the shop, reeking of exhaust, for a break from the excitement of the morning's preliminary runs.

"Hey, Keep, how 'bout a cup of mud and whatever the kid wants," Gordo called. "Throw in a couple bottles of water for the road."

"From the sounds of it, things are going well," the shopkeeper said.

"Yeah. Lots of big trucks and mud flyin' everywhere," Chester replied.

"The preliminary heats are over," Gordo put in. "Big guns will start running top of the hour. It's really something to see."

"Yeah, and Gordo and me are gonna ride, too. Can't wait to see all that mud flyin'."

"Mmmm."

"They have an area for the locals and amateurs, to troll around in. Thought it would be cool to throw some dirt around. One of the guys is letting us use his Jeep."

"Sounds like fun."

"It is," Chester chimed in, clearly enthused about powerful engines turning oversized tires deep into the mud. "Mom says I can ride if I wear a seatbelt. It's actually, a harness." He rolled his eyes.

"Good advice nonetheless," the shopkeeper answered.

Grinning, Gordo collected the bottles of water and, with Chester in tow, headed out the door.

The drivers, covered head to toe in mud, congratulated one another with wet muddy slaps on the back, their smiles showing teeth looking whiter through

Troy W. Rasmussen

the caked mud on their faces. Although the event was technically a competition with the winner taking a small cash reward and bragging rights, no one could tell that from the camaraderie of the participants. Having fun, and a great deal of it, was the focus of the day. Few displayed this more than those running the "bog".

The bog, roughly the size of a small pond, drew participants trying to cross its center without getting stuck or stalling out. Only a few attempted it, as it required specialized equipment allowing the vehicle to operate when sunk in water deeper than the engine. If a driver stalled out, a jeering group would come forward to pull him out of the sludge. Staying away from the center, drivers could opt to navigate the edges, throwing mud and water twenty feet into the air—a crowd favorite.

Driving a wreck of a Jeep borrowed from one of his cronies, Gordo took Chester toward the bog. Rolling to the edge, they paused and did a fist bump before Gordo popped the clutch, the force throwing them deep into the seats. Chester's "woohoo" was barely audible over the drone of the engine.

The Jeep slid sideways down the small embankment. Compensating, Gordo spun the wheel in the opposite direction, causing the rear tires to slip and spray a wall of mud. Gordo corrected their direction and steered the Jeep into the thick of the bog, a force that caused the seat harnesses to engage.

Mud rained down on the two adventurers, covering them and the inside of the vehicle. To Chester's chagrin, Gordo opted to maneuver the edges versus attempting a trek through the center.

"Why not?" Chester had asked earlier.

"Face it, kid," Gordo said, "you sit lower in the seat. Jeep may make it through, but it could be a different

The Shopkeeper's Journal

story for you. Face full of mud is one thing. Sittin' in it over your head is another."

Chester shrugged. "Yeah, prob'ly right. Anyways, Mom's here."

With the music blaring and his foot on the accelerator, they rounded the far edge of the bog, the acceleration sending the Jeep into a three-sixty skid.

Sheila stood then shook her head and sat back down after seeing the laughter on Chester's face. She took a deep breath thankful he was ok, yet hoping the ride was about over.

Soon after, the bog cleared in preparation of the main event with many of the locals anxious to watch the star of the show.

Boston was a six-foot-two specimen of all-American hotness complete with deep-set eyes, a rugged, youthful face and grin, and a two-day shadow of scruff covering a square jaw—a benefit not missed by members of the opposite sex, especially since he preferred to drive shirtless. With a beanie pulled over his head and a toothpick in his mouth, Boston rarely failed to capture attention.

The music to the main event started and as blasts of heavy metal guitars burst through the air, wheels began to churn mud and water as the starting line turned into a mass of roaring engine blocks and straining struts. Boston, the odds-on favorite to win the event, held back from the initial onset of over-anxious drivers pushing their trucks to max output in an effort to gain the advantage.

Drivers in front, newbies, jockeyed for position, but more experienced drivers knew position didn't matter— you were going to get covered in mud, regardless.

Troy W. Rasmussen

Boston was close enough to the pack to appear he was joining in, yet had no intention of taking part in the initial onslaught. He learned long ago that time, ego, and a heavy foot on the accelerator eliminated more than half of the participants. All that was left for those remaining was to navigate through the congestion of stalled four-wheelers and, depending on the temperament of the driver, throw out a good-natured taunt of their ineptitude as they were passed by.

At the signal to start, twenty-six of the twenty-seven four-wheeled vehicles lurched forward as their drivers fought for positions deemed momentarily better than the one they had. Boston remained where he was, engine hot.

As the music hit a guttural low, he released the clutch, his foot expertly working the brakes, and punched the gas pedal, throwing the tires into motion. When the force engaged and the torque of the motor hit, the Jeep pulled back on the rear tires like an animal preparing to spring forward in chase. Boston adjusted his sunglasses. The run was for nothing more than bragging rights of completion—and, therefore, everything.

Boston jammed the Jeep into gear, and the large knobby tires churned deeper seeking a grip to propel the vehicle forward. As the music hit an exaggerated crescendo, the Jeep lurched out of the hole it had been digging.

The course wound through multiple turns and jumps, but nothing mattered to Boston at this point except the hill.

Various trucks had either the front or rear sunk into the muck, tombstones of the attempt. Sliding past a truck with its driver and significant other standing on the roof, Boston raised a couple of fingers in salute without turning his attention from the task at hand.

260

The Shopkeeper's Journal

At the base of the hill, he slowed to nearly a crawl. Before the vehicle came to a stop, Boston punched the accelerator again and began the ascent, the churning motion rinsing the accumulated muck from the tires. As the guitar reached the pinnacle of its crescendo, his tires, whirling in sync with the beat of the music, slipped, then grabbed hold to push the vehicle toward the pinnacle. The Jeep started to slow when Boston pushed a button on the dash engaging the ARB Locker, causing the vehicle to surge forward and go airborne over the top. Bounding down the backside, Boston, a knowing grin on his face, moved his toothpick from one side of his mouth to the other.

The remainder of the ride was more a victory lap than the pursuit of the finish line. Feeding on the crowd's energy, he began turning this way, then that, sending sprays of muddied water into the air and the crowd. As he flew by the stands, he saluted the cheering horde, then brought the Jeep to a skidding halt, his toothpick flying through the air as he spit it out.

Sunday

Is there no end to the tragedy that is homelessness? Down-and-outs trudging along paths of burned-out lives, drunkenness, or insanity—hardly. For every man there is a story, tragic or otherwise, played out according to the circumstances each has been given. Some fail. Some fall, and some don't get back up. Some are only an encounter away from deciding to turn back and face life. The catalyst? Human interaction. Someone takes the time, notices,

Troy W. Rasmussen

> intervenes and finds they were the
> instrument strengthening a soul to step off
> the treadmill of invisibility.

The man entered the shop, his tentative nature and bent head common to those living on the street. What caught the shopkeeper's attention was that he seemed to enter the shop with a purpose.

Without a word, the man walked to the windows, stopped, and stood still. After several minutes he stepped closer, his gaze remaining fixed. Closer. Turning his head to peer more closely at the object of his attention, he reached out his hand and began running it slowly over the woodwork. He rapped the wood with his knuckles, leaning in to better hear the sound. He nodded his head, then rubbed his thumb along each of the layers of wood, five in all, forming the frame.

Intrigued by the man's intent observation, the shopkeeper approached and asked if he could be of assistance. Startled, the man lowered his head once more and turned to go.

"There's no need to leave, sir. I wonder if you would care for a drink."

The man stopped, his back to the shopkeeper, and replied, "I didn't mean to disturb you."

"You haven't."

"I'll be on my way."

"Is there something about the windows I should know?"

The man shuffled, tucking his head further into his heavy coat. "They're very well made. The man who did them had considerable skill. I only wanted to see up close."

"Please, sir, tell me your name and stay awhile. A cup of coffee, perhaps?"

The Shopkeeper's Journal

Looking sideways toward the windows, the man pondered the offer. At last, he replied.

"Charlie. My name's Charles, but people...used to be...people called me Charlie."

Motioning toward a table, the shopkeeper said, "Please, have a seat while I get our coffee."

Charlie seemed uneasy about this but nodded his head. So intent was his contemplation he barely noticed the shopkeeper placing two cups of coffee on the table next to him.

"Charlie?" No response. "Charlie, the coffee is ready."

Startled again, Charlie turned toward the shopkeeper, then suddenly turned away—but not before the shopkeeper noticed the left side of his face was caved in and scarred.

"No need for that," the shopkeeper said quietly. "Coffee's best when it's hot."

Charlie sat down and faced the shopkeeper, sighing.

"Just as well get it out of the way. This," he pointed to his face, "is what happened when four punks thought it would be entertaining to beat up a drunk. Boots were heavy." Charlie paused. "Surgery didn't help much, so I'm left with this ugly mug."

Taking hold of his cup, the shopkeeper smiled slightly.

"Well, then, between your ugly mug and mine sits a cup of coffee. Best get to drinking it."

"So what do ya think of a story like that?" Charlie asked.

The shopkeeper shrugged. "Explains the mug. Deeper question is what put you in the street."

"I had it all." Charlie set down his cup and leaned forward. "Beautiful wife, a boy growing strong, big

Troy W. Rasmussen

house, the whole shebang. Came home one night from workin' late to find 'em both layin' on the floor, shot dead." Charlie's stare remained fixed and distant. "Police said it was a robbery. Best they could tell she was trying to get out with my boy in her arms. Thieves probably thought…who knows what they thought?"

Charlie took a sip of his coffee. "When it was all said and done, I left. Left it all and never went back. Walked to the liquor store for a bottle and, up to a few months ago, been nursing one ever since. That's a hell all its own, but at the time, and for a time after, it was better than the hell I'd been in. Doesn't matter the size of the man, a drunk one can't fight much of anything, let alone a bunch of thugs." Charlie took a deep breath, "So he accepts his lot, stops lookin' in the mirror…stops lookin' altogether."

"Mmmm." The shopkeeper glanced toward the window.

"Contractor. That's where the money came from. Specialized in exotic wood detailing. Damn good at it."

"What are your plans?"

"Can't say I have any. Haven't been in the area long, staying at the shelter for now."

"Mmmm."

Charlie stood to go. "Thank you, sir, for the coffee and letting me 'bend your ear.'"

"If you're of a mind," the shopkeeper replied, "there may be work in the next few weeks. I'll mention your skills."

The Shopkeeper's Journal

Chapter 21

Tuesday
Sometimes, a day brings nothing
more than the easy come-and-go of people
with time to spend, never the soul to see
again. Sometimes, a day brings a visitor
whose time is spent and an old dog's soul
is revived —whether he wants it to or not.

The couple arrived with their arms around each
other, laughing. Catching their breath—and the
shopkeeper's smile—they approached the counter, arms
still linked.

"Hello!" The shopkeeper nodded.

"We're on the hunt for something totally rare,
delicate, and precious in nature…"

"From nature," the other chimed in. The two
exchanged a quick glance.

"From nature, with a touch of the exotic. Price isn't
an issue."

"By all appearances, you've found what you seek
some time ago," the shopkeeper said.

They replied, in unison. "We have." More smiles.
"Said 'I do' a few days ago. Can you help with our
search?"

The shopkeeper led them to a remote corner of the
shop where sitting on a marble pedestal under a
protective glass box, was a nautilus of fine grandeur—so
fine that, at last, the two released each other.

"It's perfect."

Troy W. Rasmussen

"It's gorgeous!"

With a click of a button, the bulb at the end of a cord turned on, casting soft light on the piece. The two stood in wordless appreciation at the soft mother-of-pearl hues of the shell and the filigreed silver wrapping around the ends and up the side. Its base was ornate silver, further supported by a block of white marble.

"Stunning," the one said, approaching for a closer look. "It reminds me of you."

"You knew we'd find it."

"We knew," said the other. As if to seal the deal, the two leaned in closer for a kiss.

"If you'll leave your contact information," said the shopkeeper with a smile, "I'll have it shipped."

The shopkeeper reached into the wine cabinet to retrieve a bottle of cabernet. "Accept this as a complement to your visit and best wishes to the future. Although... there might be another piece of artwork you'll want to take with you."

Following his gaze, the two, again with their arms around each other, saw the watercolor painter at work and walked to the edge of the easel. When they saw the painting in progress, they laughed anew.

The watercolor painting of a couple leaning with their heads together, eyes full of love and faces bright with laughter, arrived the same day as did the nautilus chosen to commemorate their union.

Later in the afternoon while cleaning the coffee machine—his preferred excuse to avoid dusting—the shopkeeper stopped, smiling at Natalia's arrival. He couldn't recall when her weekly visits had started but cherished them nonetheless.

"Hello," she said brightly.

"Ms. Natalia, how finds you this day?"

The Shopkeeper's Journal

She shook her head with a slight grin, her usual reaction to his formal greetings. "Fine, sir. My day is just fine."

Natalia reached into her pocket and pulled out something wrapped in a grease-stained napkin.

"This is going to get you in trouble, you know," she said.

"Mmmm. That depends on one's definition of trouble." He slid the package into his pocket. "How are the wedding plans coming along?"

Natalia took a deep breath and sat one hip on a stool. "Getting closer. The guest list is done."

"There are many here who consider themselves family, my dear."

Natalia smiled. "I know. I have a lot to be thankful for." She straightened. "The menu and flowers are finalized, so we're down to only a couple more details."

"Only a couple?"

"Well, a venue, for one. We had one of the churches booked but…" The shopkeeper waited. "It just doesn't seem us. Parker's left it to me. He's so supportive. 'As long as you're there it doesn't matter where we say the words.' I'm lucky to have him."

"No doubt he feels the same about you. What other places are you considering now?"

She looked dreamy. "One of the ruins at the Greene's. There's a place that sort of looks like an old castle. We're thinking a medieval theme would be fun. Parker said he'd even ride a horse." She chuckled.

"Well, then, it sounds like that detail will shortly be taken care of."

"Yeah." Natalia hesitated, then leaned forward and wrapped her hands around his. "The other is even more

Troy W. Rasmussen

important, though." She looked into his eyes. "It would mean the world if you would give me away."

To all things is the right time given.

After Natalia left, the shopkeeper removed the item she gave him from his pocket and, stepping outside, buried the beef bone in the flowerbed.

Later in the afternoon, the shopkeeper was enjoying a slow smoke of his pipe when Bacardi arrived for his ritual check of the flowerbed. Noticing the loose dirt thrown on the walk and the fair-sized hole in the flowerbed, he promptly threw down his tools and bent for a closer look.

"That damn dog," Bacardi muttered.

The shopkeeper took a satisfying puff releasing the smoke into the air before walking toward the door.

"Is there a problem?"

Bacardi uttered more expletives as he began collecting the loose soil to fill the hole. "That mangy mutt's torn up the bed again."

"Granger?" The shopkeeper asked referring to the town's stray dog.

"Who else…what else? Whatever that thing is, I've a mind to…"

"To…?" The shopkeeper waited.

"Never you mind none. Next time he comes close to my beds, I'll tear his head off."

"Mmmm. Strong reaction for a little hole in the dirt."

"Little? Hole in the. . ." Bacardi stood pointing at the still to be filled in hole. "Ain't like it's happened just this once. Seems every time I come by lately, that infernal creature's had his snout in my flowers."

"Maybe if you used a different kind of dirt?"

"Different kind of dirt! What kind of fool nonsense is that?"

268

The Shopkeeper's Journal

"Just a thought," the shopkeeper said, shrugging innocently.

Bacardi had no sooner completed repairing the damage when the object of his consternation rounded the corner and took a few tentative steps toward him. Granger sat back on his haunches, licking his chops.

"Well, look who's showed up. Come to survey your handiwork, have ya?"

Granger lowered his head at the tone.

"Don't go playin' all sorrowful with me," Bacardi pointed his shovel at the ground. "You and me's gonna go 'round if you don't keep your nose outta my business."

Granger gave a slight whimper, then stretched his paws forward, laying his head between them.

Still pointing his shovel, Bacardi bent over with narrowed eyes. "That crap ain't gonna get you nowhere with me."

Granger lifted his head, his tongue lolling in and out. Bacardi heard the familiar dull sound of his mug being set on the steps.

"Need these?" Bacardi and the dog turned their heads in unison as the shopkeeper set a bowl of water next to the mug.

"Needs a hose is what it needs."

"Mmmm." The shopkeeper raised an eyebrow before returning inside.

Looking back toward his nemesis, Bacardi said, "Seems a shame that it goes to waste." He took the few steps to the stairs and sat down with a sigh. After taking a gulp of his coffee, he looked sideways at Granger, who returned the look.

Bacardi tapped his finger on the mug.

Granger continued to pant.

269

Troy W. Rasmussen

Setting the bowl of water on the walk, Bacardi sighed. "Don't think this makes us friends or anything."

After lapping up the bowl of cool water, Granger sat next to the steps, water dripping from the hairs on his chin, as Bacardi wiped his own after sipping his drink.

Wednesday
The prodigy: ever the wonder, ever the fascination. No matter the ability, the prodigy seems to capture attention as people speculate the how and why. Both become lost in admiration when the gifted uses the gift.

The shopkeeper busied himself with entries into his ledger as the light sounds of Tameril's harp playing drifted through the shop. Taking a break from his figures, he looked up to find a young man, violin case in hand, standing in the middle of the room, listening.

The shopkeeper moved his gaze from the young man to Tameril and back again. Clearly interested, the young man set the case on the table, took out his violin, and after a few preemptory plucks of the string, placed the instrument under his chin and began to play.

The smooth sounds brought Tameril from her own reverie, but not so much as to cause her to stop playing. The two musicians played for some time before ending their set, the final notes slowing to fade.

"That's quite the talent," the shopkeeper said.

The young man turned his head toward the speaker as if waking from a dream.

Tameril gave the young man a questioning look and added, "I agree."

"Can we do another?" he asked.

The Shopkeeper's Journal

Nodding, Tameril began to play, while the young man listened to a few bars to identify the piece. Nodding, he once more lifted the instrument and joined in. As the piece progressed, so did the difficulty. The young man's arm arched high, then dropped low, as it pushed the bow across the strings, at a speed that seemed to blur both player and bow.

After a few more minutes, the shopkeeper moved down one aisle, slid a step stool in place, and reached to a top shelf. He came down with a case much like the one the young man carried. Holding it out for a better look, he blew on its surface, sending years of dust particles into the air.

Dusting.

The duo brought the piece to a close as the shopkeeper approached the young man. Standing a few feet apart, the two eyed each other for a moment before the shopkeeper lifted the case toward his guest.

"It hasn't been played for years and is probably out of tune, but with a talent like yours, this instrument's finally found a worthy companion."

Tameril tipped the harp onto its base and sat patiently, hands in her lap, observing.

Slowly, the young man took the case, placed it and his own instrument on the counter, and opened the lid, its hinges creaking. Once that was done, he dropped his hands and merely stared at the violin for a few moments. Finally, he reached in and removed it.

"It was created by Hans Krouchdaler in the late seventeenth century," the shopkeeper said. "I've been told it has incredible sound."

Running his fingers across the intricately detailed face, the young man almost seemed not to hear the

Troy W. Rasmussen

shopkeeper's words. "Most people think these designs are painted on," he said.

"Mmmm."

"They aren't. It's actually small pieces of different colored woods inlaid into the body. It took months — years maybe—to create them."

"So you know the work of Mr. Krouchdaler," the shopkeeper said.

"He studied under Joseph Meyer. The Alemanisch School, where he created this, was known for its use of intricate designs."

Tameril and the shopkeeper waited.

Turning the instrument around to view the detailed designs on the back, the young man went on.

"Some discounted his work. They felt the disruption of the body piece by the inlaid wood affected the quality of sound. They were wrong."

With his hands behind his back, the shopkeeper watched the young man tilt the instrument this way, then that. He blew on it and inspected the soundness of construction. Apparently satisfied, he brought the violin to his chin and, using his own bow, made a few tentative pulls across the strings. He continued his inspection—an adjustment here, another there—for several minutes before again setting bow to string.

Life offers a fair share of heart-stopping moments. The small group that gathered around the open doorway was privileged to enjoy this one.

When the young man finished playing the venerable instrument, he took a deep breath, placed it in its case, and closed the lid. Clearly reluctant, he turned toward the shopkeeper to hand it back.

"Thank you…" he began, but the shopkeeper only shook his head.

The Shopkeeper's Journal

"That instrument is with its rightful owner," he replied quietly. "It no longer has a place on my shelves."

Staring first at the shopkeeper, then at Tameril, the young man faltered. "I can't afford this."

"It's not for sale."

"But—"

"Where are you training?"

The young man blinked. "I'm not." He lowered both the instrument and his head. "I mostly taught myself. Just seemed natural."

The sag of his shoulders told the shopkeeper there was more to the story.

"Be that as it may, a talent such as yours needs to be fostered and developed."

The young man smiled sadly. "I know. But 'fostering' is expensive."

"Mmmm."

Tameril smiled, her gaze turning towards the shopkeeper.

"There are scholarships, I know," the young man said quickly, his gaze moving to the windows. "It's just that…"

"That…?" The shopkeeper leaned forward.

"I don't want more school," the young man confessed. "I feel ready for more one-on-one training, but…there aren't many people—well, not many around here, anyway —who can help."

"I see. And what would it take to get this one-on-one training?"

"A lot of money."

"Mmmm. Let me tell you of a girl named Jonesie."

Before leaving the shop that day, the Hans Krouchdaler violin under his arm, the young man heard the story of a girl, a rare automobile, its eventual sale,

273

Troy W. Rasmussen

and the trust set up to fund the educational development of young people.

To all things is the right time given.

> *Friday*
> Days aren't always happy. Neither are
> they always otherwise. Given their due,
> though, one finds each filled with the
> movement of life. Gordo responds again
> to the call of his spirit, this time to the
> East. Likewise, I'm told the actions of
> another revealed more than the magic
> found in a fountain.

Recognizing a change in his countenance, Bacardi watched the shopkeeper from his perch on the steps. *Only see this on days like today,* he thought. Taking a sip from his mug, he turned to gaze at the sun rising over the ridge as Gordo and the guitar player bantered back and forth about past exploits.

"India," the guitar player said. "I've never been."

Gordo shook his head, rearranging his pack and lifting it to his shoulder. "Neither have I."

"Come back healthy."

Gordo smiled his understanding.

"Come back," the shopkeeper said, the sincerity in his voice catching Gordo's attention. Bacardi took another sip, then watched the swirls of his coffee ripple to the edge of the mug. The shopkeeper gave the metal cap to a thermos full of 'mud' a final twist before setting it on the counter.

"To get you started," he said.

Gordo extended his tanned arm and stuffed the thermos through the leather ring on the side of the pack.

"Thanks, Keep."

274

The Shopkeeper's Journal

"Mmmm."

"Do me a favor?" Gordo asked. "Keep an eye on the kid."

Bacardi took a deep breath, and the shopkeeper nodded.

Gordo embraced the guitar player, gave his customary wave, and headed out the door. As he watched Gordo walk toward his next adventure, the guitar player took his own deep breath.

"See you tonight," he said to the shopkeeper. "Friend of mine is in town, and I've asked her to join us in the set."

The shopkeeper nodded, his vision blurred from a mist in his eyes, as the musician walked away.

Still watching the sun, Bacardi tipped his mug upright to drain the last of his drink. "Better get that eye looked at."

The sun rose to its peak, beating rays of heat down on the crowds milling about on Tourist Lane. Seeking refuge from both, locals sat on stone park benches fanning themselves.

Parker presented the design for the newly refurbished park, another venture of the City Council, after discussing the dilapidated area with Natalia at her bistro.

"So what's the problem?" she said.

"I'd like to see something different. Parks with playgrounds, walking paths, and gazebos are a dime a dozen."

Natalia stared at him. "You're overthinking it."

"I know."

Natalia leaned back casually.

275

Troy W. Rasmussen

"When you think of the park," she ventured, "what comes to mind?"

"Fun. Laughter. People with their kids." He shrugged his shoulders. "Like I said, fun."

"When you were young…" Natalie started, then shifted gears as Parker frowned. "Okay. When you were a younger boy—what constituted fun? What made a hot summer day less so?"

"Swimming. We used to go to the pond and swim. But the town's already got a pool. Two, if you count the one at the school."

"Not everyone can swim," she said.

"Well, no." Parker seemed thoughtful. "Sometimes the neighbor kids would come over and we'd talk our moms into letting us have water balloon fights." He sighed. "But we can't have pieces of balloons lying all over the place."

Natalia smiled patiently. "Water balloons aren't the only way to get wet."

"Yeah, there were a couple of times, you know, when the balloons were just about gone when one of us would get the idea of bypassing them all together, grab the hose…" Parker slapped the table and sat upright, "We can have a bunch of hoses kids can spray each other—"

Natalia slowly shook her head,

"What?"

"Hoses? Lying all over the park?" she said.

Parker slumped. "Maybe a fountain or something."

Natalia inclined her head. "Getting closer."

"But fountains aren't fun. Not for kids, anyway. Although I guess they could play in them from the side…" Parker jumped to his feet, the force causing his chair to slide noisily. "That's it! Fountains!"

With that, he bolted from the table and out the door. As he passed by the window he turned, giving it a slap,

276

The Shopkeeper's Journal

and blew Natalia a kiss. She shook her head and grinned. Watching him run down the street, she leaned closer to the window. *Nice butt.*

Parker sat watching as the children, their rowdiness increased by the heat, quarreled with one another. Exasperated mothers, hoping the ground-level fountains spewing random bursts of water into the air would provide entertainment and a much-needed break encouraged their offspring to "go, have fun."

The intent of the water park was missing its mark today. Thoughtfully, Parker slid off his flip-flops and walked to the edge of the fountain where two nearby children stopped their play to see what he would do.

Parker placed his barefoot over the small opening in the ground, diverting the spray of water from its upward trajectory; the two continued to watch, curious but unimpressed. With a playful grin on his face, Parker arched his eyebrows and changed the angle of his foot, causing the stream of water to splash against their bare stomachs.

Screams of delight rang through the air, and more than one mother turned, then grinned in relief.

Child's play has few rules: have fun, seize spontaneity, and make noise, all of which increase in intensity when a grownup joins in. Within seconds, Parker found himself surrounded by ten to fifteen children eager for attention and the next spray of water. He found little problem in accommodating each child's scream of "Me next!" as he expertly directed the stream of water to blast against their small bodies.

Soon, though, it became obvious he wouldn't be able to keep up with the incessant demand. The time had come to shift the strategy. Bending over the stream of

277

Troy W. Rasmussen

water, he allowed it to splash his face and head—and without hesitation, every kid followed suit. Some forgot to hold their breath and came up sputtering, but none the worse for wear. Parker's laughter turned their pouting lips into broad smiles full of life.

In their excitement, a couple of the kids slid to the ground with a wet plop. Parker picked them up, patted their behinds, and encouraged them to continue on, and they did. Seeing they were gaining one-on-one attention, others plopped to the ground, obviously hoping for "rescue"—and they got it.

After a while, Parker began ambling around the fountain area, pretending he didn't realize intermittent sprays of water were shooting up from the ground. When one did, and he was standing over it, he would jump like someone startled, grab his behind, and begin looking around for the cause. It wasn't long before the kids would scream and point when he was "inadvertently" standing over another portal. Others, mostly boys, began imitating Parker's play.

His next move was to squat down beside one of the fountain's openings, waiting for the spurt of water, which he pretended to try to catch. On the next one, he acted as if the stream had the capacity to hold his weight; when it didn't, he fell to his side, rolling in the pooling water. Clearing the water from his eyes, Parker watched the dedicated horde copy his antics, screaming with excitement.

Parker turned to better view those behind him and noticed a young boy jumping up and down in front of a woman, slapping her leg. The tears running down his contorted face told Parker the child's rage, whatever the cause, was full-blown.

Parker stood and walked the short distance to stand, soaking wet, in front of the woman and child.

The Shopkeeper's Journal

"I'm so sorry," the woman said. "I don't know what's the matter with him."

The child continued his antics until Parker moved a bit, casting his shadow across the boy. With his world momentarily darkened, the boy's focus changed and his screams of anger became sobs of curiosity. Standing still, both man and boy assessed one another, as the boy's hand slid down the woman's leg. Parker tipped his head to the left in further assessment, holding the boy's attention before slowly squatting down, his feet and one hand forming a tripod of support. The boy leaned closer to the woman, but his eyes remained on Parker. The snot running over his lip caused the boy to sniff, Parker did the same. As if to verify the action wasn't just coincidence, the boy sniffed again, as did Parker.

Tiring of the game, the boy turned his head once more toward the woman's knee, and as he did, Parker raised his free hand and snapped his fingers. Other than his eyes, which darted to the left in response to the sound, the boy's posture remained the same. Parker adjusted his position to lean closer to the boy and opened his extended hand in offering for the child to take it. The boy glanced at his mother, then back at Parker, who turned his hand at the wrist. The boy assessed the move, then reached out and placed his hand in Parker's.

Parker picked the boy up and proceeded to the edge of the fountains. Sensing the boy was comfortable, he began slowly walking through the streams of water every now and then allowing the stream to splash against the boy's leg, soaking the bottom of his shorts. Parker felt small fingers grip the back of his arm as the boy leaned out to see what caused the sensation. Parker turned his body at the waist and repeated the action. The boy leaned further. As he did, a second stream of water shot from the

Troy W. Rasmussen

ground, splashing the boy in the face causing him to grip Parker's arm and pull himself upright. Taking a breath in preparation to express his displeasure, the boy was caught off guard when instead of giving in to his antics, Parker held up his hand and with his thumb wiped the water from the boy's face. Holding the boy closer to his chest, Parker leaned forward; the boy's grip increased. With one hand around his waist and the other supporting the back of his head, Parker began to sway back and forth as the streams of water pulsed against the boy's back. Both could feel the weight of the child increase as the water soaked his clothes. The boy's grip eased as Parker continued the movement, and soon he felt the boy release altogether, allowing his arms to dangle. Small fingers began to twitch at the feel of the jet streams tickling his palms. Parker's eyes smiled as the boy watched his face.

The boy stayed with Parker for the remainder of the afternoon. Before their time together came to a close, the boy's comfort grew to the point that he would leave Parker's general vicinity, venture through the fountains on his own, and return each time to the cove of Parker's crouched body. The safety and warmth provided encouragement for his next venture out.

As they began to leave, each of the children gave and received hugs from Parker. Watching them leave, streams of water bursting around him, Parker resolved to tell Natalia he wanted kids.

Those arriving early for the Friday night goings-on lounged on the furniture like travelers stranded at an airport during a storm, the low hum of conversations about work and life for the past week a subtle drone. The band had settled in, after having started the hit-or-miss striking of a chord here or there to ensure instruments were tuned and ready for the evening's set.

The Shopkeeper's Journal

Melanie, the guitar player, and guest arrived to an exaggerated chorus of "What's up?" or "How's it goin?" As they approached the counter, the guitar player, his arm around Melanie's waist, introduced his guest to the shopkeeper.

"This is Scarlett," he said. "Scar."

"Miss Scarlett," the shopkeeper said nodding his head by way of greeting.

"Scar," she said.

"Mmmm."

Judging by her dark clothing, mood, and piercings, the average passerby might assume Scar's upbringing was checkered with incidents of abuse or neglect, maybe even exposure to life on the street. But such was not the case. Scar had, in fact, come from an affluent family. She decided early on to forego the trappings of her family's money and, instead, present an appearance and demeanor designed to squelch the inevitable assumptions she felt people would make about her.

One day shortly after her high school graduation, she packed a single bag, kissed both her parents goodbye and left home. No ugliness, no cries from confused family members, just the loving embrace from parents accustomed to her preference of experiencing life from "a darker place."

Scar didn't feel she needed explaining. Where she learned to play the keyboards, no one could say. Most that knew her would have raised their eyebrows at the discovery and likely shrugged their shoulders in a "that's Scar" fashion.

"Scar's the one I told you about earlier," the guitar player told the shopkeeper. "She's playing with the band tonight. If all goes well, she just may sing one or two."

281

Troy W. Rasmussen

Scar's steady gaze remained directed at the shopkeeper.

"What can I get you to drink?" he asked.

"Coffee," she said, looking unimpressed.

"My guess is black and strong," said the shopkeeper.

"Whatever."

"I'll have…" Melanie began.

"Something light and cool," the shopkeeper said, with a slight grin.

Melanie smiled, then turned to seek a place on one of the sofas. Scar remained where she was, her focus on the fine porcelain cup in the cove behind the counter. Steam released from the coffee machine as he poured her drink.

Taking a sip of her coffee, Scar blinked rapidly at the hint of licorice and spice. "This isn't black."

"Mmmm."

She only glared at him before turning to join the band.

The band played for over half an hour when the guitar player introduced Scar. He informed the crowd he didn't know what she had in store but was pretty sure they would enjoy it. Several people chuckled and shifted their position for a better view. Unaffected, Scar lifted her hands to the keyboard, closed her eyes, and proceeded to sing—at times, wail—a song she'd written about a wicked love.

Several women wiped tears from their cheeks at the poignant words of the song.

After the last guest left, the shopkeeper began collecting the cups and glassware inevitably left behind. He noticed with a smile that Scar's cup was empty.

Saturday
Mrs. Worthingston graced the shop
today, twin grandsons in tow. Judging by

The Shopkeeper's Journal

her demeanor, and theirs, the visit was
more one of respite than one of seeking a
specific item. Rarely have I seen ironclad
Old World sophistication so at loose ends.
Always nice to break out the fine china.

Chester, with Jax dozing on his shoulder, sat idly at
the counter twisting back and forth on a stool, the bent
straw to his drink inserted into his mouth.

The shopkeeper was just closing the sale of some
leather-bound books when he was interrupted by the
clamor of the arrival of Thomas and Cody, the
Worthingston twins. Meeting the irritated gaze of their
grandmother, the shopkeeper nodded his appreciation to
the customer, closed the register drawer, and turned to
retrieve the porcelain teacup kept for such visits.

Meanwhile, the twins proceeded to work their way
further into the shop, sticks from who-knows-where
clashing into one another in a pretense of a sword fight.
Nearing the circular steps, their screams and protests of
"me first" rang out as the two argued over an imaginary
event seemingly to take place once they reached the
stairs.

Chester's pivot on the stool left him facing the two
boys as they approached the stairs. Without removing the
straw, he uttered, "Amateurs." Then, he pointedly turned
away.

"Why in heaven's name such creatures are created is
beyond me," Mrs. Worthingston said, removing her
gloves and uncharacteristically plopping them on the
counter.

Chester pivoted once more, this time to face Mrs.
Worthingston. His eyebrows raised as if to ask, *really?*

283

Troy W. Rasmussen

"Hmpf," was all Mrs. Worthingston said before turning to face the shopkeeper. "If you please, dear sir, a cup of tea—and as quickly as you can."

"Mmmm."

Patting the back of her hair, she went on tersely. "Bloodlines aside, there should be some sort of governance, some prequel, to procreation and its possible outcomes."

The shopkeeper poured the boiling water into the cup. Chester lifted an eyebrow.

"After today there will be no more of this jockeying about," she finished. "They simply must go."

Chester restarted pivoting on the stool.

"Go?" asked the shopkeeper.

"Yes, my dear sir, go. One simply cannot endure further onslaught to the senses." Straightening with an attempt at dignity, she went on. "I'm having them and that daughter-in-law of mine relocated to the cottage on Applegate Cove."

"I see," said the shopkeeper. "Doesn't seem quite the challenge."

Widening her eyes at the comment, Mrs. Worthingston slowly extended her hand to slide her tea closer.

"A few sips," the shopkeeper went on, "and you'll…"

"My dear sir, it will take more than a few sips…" Mrs. Worthingston took a slow breath, followed by a sip of tea.

Chester and the shopkeeper remained still.

Taking another sip, then returning the cup soundlessly to the saucer, Mrs. Worthingston collected her gloves and slapped them into her palm decisively. "Now to find a workman."

"A workman?"

284

The Shopkeeper's Journal

"I'm afraid the cottage is in some disrepair," she said with a slight shake of her head. "That and more than one piece of filigreed trim work has been marred at the hands of…" She glanced again at Chester, who in response concluded his drink with a loud gurgling slurp of his straw.

The shopkeeper decided to strike while the iron was hot.

"I met a man not too long ago," he said, "with the talents you seek."

"A bright spot in a day less so," she declared. "References?"

"Mine."

Mrs. Worthingston merely nodded.

"Send your man Tuesday at 11:00. Anyone able to bring relief to this menagerie is a welcome figure, indeed. Good day."

"And to you," the shopkeeper nodded.

"Now to corral the ruffians," she said. At that, she banged her walking stick against the wood floor. Thomas and Cody raced down the stairway and out the door as loud and rambunctious as they'd arrived.

Later that evening, when the lights from the lamppost in the sitting park cast a soft glow, the shopkeeper paused in his work to witness endearment more than fifty-seven years strong.

Todd and Emily Baxter had known each other since grammar school. The friendship grew deeper during the final years of secondary school and, within a year of graduating, the two married. Lifetime unions of the young were not so uncommon then.

In love with each other and their surroundings, Todd and Emily—or "Em," Todd's pet name for Emily since

Troy W. Rasmussen

they were children—established a life together in town and rarely left. Whether by choice or providence, they never had children of their own, yet through their careers—Emily a teacher, Todd a local merchant— affected the lives of many of the local children.

Emily was the teacher everyone wanted. Her gentle yet firm approach to educating the young often found her putting in extra hours at the school or at home mentoring a student. Reading, writing, and arithmetic were building blocks Emily firmly believed every child needed to succeed in life.

Time, she often said, was another. "Give a child the time, your time, and they'll bloom like the rare flowers they are."

Nearly every time she said it, Todd would smile. "It's your time, Em, that makes the difference," he'd say. "Every day I watch that happen."

Emily would smile back, briefly place her head on his chest, and then—letting him know gently that she stood by her first opinion—would gently nudge his ribs before returning to the task at hand.

Todd's approach to furthering the educational exploits of the town's children was less formal but, in some ways, more effective than that of his wife. Rare was the child who hadn't figured out that when they came to his store and reported their scholastic achievements, Mr. Baxter, being ever so impressed, would listen for as long as they rambled. At the close of their recital, he would pull the box of hard candies from under the counter and say, "Well, a young person doing all that surely must build back their energy." Watching young hands reach in for their reward was just that for Todd, who never tired of the experience.

The year Emily retired from teaching, the senior class added an honorary tribute to the Baxters at the

The Shopkeeper's Journal

graduation ceremony. Asking both of them to come to the front, the valedictorian recited an edited version of Emily's familiar saying. "You gave us each the time, your time. Thank you for seeing the rare flower and helping each to bloom."

Todd leaned over and whispered, "Every day I watched that happen."

Johnnie Mack, the year's athletic superstar, cleared his throat and approached the podium next.

"Mr. Baxter," he said, "you didn't spend as much time with us as Mrs. Baxter." With a wide grin spreading across his face, Johnnie pulled a box of hard candies from under the podium. "But that doesn't mean we forgot the times you did." As those in attendance broke out in laughter, Todd instinctively braced himself for a nudge that, this time, didn't come.

The years passed, fifty-seven of them in stalwart union to one another, each one culminating with the two slowly dancing in the park by the shop. To this day a bronze statue of the Baxter's dancing, a project commissioned by the students of the BBC Club to better their community, stands in the corner of the park, the flowers at the base tended by a certain gardener.

Chapter 22

Monday
Postcard from India. Odd.

The shopkeeper stood reading the postcard again. *Having a great time!! India…is. Holi Festival is nothing until you've experienced it in person.* The shopkeeper turned the card over looking at the picture of a mass of crowded and wet bodies dancing in a cloud of powdered color. *Painting an elephant tomorrow. Cool celebration.*

That Gordo was enjoying his time in India wasn't a concern. Painting elephants was well within the sphere of things he would enjoy. That he sent a postcard, a totally new experience, was. The shopkeeper read the scrawl again.

"Mmmm."

"Why the concern?" Natalia asked, approaching the counter.

Wrinkling his brow further and fanning the card against his palm, he said, "Card from Gordo."

"Everything all right?"

"Appears so." Raising his gaze to meet hers, he continued, "What can I do for you today?"

"Not a thing. Just stopped by to…"

"Did you think I forgot?" he said, smiling. "About my part in the wedding?"

"No. Just reassuring myself, I guess."

"Mmmm."

Natalia took a deep breath.

The Shopkeeper's Journal

"It's finally here. Everything's been arranged. The only thing left to do is wait." She rubbed her thumbs against each other.

Placing his hands over hers, he said, "All will be well."

"How can you know that?"

"I know you... have known Parker longer. You've both got what it takes—each other." He gave her small hands a squeeze. "Besides, everyone in town knows that beau of yours. One wrong step and he'll be called to account."

She smiled.

Reaching to lift her chin, he added, "You've done well. This is just another step."

"A big one."

"Mmmm. People embracing life to the degree the two of you do are prone to larger-than-life experiences." The shopkeeper reached into the cooler, retrieved two bottles of soda, and, popping the caps, slid one toward her. He tapped his bottle against it, and then raised his in salute.

"Now, tell me all about it."

Natalia spent the next hour regaling him with details of the wedding plans. How things had been relatively small and personal until Maarten got wind of the goings-on, offered his assistance, and then took over. Not that she minded. In a way, it was good to have someone else handling the details. As she spoke, he could see her relax. And, when she finished, she stood up, leaned over the counter, and kissed his cheek.

"Thanks for the time," she said, then waved goodbye.

289

Troy W. Rasmussen

Wednesday

It starts. Only a few days left until the culmination of nuptials of our illustrious town councilman and his bride-to-be.

Illustrious. Why would anyone use such a term to describe what was once a lounging mass of inactivity? The word better describes the change in a life versus the individual. He'd laugh at my saying so. On the other hand, the description fits, part and parcel, the young woman agreeing to such an arrangement. What a darling. It will be a first for her…for him…for me.

Trudy played soft, romantic chords that drifted through the shop as Bacardi sat dumbfounded on the steps, his empty mug swinging idly from his finger. He'd seen many wonders in his time; he'd often said as much while mumbling to Granger or the plants. Yet in his estimation, all those other sights paled in comparison to what he saw now.

The shopkeeper was dusting.

Following his movements, Bacardi leaned in a bit as the shopkeeper made his way to the glass case by the door and, with a grin on his face, paused to stare.

"Same case it's always been. Gonna wipe it down, too?" Bacardi quipped.

Nothing.

"There's a rocker I'm pretty sure a guy's gotta stay on," he tried again, "otherwise, people talk."

Trudy snickered.

Seeing that his antics failed to bring the intended response, Bacardi continued his observation of the

290

The Shopkeeper's Journal

wonder before him. What he failed to notice was that the case, typically crammed with announcements and other such notices, was empty except for two: an invitation to the celebration of Parker and Natalia's wedding…and a ragged slip of paper proclaiming, *she said yes!*

That had happened one morning when Parker, as was his habit, came in ostensibly to peruse the town's posting notices. In fact, however, his intention became clear the moment he tore off a piece of paper from his notebook, wrote three simple words, and tacked it to the board in the case. The night before, he'd popped the question; that day, he had his own announcement to post.

Parker came around the corner and found himself brought up short at the sight of Bacardi…staring at the shopkeeper.

"Is everything all right?" he asked.

"Damned if I know. Started not too long ago."

"What?" Parker asked, confused.

"That." Bacardi pointed to the shopkeeper waving his feather duster over various artifacts. Parker leaned forward in earnest.

"Never seen that before."

"Never's for tits on a boar. That there's straitjacket status," Bacardi said, shaking his head.

Patting Bacardi on the shoulder, Parker stepped into the shop.

"Hello?" he said.

Turning to face his guest, the shopkeeper nodded his hello and proceeded behind the counter to store the duster.

"How are you?" Parker asked.

Not at all unaware of the reason for Parker's solicitude, the shopkeeper tilted his head and lifted an eyebrow toward Bacardi.

291

Troy W. Rasmussen

"Contrary to popular opinion, I'm doing well."

"Coulda fooled me," Bacardi muttered, blowing the dust from his empty mug.

"One may be free to choose his own actions, yet not so much the consequences," the shopkeeper retorted.

Bacardi squinted his eyes, clearly debating the cost of pursuing the conversation further. He opted to maintain the status quo. "Cup's empty," was all he said before turning back to the flowerbed.

"Now, what can I do for you?" Seeing the clouded look on Parker's face, the shopkeeper spoke a touch louder. "Parker?"

Hearing his name, Parker turned his focus to the speaker. "Yes."

The shopkeeper waited.

"I do. Well, not yet…I can't…I mean…"

"Mmmm."

In an attempt to clarify, Parker continued, "Oh, no. I didn't mean I can't…that…the wedding. No, that's all good." He looked far away again. "I have…well, actually, I don't. That's why I'm here."

Seeing a sort of panic move across the young man's face, the shopkeeper nodded encouragingly. "Go on."

"I think I messed up," Parker said.

"There's little that can't be corrected."

"I guess." Parker looked sheepish. "I got so caught up in everything I forgot…" He swallowed hard. "I forgot the wedding ring." He paused, shaky. "It's not that I can't go to any jewelry store and pick one up. But I wanted it to be special. Off-the-charts special."

The shopkeeper nodded his head toward the end of the counter. "Take a look in the bottom drawer."

Parker stepped to the row of drawers at the end of the counter, squatted down, and pulled open the drawer.

292

The Shopkeeper's Journal

"Nice collection." His fingers touched a few of the pieces. "Not really what I'm after, though."

"Is the drawer all the way out?"

Parker pulled again on the knob. "Yes."

"In the back, there's a ribbon. Give it a pull."

Parker did as instructed, then jumped involuntarily. The tension on the ribbon caused a small- hinged door, much like those one comes across when changing a battery in an appliance, to pop open. Parker leaned forward on the balls of his feet and reached in, retrieving an antique wedding band.

Trudy stopped her playing.

"Where did this come from?" Parker asked.

The shopkeeper's gaze met Trudy's.

"Some time ago," the shopkeeper began, "a young bride was given a piano commissioned just for her." The shopkeeper told Parker the tale of the piano. At its close, he nodded his head toward the one in the shop. "After the death of her husband, she never played the piano again."

Trudy moved her fingers back and forth on the edge of the piano.

Dusting.

The shopkeeper continued, "I purchased it many years ago, and it's been where it is since then. Anticipating it would sell quickly, I had it tuned. Halfway through the job, the tuner approached me with this ring in his hand. It had lodged somewhere in the hammer mechanism." The shopkeeper took the ring and buffed it quickly. "There's no proof this actually belonged to the young woman in the tale. However, when she died several years later, she did so without her wedding band on." Handing the ring back to Parker, he said, "The piano remained in the hall until it was sold at auction. I suppose it's possible the ring belonged to

Troy W. Rasmussen

someone else, but the romance of it all supports otherwise. Such is the way of legend and great loves."

"Must cost a small fortune," Parker said.

"Mmmm. For our Natalia, no greater fortune could be spent. For the young man committing his life to her…it's on the house."

Parker's eyes grew wide.

"When she asks where it came from, tell her the tale and add that it's fitting she wear such a band, as…"

"It's the way of legend and great loves," Parker finished.

To all things is the right time given.

> *Thursday*
> The bravado of young men—not for one and not for all, but given the right conditions, the ruckus of gents out and about is an exhibition of pack mentality. Comical as it can be, many an order— formal or otherwise—finds its roots based in these types of early interactions.

Lounging in the shade provided by the stones of the flowerbed, Granger was the first to react to the sudden sound. He lifted his head and ears to identify the source, clearly trying to decide if further investigation was worth the effort.

"Happens every year about this time," Bacardi said.

Granger turned a curious gaze toward the gardener.

"All's quiet as long as they keep their noses in them books." Bacardi rubbed Granger's head of matted hair. "Every time the University gives 'em time off, though, the rest of us get an education in endurance."

As he took a gulp from his mug, Bacardi watched the group of six young men proceed up the walkway, their

The Shopkeeper's Journal

loud remarks about this professor or that exam rolling along, like a heat wave expanding to fill the space.

"Ain't no sense to it," Bacardi said, noticing the dog's change in posture. "Worse than girls."

Granger, curious at the animations of neck hugging and backslapping, tilted his head in an attempt to better understand.

"Every one of 'em would roll their eyes and have sumpin' not so nice to say if a lass or two walked by acting like that." Bacardi had turned to knock his mug against the door to signal for a refill when he noticed the shopkeeper already there.

Having heard the noise outside, the shopkeeper stopped restocking a shelf and moved to the door. Bacardi took note of the hope, then disappointment, on the shopkeeper's face.

"He'll come back," he said quietly. "Always does."

The shopkeeper merely nodded his head and went back inside, behind the counter, to light his pipe. Bacardi set the mug on the step.

The smoke from the first puffs of the shopkeeper's pipe rolled up and began to dissipate as the group entered the shop as loudly as they approached it. Fanning the wooden match out with a slow shake of his hand, the shopkeeper lifted his gaze—and an eyebrow—at the spectacle. Girls sitting at a nearby table turned en masse as well.

Aware of, but seemingly unconcerned about the presence of the shopkeeper or members of the opposite sex, the group proceeded to rearrange various tables and chairs to suit their liking. Once that was accomplished, four of the group sat down and, with feet resting on tables or hung over the edge of armrests, continued on with multiple discussions of things the shopkeeper had

295

Troy W. Rasmussen

yet to ascertain. The remaining two approached the counter, laughing at one of their own private jokes.

"Afternoon, gentlemen," the shopkeeper said.

"Hey, how's it goin?" the two said, simultaneously lifting their arms in overplayed recognition of the shopkeeper.

"Well enough. Yet, by all appearances, not as well as for some." The two laughed all the louder at what they took as a jest. A third leaned back in his chair for a better view and to gauge if he wanted to change location.

"It is a great day." One of them slapped the counter in emphasis.

"Mmmm."

Looking to his compatriot, the young man said, "Finals are over and…" Turning toward the others, he leaned his elbow on the counter. "Well…finals are over."

The group raised their arms and let out a yell in chorus. The young man at the counter grinned. "Drinks on the house, if you please, sir."

"Order what you will, but you'll need to do more than take a test for them to be on the house," the shopkeeper replied.

It took the lad a few seconds to realize the shopkeeper's meaning. Then, laughing again, he slapped the counter. "Got me."

The second young man piped up. "The usuals all around. I'll handle the tab."

It wasn't uncommon for the group to frequent the shop to let off steam, relax, or on occasion to study, so the shopkeeper didn't have to ask what "the usuals" were. But as he turned to prepare their drinks, he also noticed the first speaker looking at his pipe.

"I've got it," said the young man.

"What?" asked the other.

The Shopkeeper's Journal

"What we should do, the six of us." Slapping his buddy's chest with the back of his hand, he continued, "You know, how we're always talking about all of us doing something, like secret tattoos?"

The other knit his eyebrows together.

"Pipes! We should get pipes!" The first young man pointed to the shopkeeper's pipe. "Do you sell those here?"

As if the magic word had been invoked, the other four stopped their revelry to approach the counter.

"I do." The shopkeeper nodded.

"We're really going to do this?" one asked.

"Sure, why not?" responded another.

"I've never smoked a pipe."

"Who has?"

The group continued making comments as each confirmed the decision with more counter slapping, neck squeezing, and other gestures of agreement.

Shaking his head, the shopkeeper served the drinks and, as his guests cajoled one another back to their seats, retrieved a wooden tray with some eight or nine tobacco pipes and set it down at their table. "For what it's worth, here's what I have. Choose wisely."

"Wisely? Why wisely?" one said, grabbing a pipe.

"Every pipe's different. Has its own personality."

Another young man laughed. "What's mine—happy or sad?"

His companions merely groaned.

"What?" the young man asked, feigning ignorance.

"You'll find tobacco selections in the humidor," the shopkeeper said, turning to go.

"What's the best one?"

Troy W. Rasmussen

"Depends." Assessing the group, he said, "For the intents and purposes of this bunch, I'd recommend a cherry-flavored blend. No need to push things further."

"Then cherry it is. Bring us some of that."

"By all means," the shopkeeper said. Returning with a small bowl of tobacco, the shopkeeper bent toward the girls with a quick, "This ought to be rich."

Without further instruction, the group proceeded to pack and light their pipes, and the shop began to fill with heavy clouds of smoke as the eager group puffed away at their respective pipes. Soon the bowls glowed hot, as did the smoke drawn through them, causing several in the group to cough and fan the air or flinch at the sting of a burned lip, drawing snickers from onlookers.

The young men were undeterred. Convinced they had mastered the art, each one leaned back, placed his feet on the coffee table, and proceeded to puff away, the very picture of youngsters playing grownup.

Every now and again, the shopkeeper noticed one of the girls steal a glance at the goings-on, but the boys paid no attention. Once the covert op was completed, the information gathered during the visual reconnaissance was relayed to the others. Before long, looks of exasperation prevailed over interest in the young men—who definitely had no eyes for the girls watching them.

Instead, they discussed the latest breakthroughs in technology, specifically 3-D printing. After several minutes of listening, the girls, reaching the conclusion the boys hadn't and probably wouldn't notice them, collected their items to leave. One of them delivered the parting shot: "Might as well start printing out our own."

Saturday
Closed the shop today. Our dear
Natalia met her love at the ruins of

The Shopkeeper's Journal

Matfield Greene, committing her life to
his, and heard him do the same in return.
How promising young love. How
inspiring the energy and anticipation. How
honored an old man to hand her hand to
another.

The morning started with the steam from a fresh
batch of coffee billowing into the air as the bell above the
door gave a tentative ring. The shopkeeper smiled at
seeing Natalia attempting to enter without making noise.

"Coffee's fresh," he said.

"You're not open yet."

The shopkeeper sensed there was more. "I won't be.
Today, I'm giving one of the world's loveliest creatures
away."

Taking the cup of coffee, Natalia shrugged, and set it
down without taking a drink.

"It won't all fall apart," he said, watching her rotate
the cup back and forth in her palms.

"How do you know?"

The shopkeeper wrapped his hands around hers and
said, "Because you're not that person any longer. You
changed course, my dear, and that took strength. It took
even more to accomplish all you have, to be where you
are today. You're no longer the type to turn back…to let
it fall apart." He reached out to lift her chin. "You won't
and, therefore, it won't."

She bent to kiss his hand. "You are dear to me. How
could I ever have done it without you?"

"Mmmm. There are those with reason to say the
same about you." He reached to the side. "Once-in-a-
lifetime events happen every day, and it's only fitting we
have another one."

299

Troy W. Rasmussen

Her eyes lit up. "Is that what I think it is?"

"It is."

She was like a gleeful child as he slid the cherry torte to a place between them. It was a fitting accompaniment to their coffee and a chat about memories.

After a time, Natalia prepared to leave—only to see the shopkeeper walk from behind the counter and hand her a small wrapped box. When she opened it, she found a key.

"A key? What's that about?" she asked.

"There's a place on the edge of town," he said, tapping the box. "That's to the front door. Needs a bit of work, but that won't be an issue for the two of you." He leaned forward and kissed her forehead. "I've never had a daughter. You changed that."

Natalia's eyes filled with tears. "That means so much. But—a house? I don't know what to say…"

The shopkeeper merely nodded.

She smiled as she left. "Thank you. From us both."

By midafternoon, guests were milling about outside, some in costume coinciding with the medieval theme. Insisting every detail be as authentic as possible, Maarten had hired artists and entertainers specializing in period productions and placed them throughout the grounds. Fire-breathers, jugglers, dancers, metal artisans, and grubby children selling roasted turkey legs all contributed to the ambiance of a Renaissance festival.

The shopkeeper walked through the throng, greeting townspeople and shaking hands. It hadn't taken long for word to get out he was giving Natalia away—thus, he was treated as the father of the bride. He didn't mind. Nor did he mind his costume, that of a wealthy merchant. Stopping at one of the booths for a drink, he tilted his

The Shopkeeper's Journal

head, the feathers in his hat following suit, and silently commended Maarten; he'd once again worked his magic.

"I'm well aware of what you're capable of," he had said to Maarten during an earlier discussion. "Natalia's given us the basics. I leave to you the putting together of it all."

"It's the details," Maarten exclaimed with some exasperation. "The details drive an event like this. Don't get me wrong, I'm happy to be a part, it's just…"

"There will be no sparing of expense," the shopkeeper said, understanding Maarten's hesitation. Then he chuckled. "Not that you could if you wanted to."

"Carte blanche fares best, I always say."

Now, grinning at the memory, the shopkeeper lifted his wooden mug. "Here's to *carte blanche."*

He'd just finished his drink when a trumpet sounded outside the ruins' main door. Turning in unison toward the blast, guests strained this way then that, some on tiptoe, to see what was to happen next. The enormous arched wooden gate drew open, and a brilliantly costumed herald stepped forth.

"Hear ye, hear ye. The lord of this land announces and invites you to attend the union ceremony of the Lady Natalia to the most high and honorable Lord Parker."

The shopkeeper, on cue, began making his way to his assigned post as good-natured laughter swept through the crowd.

The Herald (actually a local high school student) went on. "Does anyone know where the lord of this land is?"

"The lord," the shopkeeper called out, "like any other facing what he is today, was at the tent of mead bolstering his courage." Laughter rippled through the

301

Troy W. Rasmussen

crowd anew, and many in the crowd reached out to slap the shopkeeper's shoulders in well-wishing.

At last, he arrived at the landing, then turned and addressed the crowd one more time. "Now that the lord's arrived, he's of a mind to go have another."

Maarten wished he'd had one, maybe two. But he had to admit, the shopkeeper was doing a terrific job playing his part.

"My lords, my ladies, my guests..." the shopkeeper proclaimed, "...welcome one, welcome all. I am honored you have come." At this, the trumpets sounded and the gate was pulled to its fully open position.

It took several minutes for the crowd to meander through the gate, down stone corridors lit by oversized candles in wrought iron holders, and into the main hall. Actors dressed as squires encouraged people to fill in the area, even though it had no seats, reassuring them they wouldn't be standing long.

Most of the people didn't seem to care about standing; they were too mesmerized by their surroundings. Twenty-foot-high balconies supported by massive stone archways flanked the space on either side. A large cathedral arch, fifteen feet across and thirty feet high, gave entry to a winding stone stairway wrapping up and around to the second and third stories of the edifice. Plaster and stone from the walls and ceiling had cracked and fallen loose in some areas, yet an enormous circular stained glass window, nearly a full story in height, remained intact. Maarten had insisted the window be meticulously cleaned inside and out...for an effect he hoped would "wow" the audience at the right moment.

In the midst of the chatter, the oohs and the ahhs, trumpeters, five to a side, stepped to the edge of the balcony, raised their horns, and blasted out a full-volume

The Shopkeeper's Journal

fanfare to announce the arrival of the King—in this case, Parker.

The heavy wooden door at the entrance of the hall slammed open with a thundering bang, drawing the crowd's attention. At that point, they heard the sound of the Welded Roses playing a majestic march, that of an enormous warhorse carrying its proud and worthy rider. Chester led the way, calling, "Make way, make way, for the Lord cometh!"

The black Friesian horse stomped through the galley toward the front of the hall, its heavily muscled legs lifting high on each step, its hooves crashing against the stone floor. An entourage of nobles, squires, and standard-bearers behind him began to fill the hall with shouts of praise and honor, and the crowd soon joined in as Chester urged them to.

Reaching the base of the stairs, Parker slid off the horse and, with a wave of his heavy brocade robe, prepared to ascend the stairs toward the waiting clergy.

Music throbbing, trumpets blaring, lighting following him, he rose step by step to his post, where he was illuminated by a single spotlight. Parker reflected how, at the rehearsal, it all felt sort of comical. Standing in full regalia, he no longer agreed. It was real—very real. He had found the rare gem, asked her to be his own, and sworn himself true. Noble, indeed.

Those playing the part of squires led horse and host to a smaller area of the hall, the stone wall providing a break in the line of sight which aided in keeping the animals calm. In the stillness following Parker's entrance, people up front could hear soft, encouraging tones of handlers as they stroked the noses of excited horses.

Troy W. Rasmussen

A few minutes passed before the music changed, softening in the signal of Natalia's arrival. The shopkeeper straightened; the time had arrived. Natalia turned to look at him as her entourage began its graceful procession through the hall. He smiled and winked, sending a sense of ease through her before lifting his arm, patting her hand as she took it.

"Not every day will be filled with magic like today," he said, "but those that are make up for the ones that aren't. Hold on to those, Natalia. Seek them out. Create them. Live them as you were meant to."

Natalia caught her breath at the words, then nodded that she was ready.

Chester dutifully cleared Natalia's maidens from the area as the shopkeeper leaned in to once again kiss her forehead. "Go now, my dearest. The magic of your future awaits, and today you meet it head-on."

Natalia threw her arms around his neck as he wrapped her in a hug. "I love you."

"Mmmm."

With a respectful bow, the shopkeeper relinquished his hold, and Natalia began her ascent up the stairs. At long last, or so it seemed, she reached Parker, whose smile echoed her own.

The clergy intoned, "Do you confirm before those present that you have found your true love? Do you commit your life to theirs in all it entails?"

"I have and I do," Parker said.

Looking at him—the set of his jaw, the tear forming in his eyes —Natalia blinked back tears in her own. "I have and I do," she replied.

Later, people would reminisce about the romantic day. They'd even argue, good-naturedly, about what moment was the pinnacle. In the end, most agreed that the sun's rays, coming through the massive stained glass
304

The Shopkeeper's Journal

window as Parker and Natalia kissed, was a moment tough to beat.

Troy W. Rasmussen

Chapter 23

Monday
How captivating is the wonderment children find in the remedial. To those not yet callused by life, something as simple as chasing the shade is a game, a momentary challenge, with the results one day washed away by the rain.

The late afternoon light was making its daily pass across the windows, and the shopkeeper restocking the wine cabinet, as a family entered the shop. Although the day wasn't hot, they were visibly refreshed stepping into the cooler interior of the shop, sheltered as it was by eighteen-inch limestone walls.

"Good afternoon," said the shopkeeper.

"Hello," the parents said in unison.

"Heeelllooo," said one boy, clearly the youngest of the three children the couple had in tow.

"Well, hello to you, young man. And what might your name be?"

"Maximus. Max for short," replied the boy.

"Well Maximus, Max for short, how can I be of service?"

Watching the two older children as they moved deeper into the shop, the woman spoke up. "I'm hoping you have some lamps. Preferably of Victorian design. We're redoing a parlor and have made it a goal to find something extraordinary for a table that once belonged to my great-grandmother."

The Shopkeeper's Journal

"Lamps I have. As to extraordinary, I'll leave it to you to decide," the shopkeeper said with a grin. He pointed them in the direction where various lamps could be found, then turned toward the door to find Max standing fast.

"Mmmm."

Walking behind the counter, the shopkeeper noticed that once Max's parents moved deeper into the shop, Max turned to stand in the doorway, facing outside. Moments later, whatever had caught his attention led him out the door and into the sitting park next to the shop.

"Max," called the woman, but there was no answer.

"My guess, ma'am," murmured the shopkeeper, "is that he hasn't heard you."

A look of fear shot over her face as she made for the door.

"All is well, don't worry." He smiled. "Seems our young wanderer has found entertainment elsewhere. I'll keep an eye on him while you hunt the extraordinary."

Grinning sheepishly, she thanked him and resumed her shopping.

The shopkeeper moved from behind the counter to the windows, pulled out and lit his pipe and, while sending puffs of smoke into the air, stuck his hands in his pocket to watch the exuberant Max.

Max wasn't sure what the park had to offer or if it would be fun but, in his experience, parks delivered. Standing with his hands on his head, the boy surveyed his surroundings. Just then, a cloud drifting overhead blocked out the sun. Not realizing what caused the phenomenon, he stuck out his neck, his eyes tracking the line of the shade caused by the cloud floating by.

Soon enough, the small cloud moved on in its journey, allowing the light to shine again. Moments later

307

Troy W. Rasmussen

another cloud drifted by, bringing into Max's world another line of shade.

Amused by the young boy's curiosity, the shopkeeper leaned further back on his heels and waited in his own anticipation of Max's next move.

As the shopkeeper watched, the boy stuck his hand in his pocket and pulled out a large, well-used piece of sidewalk chalk the size of a small tube of toothpaste. This, he used to trace a line at the edge of the cloud shade. As the cloud moved on in its travels, so did Max, stopping every few steps to bend over and trace another line. Eventually, he stopped the chase and turned to observe the lines, his small thumb rubbing back and forth on the rough-hewn edge of the chalk.

Max stood surveying his handiwork for several minutes before stuffing the chalk back in his pocket and walking toward the shop again. At the steps, he turned and sat down, his chin in his hands, apparently waiting— for what, the shopkeeper was unable to pinpoint. The answer came with the arrival of the next cloud.

As it passed overhead, its shadow line moving slowly toward the park, Max jumped up and pulled out his piece of chalk once more. When the edge of the shade reached roughly the same place as the first line, he repeated his earlier task, methodically following the cloud through the park.

In the time it took his parents to find and purchase a Hector Guimard lamp, with its elegant hanging crystals, Max had repeated the process of chasing the shade and making a line several times.

At the door, the woman turned and thanked the shopkeeper for keeping an eye on Max. As the family moved toward the park, the shopkeeper heard him ask, "Do ya s'pose if it happened enough, all the lines would fill in and touch?"

The Shopkeeper's Journal

Noticing the lines on the walkway, his mother smiled and ruffled her son's hair. "Eventually, yes. At some point, all things come together and take shape."

The shopkeeper thought it most fitting.

True to his assertion that the shop didn't close until everyone had left, the shopkeeper waited for the last customers to file out before he shut the door, turning the key and hearing its familiar rustic sound. Bacardi, cart loaded with the tools of his trade, turned toward the shopkeeper, tapped the brim of his hat with his forefinger, then headed down the walkway.

THE END

Troy W. Rasmussen

Acknowledgements

Things to the magnitude of creating a book are not a singular effort. How does one thank those who put in as much, if not more, effort to the final product? Like this…

A monumental thanks to my wife, Stacey J. Rasmussen Without your driving force, this story may never have seen the press. Your love, encouragement and patience through this process were unmatched. From your declaration, "It's time to start writing your stories," through all of the "you'll get it," to your "honey it's beautiful"…I love you.

A big thanks from Dad to: Montana, McKenna, and Mahagony (The 3Ms)
You girls, along with your mom, are who this story was written for. Who knew that telling you stories when you were little would lead to this? You are the light of my life. Thanks for all the hugs and encouragement. Papa loves you.

To Janet Butler and the team at The Book Butchers Janet, I can only imagine what it took to edit the manuscript of a first time author. I'm grinning right now at the recommendations you would make for this page alone. Try as I might, I couldn't find a misplaced modifier to throw in here.

310

The Shopkeeper's Journal

Thanks to Judith Reveal for your efforts on the initial edit and encouraging words.

To Karla Savard, Cile Smith, Ruth McCaleb, and Janna Chamberlin
Beta reader extraordinaires all! (Janet just poured another glass of wine) You took on this project without having met its creator and I cannot thank you enough for your time and contribution to this project.

"Ms. Susie" Bright
Lady, no one does "porch talk" like you. Thanks for all your encouragement and kind words. The book aside, your love and friendship mean a great deal. You and Butch are the best!

Made in the USA
Columbia, SC
11 March 2018